MURDER
AT THE
KENTUCKY
DERBY

MURDER
AT THE
KENTUCKY
DERBY

Charles Parmer

COACHWHIP PUBLICATIONS
Greenville, Ohio

To
Noma and John Wesley Graham

Murder at the Kentucky Derby, by Charles Parmer
© 2023 Coachwhip Publications edition

First published 1942
Charles Brower Parmer, 1893-1958
CoachwhipBooks.com

ISBN 1-61646-552-2
ISBN-13 978-1-61646-552-0

1

"Will you slow down—for one split second?"

The compactly built chap was getting red in the face. He leaned forward, snapped his words into the receiver. "You don't say who you are—or what you want. How do I know you aren't a phony?"

Strident tones crackled back through the transmitter so loudly that the lurch-shouldered fellow sitting near the window peered over his paper. He rubbed his jutting chin and listened.

"Well, I'm damned." The French phone clicked down on its hook. Roderick Austen gripped the burnt-walnut table that served as desk and gave it a shake. "Of all the crazy—" Then sitting back in his chair abruptly, "Trigg!" he called.

George Trigg dropped the sports sheet he was spelling. "Yes sir?"

"You give this phone number to anyone?" The deep voice was serious.

"No sir, Major. You know I ain't." The little man shuffled over, his left shoulder poked forward. He was standing tense. "Why—why—?"

"One minute." Austen picked up the receiver. The snap in his alert blue eyes, the set of his square chin, the bulging of the fighter's chest—all gave impression of a high-geared dynamo whirring into action. He spun the dial. "Opera-tor—chief operator." Then, after a pause, "Roderick Austen speaking. Investigator, Racing Commission. Please have all incoming calls traced—until further notice. Especially any calls from a woman."

He snapped the phone back on its prong, turned to the waiting man. "I've never caught you in a lie, Trigg. Don't let me. But a woman just called—lady, by Jove!—badly frightened one. Said she knew I was a specialist in race-track matters. Wouldn't tell her name. Wanted to engage my services. Would send proof of her intentions. How the deuce'd she get my number?"

Roderick Austen swung to his feet, walked back and forth behind the table.

"Women is bad medicine—and women and racin' don't mix," George Trigg added. His small gray eyes measured the broad-shouldered, lean-hipped man who moved with such swiftness. "I allus wonder why one ain't gone after you—"

"Cut it, Trigg." Austen frowned impatiently.

"Didn't mean nothin', sir."

"This girl is close to somebody in the racing know. Something's stirring. I don't know what. But I don't like it. The Derby's being run tomorrow—"

A deep bell sounded at the back of the apartment. The apartment was half the floor of an old house which had been made over, and the two men were standing in what had been the library. Sets of books still lined the dark-stained walls, and a low brass lamp with green glass shade stood in the table's center.

"That'll be Slenk, sir," Trigg said. He shambled to the wall, pressed the button that released the street door, then opened the hall door. He stepped out, half closing it behind him.

Austen's keen ears caught the tread of light feet on the thinly carpeted hall floor and Trigg's voice, surprised:

"Oh, you? You can't come in. This be a private meetin'—"

A high-pitched voice protested, "I—I've got to see him. Tell him—"

"Just a minute." The door opened fully; Trigg looked around it. "You want-a see—"

"I heard. Let him come in—one minute."

A youngster—he might have been eighteen; he could have been twenty-two—crossed the threshold. A slight lad in loose-fitting clothes and with well-spaced blue eyes under wayward sandy hair.

"Hello there, Danny!" Austen drew the boy into the big room. "What brings you here, son?"

"Major Austen"—the boy's words came in urgent tones—"can I see you—alone? I—got to."

Austen pushed the cuff back from his wrist watch. "For just one minute, Danny. Trigg!"

The old fellow nodded. He went into an adjoining room, closed the door, and stood with his back against it.

"It's about Red Moon, sir," the youth began in a half whisper.

"You boys hear everything." Austen looked appraisingly at the lad, who turned a hat awkwardly in his hands. Strong, firm hands, large for his body—hands through whose skill so many horses had run to victory.

"Slenk promised me I could ride Red Moon in the Derby, Major. Now I hear somebody else is goin' to get the horse."

"And if somebody else does?"

"I want to know if there ain't some way you could get me the mount."

Austen shook his head. "Impossible, son. That would be up to the new owner. You'd have to sell yourself."

"Then, sir"—with great eagerness—"could I set in the meetin'?"

Austen laughed outright. "You heard about this meeting too! I'm afraid your presence would be irregular." He sobered.

"Major Austen"—the boy's face had gone grave; there was the light of fear in his eyes; he dropped his voice still lower—"there's strange things goin' on, sir." Then his face shut as if a mask had slipped over it.

"What do you mean, Danny?" Austen leaned forward on the edge of the table where he was sitting.

"Er—nothing, sir." The jockey's face again was full of fright. "I—I ain't told you nothin', sir. Nothin'."

Austen watched the boy for an instant. "Are you sure you have nothing to tell me, Danny?"

"No sir, no sir," Barton repeated. He looked anxiously at the door behind him. "I—I ain't told you nothin', Major Austen, have I?"

Austen whistled a tune as he walked twice back and forth behind the desk. He stopped beside the boy, put a hand on his shoulder. "You've told me a lot, but you don't know it." The jockey stood with eyes lowered, as if nothing could budge him from secrecy.

"On second thought," Austen said, "I think you may sit in, Danny. But be careful, and when it's over—" Austen broke off as the house bell rang again. "Trigg!"

The inner door opened. Trigg returned to the room. "That better be Slenk," he growled. "I'll get it, Major." He went outside, closing the door behind him.

"You can speak to the man who gets Red Moon, Danny. Sit over there." Austen indicated a chair in a far corner, to the left of the door. He touched his blue four-in-hand quickly. It was five o'clock—would be Derby time tomorrow—and dusk was creeping into the study. He flashed on the green table light. He stared down at his wrist watch.

He spoke softly, but the words carried to the boy in the far corner. "I wonder, Danny—" he began. He heard the rider's feet shuffling nervously on the hardwood floor beyond the rug's edge, waited for him to speak.

"I—I ain't done nothin', Major," Barton said in a voice so low that it seemed to drift in from the gloom beyond the lamp's circle of brilliance.

"I wonder if you had that girl telephone me, Danny," Austen said quietly, waited for a second, "and why."

An instant's silence. Then another foot shuffling. "I ain't done nothin', Major—and I ain't told nothin', neither."

The muffled cacophony of a city celebrating Derby week drifted up from the street—sounds deadened by the thick walls and closed windows: the sharp honking of impatient horns, the rumblings of heavy trucks, the drone of a plane overhead, strains of a marching band far off.

"That's the trouble, Danny." Austen's voice was stern. "You haven't told a thing—on purpose." He walked to the boy's chair, looked down at him sharply. "What does that girl want, Danny—the one who telephoned me?"

The boy crouched back in the chair, his eyes darting nervously about as if looking for a way to escape. "I told you, Major," he said, wetting his dry lips with his tongue, "I don't know nothin', sir."

Sounds of a scuffle broke in from the hallway. The door was pushed open violently and flung wide.

2

Across the threshold, in the hall's gloom, stood two men. One was Trigg, his left shoulder jutting forward.

Trigg had a hand on the wrist of another undersized chap—a man of thirty or so. "Here be Slenk. I just grabbed him so he won't run off again. He don't like to be grabbed."

Austen frowned. "Bring him in."

"In you go!" Trigg flung the man into the room, closed the door behind them.

Guy Slenk's splotched face showed he had lived hard and rough. A vacuous grin spread over its wind-swept surface. He pulled off a soggy cap, revealing a half-bald head with sandy hairs sprouting around the perimeter. Yellow buck teeth caught a gleam of light. The man recognized Roderick Austen. His face sobered.

"So it's you, Slenk! Sit down. You've caused the Racing Commission enough trouble for a lifetime."

"Yes sir. I allus says a man's got to—"

"Save it!" Austen snapped. "Sit down and don't speak until I say to."

"Yes sir!" Guy Slenk agreed in a squeaky voice. "I allus say— *Ouch!*"

He leaned over, clutched his right shin with both hands an instant. George Trigg had kicked him sharply. "Shut your trap—sit down," Trigg growled.

11

"You—you—"

"Shut up!"

"Oh—a'right, a'right!" Slenk looked around, saw Danny Barton, the jockey, backed off from him, took a chair in an opposite corner.

Austen noted that the trainer was dressed—save for the soggy cap—in what he believed to be fashion's height: in a swagger-cut suit of light gray; pearl-buttoned, gray-topped shoes; a flaming purple tie against an orange shirt, and on his hands a new pair of light mocha gloves.

Trigg lugged out a huge silver-cased split-second timer. "You're two minutes late," Trigg said, inspecting it, putting it back in his vest pocket.

"I'd-a—a-been on time, but I had to get a—a pair of new gloves," the trainer apologized.

"Got to have gloves," Trigg sneered, "even if you ain't got the price of oats."

Another loud ring on the bell. A moment later two other men stood in the doorway.

"On time, Major?" The question was asked by the first one—a fellow dressed in soft tweeds and just getting middle-aged spread. His clothes were too form-fitting, his jowls too red, the look in his brown eyes too arrogant.

Austen pulled a finely chased split-second chronometer from his pocket.

"Make it three minutes, thirteen and four fifths seconds late," he said.

"Sorry—but had to pick up Dr. Fellowes. You know each other?—Dr. Ralph Fellowes, Major Austen."

"Yes, how do you do?" Austen nodded to the man—a studious-looking person in his middling forties, more quietly dressed than the horseman. Austen remembered reading that Fellowes had inherited a profitable whisky distillery just before getting his M.D., that he had been kept so busy managing his property since that he had never practiced.

"You connected with this, Dr. Fellowes?"

"No, I'm not, but Madison insisted I come along."

"He is connected with it too," Madison spoke sharply. "He's my witness."

"I see." Austen put the watch back in his pocket. "Come in and have chairs."

The men crossed the threshold. Austen closed the door.

Madison said: "What's the idea of making us run out here? Why not meet in the Commission's office?"

"Where half the sports writers of America are camping this minute—waiting for something to happen?" Austen demanded. "We'd rather keep these matters quiet."

"So that's it. I get you." Madison took the easiest chair, motioned his companion to one by his side.

"No use getting the public upset," Austen went on.

"Course not. Well, I'm ready to start."

"We'll wait a minute."

"Wait for what? We are here. See you caught Slenk." He ignored the jockey, Barton. "Who else is concerned in this Derby business?"

"You forget that Sam Bosun, through a Chicago attorney, filed a claim for Red Moon. I—"

He stopped speaking as a blast of music came up from the street. He stepped to the broad window, pressed his face against the glass. Heading from the near-by depot was one of the many parades of Derby week. It was moving toward the hotel section. A red-coated band, with drum major in black shako twirling a golden cane, was blaring Sousa's "Stars and Stripes Forever." Behind, marching in column of fours, were half a thousand men, shouting, waving hats. At least a score of banners were being carried in line: banners bearing two words in yellow against a red background:

GOLDEN RULER

Madison, now at Austen's side, scoffed. "Darn fools! Their nag hasn't a Chinaman's chance tomorrow."

"No?" Austen turned back to the men in the room. "That's what they say every year about some outsider." He shrugged. "Look at the outsiders who've won! Favorites come in first less than half the time. Every horse has a chance," he said.

"Every one except—" Madison looked at Austen. "All right, forget it!" He sat down. "Let's begin."

"You know Sam Bosun claims he holds a written option on Red Moon?" Austen asked.

"A written option? I have the winning option. Why wait? There'd been no foolishness if this crook Slenk—"

"Now you wait!" The trainer leaned forward on his chair.

"Yes, I said crook." Madison turned so his right shoulder greeted Slenk. "My option was due four days ago. I tried to take it up. You turned yellow. Skipped over the state line so I couldn't serve papers on you. I had to appeal to the Commission to get justice."

"Please!" Austen raised a hand. "No quarreling."

A firm peal on the bell. "Trigg, open up."

George Trigg, walking with his peculiar shuffle, went out to answer the summons. Madison spoke casually:

"Ralph, think I'll throw a party for her tonight. Celebrate getting Red Moon."

Fellowes said something as George Trigg raised his voice at the door. "Women ain't allowed!"

"One side, please." The voice of a stranger.

Austen called: "What's going on?"

The door swung back. In popped Trigg, his left shoulder leading the way. Behind him stood a man and a woman. Austen noted that either would attract attention anywhere.

The man was sleek and powerfully built. A jagged scar zigzagged across his swarthy right cheek. His black hair gleamed as if from a pasting of bear's grease. There was a surly twist to his bladed lips. His opaque Chinese-shaped eyes told nothing. He was dressed slightly in advance of spring styles. A huge, oblong black pearl stood out against his gray tie.

The woman had the curves and the beauty of a poster girl: platinum hair, large sea-blue eyes, bright cheeks, a figure of soft, undulating curves, sheathed in something of filmy blue. She was twenty in the soft twilight. Perhaps twenty-five, or older, in the light of midday.

She looked hesitantly at Austen for a split second, then her glance swept to Henry Madison. She nodded and smiled. Austen saw the sportsman draw his shoulders up, strut like an old turkey buzzard, and smile back. Then Madison whispered a word to Fellowes and smiled again at the platinum-haired one.

The strange man's eyes fastened on the broad-shouldered, lean-hipped racing investigator.

"Major Austen." He spoke the words as a fact—not a question.

Austen nodded.

The man's bladed lips smiled. "Had the impression you were a much older man," he said pleasantly. "We are on time, I believe. I—"

Madison broke in: "How many minutes late is that, my good man?"

The man went on, ignoring Madison: "I am Mr. Doyle, Mr. Rock Doyle, of Chicago. Attorney. Representing Mr. Bosun."

"You are on time, Doyle, but as for the young lady—"

"My secretary." Spoken suavely.

"She won't be needed. This meeting is off the record."

"But as a witness to the proceedings—"

"My decision will be final."

Austen glanced at the girl. She was studying him, as if trying to make up her mind about something. Then a light came into her eyes. She made a movement as if to speak. The man Doyle was too quick. "I'll do the talking," he said in low tones. She took a step backward.

Austen went over to her. "Believe you wanted to say something?" He smiled encouragement, but Doyle closed the incident. "That is all," he said sharply to the girl. "You may go."

He waved her out and closed the door himself behind her.

Madison looked at Fellowes, raised eyebrows an instant. Fellowes scowled and said nothing.

"Shall we begin?" Mr. Rock Doyle asked, his back against the closed door.

3

"Extry! Extry! Derby sen-sa-shun! Extry!"

The men in the room moved forward in their seats, craning necks to hear.

"What the devil!" said Madison.

"Extry! Extry!"

"We'll find out." Austen opened the window. "Here, lad!" He tossed a quarter down. "Keep that—and keep your paper. Just call out the headlines."

"Thanks, boss! It says here"—a freckled-faced boy with red hair and no hat held up his papers—

> "'SIR HUBERT SCRATCHED!
> Khayyam Colt Goes Lame
> On Eve of Racing Classic'

"And it says"—the boy now was looking at the finer print—"it says he won't go to the post. That's 'bout all, boss."

"Thanks—and good luck."

Austen closed the casement. "That's that," he said as if to himself, but the men heard him. "One horse the favorite had to fear—and now he won't start." Then:

"Gentlemen!" Austen swung to his ladder-back chair behind the table. "Let's make this short, if not sweet.

17

Reason for this meeting: to determine who owns Red Moon. Right?"

All nodded their heads save Guy Slenk, who was studying his new mocha gloves.

"At present Red Moon—the Derby favorite—is in your barn. Eh, Slenk?"

The trainer looked up. "Yeah." Then he tugged at a glove.

"You, Madison, have an option to buy the colt for five thousand dollars?"

"I have—and a witness to the transaction."

"And—you"—to— Doyle—"representing— Sam Bosun, claim—"

"We hold an option to purchase the colt for fifteen thousand dollars."

"I see. You, Madison—"

"I complained to the Commission yesterday that I tried to exercise my option; that Slenk refused to recognize it and slipped off so I couldn't get court action. I swear it."

"You asked the Commission to determine ownership of the horse before the Derby's run?"

"I did."

Doyle glanced up, spoke quickly: "I appealed too. It's a matter of record."

Madison turned on him. "Where do you come in?"

Smiling, his long eyes narrowed, Doyle took a paper from his pocket and gave it to Roderick Austen, ignoring Madison.

"I believe you will find that's an option—in writing"— he stressed the words—"to buy Red Moon for fifteen thousand dollars on May first."

Austen glanced around. "All this is off the record. You don't have to agree, but if you remain here and take part in this discussion it's understood you do agree to my ruling. Understood?"

Slowly the heads nodded.

"Good!" Austen picked up the written option, glanced at it, and passed it to Slenk.

"Your signature?"

The trainer focused his eyes. "Yeah, that's mine."

"You gave this option on January second in return for five hundred cash."

"Yeah."

Madison straightened. "You dirty swine!"

Slenk tried to look him in the eyes. He failed.

"This option is good—far as it goes," Austen said, laying it back on the table. "What about yours, Madison?"

"My option was taken four months earlier—invalidates that one."

"Let's see yours," Doyle demanded.

"I'm not talking to you, sir!"

"You haven't got it!"

Madison's face flushed. He said with deadly slowness, "You are a damned liar—a cheap shyster liar."

Rock Doyle was on his feet. The scar stood out like a lightning streak as red poured into his swarthy face.

"I demand instant retraction."

"I don't apologize to pigs."

"Henry—shut up!" Fellowes was pressing the sportsman's arm. "Shut up!"

Madison shook himself free. Doyle, standing above him, said: "I'll kill you for that."

The horseman looked up, sneered, "Oh no, you won't. Haven't got the nerve. Besides, you are a damned liar." He turned his head as if dismissing an insolent menial.

Austen was between them now. "Cut it. We're here for facts only. When did you get this option, Doyle? Sit down before you answer."

Doyle sat down, carefully adjusted each trouser leg to preserve the crease, then answered:

"My friend Sam Bosun and I—we were returning from Palm Beach; it had been Christmas—"

Madison broke in: "Don't tell us that Gypsy owner has enough money to buy a Derby colt—or hire a mouthpiece like you!"

Austen made a warning gesture. Madison sat back in his chair. Doyle continued:

"We stopped at a track downstate where Guy Slenk was wintering Red Moon. We'd heard the hide was coming along fine, and if you want the facts, Major Austen, we understood Slenk—as usual—needed money."

"Well, that was my business," Slenk broke in from his side of the room.

"We made it ours before we left." Doyle spoke easily. "Slenk wanted to borrow five hundred. Bosun wanted an option on the colt, so—we reached terms. I drew up the paper. There it is. Says we can have the colt May first for fifteen thousand if we want him, and we wanted him May first and we want him now."

"Well?" Austen prompted.

"I went to Slenk a few days ago—May first—to take up this option. The colt had developed into true Derby caliber. Slenk refused to accept the option. Next day he had disappeared. So we appealed to the Commission." He touched his breast pocket.

"Inside here," Rock Doyle finished, "I have fifteen thousand, cash money—not a check—and we want the colt. Do we get Red Moon?"

"One minute." To Madison: "What have you to say?"

"I might say, Austen"—Madison leaned back, spoke impressively—"there's something funny about this business. Mr.—er—er— What's the name?" He glanced toward the attorney.

"Mr. Doyle."

"Quite right. Thank you. Something funny about this Doyle man's transaction. How does Sam Bosun, a Gypsy owner from Poverty Row, who never had two bales of hay at one time, suddenly blossom out with a high-tongued attorney and fifteen thousand in cash—not a check? Think this itself merits investigation."

"I demand—"

"Shut up, Doyle! Wait till I finish." Madison turned to Austen. "I charge that Bosun is not the owner of the option. That he's a dummy. That Doyle is representing a group of—"

"That's not true!"

"Don't tell me you don't represent—"

"Quiet—everybody!" Austen called. "Sit down, Doyle. Keep quiet, Madison."

Doyle and Madison glared at each other. Then the lawyer sat down, again adjusted knife-edged trousers over knees. Madison compressed his lips an instant, then grinned. He said:

"Takes seven generations before you can sit down without doing that!"

Doyle's head went back at the insult. He said nothing. Austen said: "Now state your case, Madison." The sportsman nodded. He was his assured self.

"You understand I have one of the biggest stables in the state," he said. "Some years ago this man Guy Slenk was an exercise boy for me. Then I made him into a jockey. Pretty good too. That right, Slenk?"

"Oh, er—yes sir—I sure was."

"Yes, you were. Then you went the way of all white trash—"

"Look-a here! I won't—"

"Shut up! I'm talking! Well, we won't go into that. Anyway, Slenk got too heavy to ride. So I helped him get a trainer's license. Since then he's been on his own, making a living. Well, Austen, you know how these Gypsy owners get by—borrow a bag of oats." Madison called over his shoulder, "You borrowed more from me than oats, didn't you, Slenk?"

"Get on with the option matter, Madison," Austen warned.

"Very well. Last August Fellowes and I were at the Saratoga sales together. Two-year-old colt with Man o' War blood on his dam's side was led in one night—after yearlings had been sold. Was tossed in—sort of a soupçon—if you know what I mean. He had never started—been tied up in an estate. I saw possibilities in him, so started bidding. Then Slenk began bidding. I've always felt sorry for him. Had a poor start in life."

"Look-a here, Mr. Madison"—Slenk was on his feet at last—"I stood a lot, but you goin' too far—"

Austen broke in: "He's right, Madison. Go on with your statement. And you, Slenk, sit down!"

Slenk sat down slowly. Madison went on:

"I saw Slenk wanted the colt—nobody else did. I thought I'd favor him. I quit bidding—colt knocked down to him for eight hundred—and he didn't have eight hundred."

"I had six seventy-five," Slenk growled.

Madison ignored him. "You know Saratoga sales, Austen: cash on the barrelhead if you have no credit. Slenk's credit—we won't go into that. He came over. What did he say, Dr. Fellowes?"

The physician cleared his throat. "Why, he—ah—"

"Go on—tell 'em. You were there!"

"Slenk wanted to borrow one hundred twenty-five dollars."

"Right. What did I say—exact words?"

"Exact words—I can't swear to them." Fellowes frowned.

"Well, what was the sense of what I said?" Madison was irritated.

"You thought he was—ah—slow in repaying."

Madison had turned, was facing the other man. "Will you please tell what took place? You remember, don't you?"

"Please—I don't like that, Madison. You said—as well as I remember—that you didn't—"

"Wouldn't!"

"Yes—wouldn't lend him money. You'd pay it for an option on the colt."

"Pretty cheap!" Rock Doyle nodded his head.

"Sir!" from Madison.

Rock Doyle nodded again, but his lips stayed closed.

"Mr. Madison, here," Fellowes went on, "gave Slenk the money—in cash—payment for an option to buy the colt by May first for five thousand if it developed into Derby caliber."

Austen spoke: "Put that option in writing?"

"Course not!" Madison bristled. "You know the turf, Austen. Nine tenths of the transactions are by word of mouth. Besides, I had Fellowes as a witness."

"It ain't so!" The words were blurted out by Slenk.

"What?" The exclamation came from Madison. He whirled around.

Slenk was on his feet. "Look here, Major, this here colt's worth twenty-five thousand. This here Madison can't steal him for five thou—" He stopped; his jaw dropped in amazement, for Madison turned a sudden devastating flow of invective on him: a stream of lurid charges, mainly concerned with the trainer's maternal ancestry, ancient and medieval and modern.

The trainer's gloved hands went up. "You can't call my mammy that—I'll kill you!"

"Shut up, rat!"

Austen stepped in front of Slenk, pushed him into his chair. He turned around. "Keep quiet. I'm going to talk. When each of you—Doyle, Madison—tried to enforce your options, you say Slenk ran away." He turned around, backed off from the trainer. "What did you run for, Slenk?"

Silence.

"Come on. Why?"

"If a coupla rich guys was tryin' to steal your colt—"

"Then you did give those options!"

Again silence.

"And you ran into another state so those options couldn't be exercised!"

Sullenly the trainer rubbed his hands together. "Aw, sure."

George Trigg spoke up from beside Austen: "I found you in that there gamblin' joint—yanked you back too."

Slenk stared at the floor. Austen said:

"The facts are established. Everyone agree to stand by my decision? Speak up—or shut up!"

He glanced from man to man. Slowly Madison's head nodded, then Doyle's. "What about you, Slenk?"

Slenk glared. "What else can I do?"

"Do you—or not?"

At last the trainer spoke. "Yeah," he said.

"Very well. The colt, Red Moon, goes to Madison, who had the first option. Madison, have you a certified check?"

"I have."

He passed the paper. "Slenk," said Austen, "make out a bill of sale." Slenk went to the table, began writing laboriously. At that moment a figure emerged from a far corner—a figure that had been lost in the evening shadows.

It was Danny Barton, the jockey. He stepped into the center of that dusk-darkened room.

"Please, if Red Moon's going to win tomorrow I—I got a lot to say!"

4

"Huh! Wondered what you were doing here." Henry Madison spoke first. "Could hardly see you—in the corner."

Austen stepped to the wall, turned an old-fashioned switch. A chandelier in the ceiling's center lighted up. Danny Barton's eyes blinked—once. Hands, holding his hat, shook, then steadied themselves. He looked up at the sportsman.

"Well?" said Madison.

"It's this way, Mr. Madison: Guy Slenk engaged me to ride Red Moon in the Derby. I want to ask, sir—if—if I go with the colt."

"You do not. My contract jockey rides for me tomorrow."

Barton threw his thin shoulders back. "I was spoken for this mount last fall," he added. "I turned down a dozen other offers—"

"Hard luck."

"Now it's too late to get the leg up on another entry—all of 'em have their jocks."

"Too bad."

Barton turned a drawn face on Slenk. "You said you'd fix it up for me to ride if anybody else got Red Moon."

The trainer looked up and glared. "Pipe down! Don't you see I got troubles?"

"I don't want to mix in, Madison," Austen spoke casually, "but the lad has a moral claim—"

"Moral claim? To hell with it! Tend to your own business."

"It is my business—seeing that horses on our track run to win."

"What's this? No damned flatfoot can tell me—"

"Careful, there!" Austen stepped up to Madison. "You'd better be careful, Madison."

"Say!" Madison moved back, looked at his companion. "What do you know?—this flatfoot's getting touchy."

"Suggest you listen to Barton, Madison." Austen was intent on the job in hand. "Go on—speak up, boy."

"I got somethin' to tell you, Mr. Madison—somethin' you don't know about that colt." The jockey spoke rapidly.

"Nothing you can tell me!"

"Yes, there is! I can tell you how to win with him—nobody else knows that!"

"What're you talking about!"

"Mr. Madison, you know this colt never started till Slenk trained him. And he never won 'cept when I rode him. Look up the past performances!"

"Slenk have him pulled?"

"Course not! He was tryin' to win, but I was the only boy who learned how to handle Red Moon. It's my secret! That's why Slenk wanted me to ride him in the Derby. I never lost when I rode him. I won that mile and a sixteenth at Keeneland with him 'leven days ago."

"A clown could have won with him that day! Colt was on edge—and the best horse in the race."

"Naw, he warn't the best horse, but I got more speed out of him. I'll get the speed tomorrow too; he'll sulk for any other boy."

"You're crazy!" The horseman turned his shoulder.

"I've watched the colt, Madison," Austen explained. "I believe the boy's telling the truth."

Madison whirled around. "It'll be my loss—not yours—if he doesn't win."

"Your loss—and the loss of thousands of others."

"How so?"

"Last winter, when Derby nominations were made, Slenk told the papers Barton would ride. You know what happened. In a hundred cities women and men began betting in the future books, betting on Red Moon. And why? Because they knew Barton never took a mount unless he felt he could win."

"And I think Red Moon's going to win," Madison broke in, "with my contract jock on him."

"Don't think so, Madison. And I think the public has a right to a run for its money."

"Just a minute, young man!" Madison looked Austen over insolently. "You're overstepping your duties. I have a right to put the jock I want on my horse. I want my boy because I think he can win with this colt. Even if I didn't think so I'm under no obligation to wet-nurse fools—and only fools bet on horse races. You know I never bet." Madison strutted. "I get my thrill out of winning big stakes."

"Mr. Madison," Barton broke in with growing boldness, "will you listen if I show you how to save sixty-five hundred dollars?"

"Huh?"

"Winnin' rider by custom gets ten per cent of the purse, don't he? Derby'll be worth about sixty-five thousand dollars to the winner tomorrow."

"Well?" Madison growled as the boy hesitated.

"I—I had a few dollars saved in January. The day the bookies began takin' bets on the Derby I—I got a good bet down. At good odds too. I—I stand to win a lot of money

if Red Moon wins. So I'll ride him for you for nothin'—
and I'll win!"

Madison looked at him coldly. "Huh! You rode a race
for me at New Orleans once that I didn't like."

"I know," Barton shot back, "and I didn't like it either.
I had to sweat off five pounds in a hurry to make the
lightweight. I was so weak I couldn't hold him against the
rail—he run out on the turn."

"Bosh! You're not fit to ride a ring-boned jackass, you
hillbilly!"

"Mr. Madison!"

"How do I know you won't pull Red Moon?"

"It's—it's—it's a lie if you think that!"

Utter silence for an instant. Then Madison's right arm
shot out. The open palm of his hand crashed into the
rider's face.

Danny Barton fell back. His shoulder struck the wall.
He leaned against it in a half crouch for an instant. A bit
of red trickled from his nose. He straightened up slowly,
his face a dark red.

Austen reached out, seized Madison's shoulders. "I'll be
damned! You weigh more than two hundred—"

The sportsman drew in a deep breath. His face now was
red. "Sorry, sorry," he muttered. "I—I just can't stand—
anyone—calling me a liar."

Fellowes, who had been standing to one side, came up.
"It's time you were leaving," he said in an odd voice.

"All right." Madison looked around at the jockey. Barton had a handkerchief to his nose. He blew his nose,
held the handkerchief there a moment, then put it in his
pocket.

Madison's hand went out. "Shake, Barton? Sorry,
y'know." But the boy didn't take the outstretched hand.
He picked up his hat, went to the door, stood there a

moment, again put his handkerchief to his nose—a hand-kerchief now half red—then put the handkerchief back in his pocket. He opened the door, started through it, then turned around, said quietly:

"You hit me once, Mr. Madison. You won't live to hit me again."

He walked out, closed the door behind him.

"Well, well!" Madison blustered. "Guess you all heard the threat?"

"I saw the blow too," Austen said evenly.

Madison flushed. He turned to his companion. "Come on—we're here too long."

"I'll say so!" Fellowes muttered. "This time you've gone too far."

"All right—all right. Where's that bill of sale?"

Slenk gave it to him. Madison took it, held it at arm's length, puckered his eyes, and nodded. He put the paper in a pin-seal billfold.

Rock Doyle, who had been standing on the other side of the table—calm and silent—spoke now: "I'll give you thirty thousand for Red Moon—thirty thousand cash."

"Not interested," said Madison without looking at him.

"And twenty per cent of what he wins tomorrow."

"The answer is no." Madison was putting on a pair of old pigskin gloves.

"Forty per cent of his win."

Madison turned to his companion. "Come on, Ralph," he said, and after nodding to Austen he and the physician left the room.

Rock Doyle took up his hat. "Thank you, Major Austen, for your trouble."

Austen bowed and watched Doyle go out the door. Slenk got up, looked around warily, scowled at George Trigg. He turned, slammed through the door.

"That's that!" Austen said, sitting in the chair behind the table.

The phone bell rang once. Then twice. Austen picked up the receiver.

"Yes?"

Trigg stood by, eyes on his boss's face.

Austen's brow creased into a frown. "One minute, please!" His free hand doubled into a fist, struck the table.

"Do you know what you are talking about, young lady? . . . You certain of that?" His manner became swift and direct. "Then don't tell me—tell the police. And if you'll wait one minute—" His left hand covered the transmitter; he spoke in low tones to Trigg: "Run out and stop Madison. Bring him back here." Then, into the transmitter, "Just hold the line for a second or so. I'm going to let you tell that to Mr. Madison himself—tell him that someone is going to kill him tonight. He'll be interested."

5

A click sounded over the wire just as George Trigg shuffled fast through the doorway.

"Hello!" No response. Austen jiggled the hook. Then came the drone on the wire, indicating the line was free for a call. The woman had hung up.

Austen waited a moment. The bell sounded. He lifted the receiver. "The telephone office, sir. Speak with Mr. Roderick Austen, please."

"This is he."

"You wished your incoming calls traced, sir?"

"Yes. That last call—"

"It was made by a woman. From a pay station in the Brown Hotel. It did not pass through the hotel switchboard."

"Thank you."

Austen frowned with annoyance, pushed the phone from him. He was staring at it when Trigg came in, puffing.

"He—he got away," the ex-jockey gasped.

"Get your breath and tell it."

Trigg puffed like a locomotive's exhaust.

"His car—Madison's—parked halfway down block. Saw him—I did—getting in—"

"Take your time. And where was Fellowes?"

31

"Fellowes? Oh, he was walking around the side of the car."

"Did he get in with Madison?"

"I—guess so. Wait—he could-a crossed the street. Lot o' people movin' around."

"Go on."

"When I—I was a hunnerd feet away the Doyle man stopped Madison, as Madison was slippin' behind the wheel. Madison looked out—face was ugly. Must-a cussed Doyle."

"What makes you think so?"

"Well, I see Doyle double up his fists—like he was fixin' to fight. Madison drove off. That quick, a-fore I could stop him. I hollered. No good."

"Then what?"

"Doyle hopped into a car parked right behind Madison's—drove after him."

"Why didn't you hop a ride—catch Madison?"

"I—I didn't think."

"I see." Austen's lips shut tightly.

"That was the—the gal, Major? That last call?"

Austen nodded. "The girl," he corrected. "Same one."

"What'd she want?"

Austen answered obliquely, as if speaking to himself:

"Said if I'd stay right here for twenty minutes—how in thunder did she get this address?—that she'd send me proof she wasn't joking. Then she hung up."

"Wasn't jokin' about what, Major?"

"About somebody gunning for Madison."

"Humph! Three men here this afternoon want to kill him." Trigg's head nodded sagely. "That's no joke, neither."

"The girl says this is no joke." His hand grasped the telephone.

"She tryin' to save Madison?"

Austen glanced up, with his free hand rubbed his thick brown hair. "I gather she's trying to protect some friend—a friend who evidently wants to rub Madison out."

"Ah!" Trigg's lantern jaw dropped wide. "She's got a feller—'fraid he'll be caught—wants you to protect him while he—he—"

"No, wants me to stop her boy friend, I'd say." He lifted the phone receiver.

"Then why don't she spill everythin'? Why this secret-meetin' business?"

"You ask!" Austen broke in, then dialed the number of the Pendennis Club. A moment later: "Please page Mr. Shepherd Thomas of Chicago. You may find him in the grill."

After a short time:

"'Lo, Shep—Rod Austen. . . . Fine! . . . If you can leave the gang long enough—or bring 'em with you if you want to"—he grinned into the transmitter—"you might care to drop in—got a private place. . . . Oh no, nothing important at all! Would like to ask you a question, Shep, about the boys in Chicago. . . . Swell, thanks—no rush!"

He disconnected, grinned again, and spoke aloud:

"He'll be here in the shake of a hungry dog's tail. He can scent a yarn a mile off." And to Trigg: "You know Shep Thomas?"

"Jees, yes. He liked the *leppers*. When I was ridin' for old Ed Corrigan at Hawthorne he ust-a come out—"

"Didn't know he was that old."

"He's no spring chicken! He—"

Austen nodded, raised a hand for silence, again lifted the phone, and dialed Madison's home. A servant answered. Mr. Madison had just been there and had just left. Said he had business to tend to—didn't say where he was going.

That was that. Then the doorbell rang. Austen waved his thumb. Trigg shambled happily out to answer it.

Austen heard him greeting Shep Thomas, then the two coming down the hallway.

A tall, thin chap sauntered into the room, his clothes hanging carelessly on him. He was of middling years and thinning light hair, with eyes sharp as his long nose.

"'Lo, fellow, why didn't you bring the gang along?"

"Huh? And let 'em in on a big beat? Not that crazy! How you been?"

Austen waved him to a chair. Trigg closed the door. "Sorry, I got no liquor."

"Don't need it, my friend!" Shep Thomas threw himself back in a chair and closed his eyes a second. A look of contentment crossed his long, lean face.

"I just met eleven hundred Kentucky Colonels." He spoke in crisp accents. "Each wanted to give me a drink. Hospitality—my word!" His eyes opened. "Got a few admirals loose around here?"

His face sobered. He leaned forward, and a different Shep Thomas spoke.

"Thanks, but no drinks till after the Derby." His deep-set blue eyes narrowed an instant under jutting eyebrows: "Rod—what's up?"

Austen was silent a moment. He said thoughtfully:

"Shep, my business is to keep racing straight—not to catch murderers."

"Who's been killed?"

"That's the point—nobody. But there's something in the wind, and it isn't attar of roses. I thought you might sniff out a fact or two. You're the murder expert of the Chicago press."

"Rather see a horse race any day!" He looked around. "Huh! Something's happened in this room—a few minutes ago."

Thomas was like a bird dog on the scent.

"I feel it—and I see things." He peered around. "Rug's rumpled—chairs skewed round. Your table—you're more orderly than that! Pen here—ink bottle there—why no fountain pen? Ink blotches just spilt—by somebody else, 'cause you don't spill ink—but your fingers rubbed across that ink not long ago."

"Why not long ago?"

"Simple—primary. Oh lud! You wash your hands four or five times daily! They're still ink-stained."

So they were. Austen noticed it for the first time. "Go on, boy," he said. "You're good."

"Agreement had to be signed—in secrecy, or you'd been in Commission's office. And why didn't you—?" He paused, looked intently at Austen.

"Why what?"

"Why didn't you give the man your fountain pen? I know!" He raised a finger like a teacher to a pupil. "Trainers have heavy hands, don't they? Would have ruined your pen. Right?" Austen said nothing.

Thomas went on:

"So it's about the Derby! See that window, Austen? If you look through that window and look through a lot of houses you'll see Churchill Downs. In a little while they're going to tuck in at the Downs, but it'll be broken slumber! America's greatest race tomorrow—a fistful of champion three-year-olds, a purse of seventy-five thousand dollars. Some owners been trying to win that race for years. There'll be a hundred thousand jamming stands and rails—were ninety-five thousand there last Derby day—remember?"

Austen nodded. Said softly: "Go on, poet, what could you do on two drinks?"

"Never mind. A lot more climbed the fences and sat on stable roofs. Yes sir—one of the great races of the world is about to be run, and—and—" His manner changed again.

He leaned forward, asked quietly: "Any dirty work, Austen? There never has been—"

"And there never will be!" Austen broke in with force. "But there's something stirring. On the surface it has no bearing on the Derby—save that a man mentioned owns a couple of Derby hopes. And he—"

"And somebody wants to kill him!"

Austen nodded.

Thomas nodded. "I can name him. Madison—right?"

"How'd you guess?"

"Didn't guess—just put known facts together, got the answer. Madison's hot-tempered; Madison's arrogant; Madison's filthy rich—filthy nasty—always chasing skirts. Only thing in his favor is that he runs his horses to win. He does do that. His one hope of heaven. I'd say a lady is mixed up in it, so spill it all from the start, m'lad!"

Austen told him all. Thomas nodded. "I guessed it!" Then, "The skunk—hitting Danny Barton. That's the best jock in America, got the finest hands and seat. He can win with Red Moon. Doubt if anybody else can."

"Good story, Shep?"

"I'll say it is." His body moved toward the phone.

"Wait—your paper doesn't go to press for several hours, and the Press Department will release it to everybody. That is, the bare facts—that Red Moon runs in Madison's colors."

Thomas was disappointed. "Can't I tell what happened here?"

"Well, er—"

"Sure, we'll fix that up!" Thomas swept over Austen's hesitation. "But look here—something funny about this. About Sam Bosun having fifteen thousand to pay for a horse. He's been racing in Chicago for years."

"Go on! I knew you could fill in the pieces."

"He's always broke. Nothing but a cheap-selling plater or two in his barn. Wait! Not so funny, either. Say—" He looked keenly at Austen. "Now I know what you got me over here for! Yep, and I'll tell you. Bosun—he's just a tool."

"Sure," Austen agreed. "He's out of the picture now. Yet—"

"Anything can happen, eh? And you want to see it don't happen! Right?"

Austen nodded. "Go on, boy."

"Tell you what I know: Last month sixty grand, sixty thousand smackers—sixty thousand bucks to you—were bet in the Big Store in Chicago. On Red Moon—to win the Derby. You know the Big Store—biggest gambling joint in America."

Austen nodded. Shep Thomas continued:

"They take bets on world series, football games, on races—and specialize in taking future bets on the Derby. The Big Store—I happen to know—laid five to one against Red Moon's chances. That's liberal odds against the favorite—a week before the race. Now I understand." He slapped his thin thigh. "Get it?"

Austen played dumb. "Get what?"

"Easy! Future betting is play or pay—that is, you bet your money, and if the horse wins you are paid; if he loses you lose; but there's this big catch—and that's why they give you bigger than post-time odds:

"If the horse is scratched—doesn't start for any reason—you don't get your money back. You lose the coin you put up. Can't you see the Big Store laying its plans? Red Moon was the fall champion among two-year-olds—"

"After Danny Barton made a winner of him."

"Sure. And Red Moon became winter favorite. Can't you see a crook like Bosun acting as a tool? Have him take an option on the horse and plan to take up that option at the last minute if the colt stands out, in the meanwhile taking all bets offered? So"—Thomas' voice showed excitement—"sixty thousand is bet on Red Moon in the Big Store. The Big Store wants to take up that option and scratch Red Moon out of the race. It's perfectly willing to put up the fifteen thousand. But Madison beat 'em to the horse."

"Who's Rock Doyle?"

"Where you been these years?"

"Not in Chicago."

"So I gathered. He's a Levantine—brought to Chi as a babe. Fought way through school. Took good Irish name of Doyle for political purposes. He's an undercover man—an adviser in politics. And, I happen to know, the shyster who advises the Big Store."

"Fine! Now where does the woman come in—the one who's been telephoning me?"

"Simple! The platinum blonde with Doyle—maybe." He hesitated a minute. "You didn't hear her voice. You saw her recognize Madison. Maybe Madison and Doyle been scrapping over her—maybe Doyle had threatened before to kill Madison. Maybe the girl really loves Doyle—while flirting with Madison. Maybe not. But wants to protect Doyle—" He broke off as the house bell rang.

Shortly Trigg ushered in a rheumy-eyed old messenger who said, "Western Union for Major Austen—that is, pers'nal message."

He handed Austen an envelope stamped Brown Hotel.

"Sign here, mister."

Austen signed. Gave him a quarter. "Wait a second." He tore open the envelope; a batch of green bank notes fell out.

"Great lud!" said Shep Thomas as the bills cascaded to the floor.

6

Austen stooped, picked up four fifty-dollar bills, one ten-dollar note, and a crumpled dollar bill. Nothing else had been sent with the money—no message of any kind. Austen looked at the torn envelope: his name and address were printed in ink—not written on it.

"Who gave you this to deliver, Cap?"

"I dunno."

"A woman. I know." Austen spoke quickly over his shoulder to Thomas and Trigg. "Last time she phoned—from the Brown Hotel tool—she said if I stayed here twenty minutes she'd send evidence that she was serious. I'll say she is." Then, to the messenger: "It was a woman?"

"Well, yes, mister. I was head of the line. They send three-four of us there—for Derby time. A young'un—had one of them newfangled veils, couldn't see her face plain—come in. I heard her say: 'Deliver to Mr.—Major Rod—Rod—'"

"Roderick?"

"'Roderick Austen.' She give the envelope to the clerk, told him your number—but it's already printed there—give him a dollar bill, said give me the change, then she was back in the crowd, quick-like. Awful jam there tonight, Derby folk—"

"How was she dressed?"

"I—I don't rec'lect."

"Know her if you saw her again?"

"I—I didn't see her. That veil—her face—I mean—"

"That's all, Cap. Thank you." Trigg hurried the old man out and was back in a flash.

Austen sat fingering the bills. "See this money? From the woman who was phoning me—of course. Can you feature a girl, scared and trying to protect her man, grabbing every cent she had and shipping it to a detective she don't even know as a retainer?"

He held up a hand. "Don't ask me why she did it this way, why she won't even say who she is, but I've a notion I'll hear again—soon. Wait."

He reached for the phone and dialed Madison's house. No answer. "H'm'm. That's funny. Always a couple of servants there."

Again he dialed; again no answer.

Austen thought a moment; no one spoke. Then, "I was a fool to take that envelope—to open it."

"Why, Major?" Trigg asked.

"It obligates me to help her, and I've got no business mixing in anything that's not connected with racing."

"I'd say there's plenty of racing in this." Shep Thomas spoke with a drawl, a habit when he was thinking deeply.

"Trigg, I've been left at the post," Austen said suddenly, ignoring Thomas.

"How come, Major?"

"Should have been watching that woman—with Rock Doyle. Remember? He sent her away. I've an idea she'll show up, herself—at Madison's tonight. If she does, cover her."

"Tail her?"

"Yep. Follow her—cover her—shadow her—let me know what happens."

Trigg had been gone five minutes—five minutes of thought for Thomas and Austen—when the telephone rang.

It was the unknown girl again. Her voice came in throaty contralto tones: "You believe me now, don't you? You have my retainer by this time."

"Look here, young woman"—Austen's voice was sharp—"this has gone too far! If you won't come here tell me where to meet you."

"Major Austen"—a note of anxiety in her tones—"this afternoon I could have met you—alone. Now—impossible. But if Henry Madison is murdered tonight I know the wrong man will be caught—" Her voice broke off. At the same instant Austen heard an overtone, as if someone were speaking behind her. He thought he heard ". . . *fifteen minutes* . . ." That was all. Evidently she placed her hand over the transmitter.

"Heh—what's this?"

She answered him in gay tones, "Darling, I'll call you in exactly forty-five minutes!"

The phone clicked off.

Austen drew in a deep breath, then smiled at the newspaper reporter. "Figure this one out, big boy." He recounted her words. Then the phone sounded again. The chief operator: that last call was from a wagon diner in the heart of the city. About eight minutes' walk from the Brown Hotel, Austen figured. So the girl was changing her base of operations!

Shep Thomas sat rubbing his hands together slowly, saying nothing.

"Tried to tip Madison off—couldn't reach him," Austen said.

"Huh! Wouldn't be the first time somebody gunned after him—over a skirt," the reporter added. "The fellow's always in danger of somebody taking a pot shot. He knows it."

"I've got to make out a report on this afternoon's meeting for the Commission," Austen said, opening his portable typewriter. "If you want to stick around—but I don't want to keep you from the Kentucky Colonels." Austen grinned.

"Try and throw me out." Thomas grinned back. "I've an idea that phone is going to ring again, so I'm standing by." He threw a leg over the chair's arm, settled himself comfortably.

Austen typed his report, then looked up, saying:

"Shep, I'm doubly dumb tonight."

Shep opened an eye. "How so?"

"I should have tipped the cops off—that Madison has been threatened."

"And be laughed at for your trouble? I know cops, my friend, and they know Henry Madison. They know the guy's going to be bumped off someday, so why worry?"

"Just the same—" Austen dialed police headquarters.

"Give me the desk." He got it. "Sergeant? Roderick Austen speaking. I think you should be warned, Sarge, that someone may take a crack at Henry Madison tonight—"

The desk sergeant interrupted him. Austen's hand gripped the receiver tighter; he looked quickly at Shep Thomas. The newspaperman was already sitting forward on the edge of his chair.

Austen said: "You sure, Sarge? . . . Who did it? . . . Oh, he did! Sure of that too? . . . Well, thanks, Sarge." He disconnected.

The investigator turned to his guest. "Well, Shep—" As he spoke those two words the phone jangled. Austen grabbed the receiver.

"Yes?" It was the vibrant voice of the girl again. Austen took the offensive. "You called on time—to the split second," he said. "Certainly I shall take your case. Henry Madison has just been killed."

Austen heard Thomas' chair go back. The reporter was standing over him as he repeated, "I say, Henry Madison has just been killed."

A gasp came over the wire.

Austen spoke again: "And they caught your man at the scene—police say."

Sharp resonance came into the girl's tones, so sharp that Shep Thomas, a hand on Austen's shoulder, heard her words:

"My man?" she repeated.

"That's what they say."

"Who—what man?" The question came in incredulous tones. "Who is he—his name?"

"The jock—Danny Barton."

"Barton? Danny Barton—the rider?"

"Yes—so police say."

A sigh of relief broke over the wire. Then, "Thank God, thank God!"

The phone clicked off.

7

Shep Thomas shook Austen's shoulder in excitement. "Heh, Major—that on the level? Madison's been killed?"

"I hope you heard. I held the receiver up for you, Shep."

"Gimme that phone!"

As he seized it the phone bell rang again. Thomas shouted into the transmitter, "Hello—hello—get off the line! Give me the *Courier* office— Oh Hades!"

In disgust he passed the receiver to Austen. "It's the chief operator. Make her get off, Major."

The operator reported the last call as coming from a pay station in the wagon diner.

"Thanks," Austen said, giving the instrument to the newspaperman.

"Heh! The *Courier* office—quick. I don't know the number. You do; give it to me!" Leaning over the table, he held the instrument in one hand, pounded the table with the other. At last:

"*Courier?* City desk—quick." His feet quit moving; he ceased pounding the table. A high-powered reporter was going into action. He said to Austen over the receiver: "My copy's being syndicated. *Courier* takes it. I'll give 'em a flash and a bulletin. They'll put it on the wires for Chicago." Then:

"City desk? Shep Thomas speaking. Got anything on Henry Madison's murder? No, then here goes!

"FLASH! Henry Madison, leading turfman, killed; Jockey Barton held—on Kentucky Derby eve. Now get ready for bulletin."

In the *Courier* office the eye-shaded city editor was calling for an extra even as he penciled the flash for the telegraph lines. Lifting his shade, glancing over his spectacles, he was calling: "Frierson—take number two. Henry Madison killed—Shep Thomas on the wire."

And in Austen's apartment Shep Thomas began barking out his story:

"You can take this as I give it to you, fellow:

"Henry Madison, America's foremost turfman, was shot and killed tonight shortly after he obtained possession of Red Moon, favorite in tomorrow's Kentucky Derby.

"Daniel Barton, last season's leading jockey, was caught at the scene of the crime and is held by police for investigation.

"Madison's death, which occurred shortly after nightfall— Heh? . . . Wait!" He covered the instrument, asked Austen, "At Madison's home?"

Austen nodded. "Cops said on his place—in his office —a little one-room structure to one side of his residence."

"Thanks." Thomas lifted his receiver, went on: "Hello? Yes, his body was found in his office, a one-room structure to one side of his house. You'll know it. . . . No, I don't know all about Barton yet. Hell's bells, man, I've just given you the flash. Now take what led up to the man's murder—and maybe Barton didn't do it; I just said the cops caught him at the scene of the crime.

"Madison's death followed a secret meeting this afternoon in the apartment of Major Roderick Austen, investigator for the Racing Commission.

"This meeting was called to determine ownership of the colt, Red Moon. While registered in the name of Guy Slenk, both Henry Madison and Sam Bosun, a Gypsy trainer from Poverty Row, claimed to have options on the colt.

"Madison to buy for five thousand dollars—Bosun to buy for fifteen thousand dollars. . . . Hell's bells, man, I don't know how Bosun got that dough—don't ask me!" He turned an agonized face on Austen a minute, said: "Smart guy, he is." Then:

"Come on—here goes: Slenk had refused to accept either option and had fled across the state line. He was caught, brought back, and was present at the afternoon's meeting.

"At this meeting Madison was threatened with death three times: by Guy Slenk, by Rock Doyle—Chicago lawyer representing Sam Bosun—and by Barton. Slenk and Doyle both argued with Madison about the colt's ownership. Jockey Barton had a discussion about riding the nag in tomorrow's Derby.

"Barton had been promised the leg up by Slenk—then Slenk lost the colt to Madison, the Commission ruling that Madison had the right to exercise his option.

"Madison said his contract jock would ride Red Moon. Barton and Madison had words. Madison, who weighs more than two hundred, slapped Barton against the wall—Barton rides at one hundred and eight. Madison apologized; Barton refused to shake hands. Said, as he went out the door, 'You won't live to hit me again.'

"It is said on good authority that Sam Bosun—who didn't get his hands on Red Moon—was only a tool of a Chicago gambling syndicate. . . . All right, all right, don't print that if you don't want to!

"Now I'm hopping down to the police station. Might shoot out an extra, and don't forget to gimme my by-line

—get me? It's Shep Thomas, in case you've forgotten. And thanks, fellow!"

He put the phone down and mopped his face.

"Major, you sure gave me a beat—thanks."

"Quick work, Shep, but didn't you lay it pretty hard on Barton?"

"Huh? I thought I gave him a break. Why, man, this is going to be one of the big yarns of the year—old Henry Madison killed at last! Know what they do and say in the Kentucky hills when such a man is killed?"

"No—what?"

"They let the sweetheart or husband go free, and the jury says: 'The deceased should have went!' Same goes for Madison, but something in my bones says Barton is innocent. Let's work on this together—what say?"

Austen reached for his hat. "We are—already. Even if this unknown girl hadn't phoned me I'd investigate for the Racing Commission. Barton's one of our own. We don't want him railroaded—if innocent. Let's go."

As they went down the hallway he explained:

"Barton's not the killer kind. He may have got mad, taken a drink, gone to Madison's house to argue the riding of Red Moon. He stands to take a lot in the future books if Red Moon wins, you know. And remember, Shep, a lot of men have wanted to kill Madison at one time or another."

"Yeah, but they say they caught this fellow with the goods."

"Sure—the cops say it. Smart thing to do—nab a man instantly—but the boy may have reached the place just as someone else killed the turfman and ran."

"Oh, sure." They got into Austen's car, started for police headquarters. Shep Thomas added: "There's the woman too. She wanted somebody protected—somebody who was gunning for Madison. Say! May have been her man who bumped Madison off!"

"Yep, it might." Austen tooled around a stalled truck.

"Your phone's unlisted—how'd she get your number?"

"I've been wondering."

"I can tell you—a ten-spot did it."

"When and how?"

"Don't know when, but if it was Doyle's secretary—well, Doyle could have got it from the Commission."

"They wouldn't give it to the President himself."

"Not officially," Thomas conceded. "but a ten-spot to some poor devil in the office. Ten-spots are magic workers sometimes. Then the woman gets it from Doyle."

"If it's that girl," Austen reminded him.

"Yes, if. Cinch she isn't his secretary. Well, maybe she is! Who am I to say?"

"May not have been the platinum blonde at all. My mind's open on that."

"So's mine—just hunching."

They parked around the corner from police headquarters, and Austen led the way into the detectives' quarters. He knew the captain of detectives was on sick leave; that an assistant was sitting in. The latter—large and heavy-jowled, with a big link watch chain across his vest—met them genially.

"Hel-lo, Major! Thought you'd be showin' up! You racetrack fellows stick together, eh? But it's no use, Major. This is an open-and-shut case—and right now it's shut."

"Yes? As a little favor to me, Captain"—he gave the assistant the courtesy title—"wish you'd tell us all about it. This is Shepherd Thomas—"

"Not tellin' a thing to the press; they just got a whiff of it. We say Madison's killed dead; Barton's arrested at the scene with a pistol—and sayin' nothin' else tonight."

"Shep—he's not even a local man—Chicago fellow—"

"Oh, he is! Bring him right in. We'll show him a thing or two. Come in the front office, Major. But it's no use.

One of my flatfoots was on the job. Caught this kid Barton doin' the deed."

"Caught him killing Madison?"

"Well, same thing—almost. Come in." He shut the door to the private office. "The officer's makin' out his report. I'll let you talk to him in a minute."

8

The patrolman who had brought Danny Barton to the station house was dictating the end of his report. A stolid, beefy-faced man, huge in build, he ballooned now with importance.

". . . and that's how I caught the murderer."

"Swell, Tiny." The captain's tone was warm. "Now here's Major Austen, the gimlet eye of the Racin' Commission. He's come to help you find the man who killed Madison. He's got a friend too."

"They're too late," Tiny stated with dignity. "I caught the lad red-handed meself, and with a gat in his breeches pocket at that."

Austen began with diplomacy: "One thing I always liked about you, Tiny, is that you are always on the job. Now you know everything affecting racing. Well, I've got to make a report to the Commission. Now, like a good fellow, tell us everything."

The big cop's jaws worked thoughtfully. "Cap, want to show him the report?"

"I'd rather have you tell it to me, Tiny." Austen spoke quickly.

"All right, Cap?"

The acting head nodded. "Well, sir, it was about eight-ten—well, make it eight-twenty; mebbe eight twenty-five.

51

I pull my box for the eight o'clock call when I'm walkin', slow-like, down the Shore Road—keepin' my eyes peeled.

"Madison, God rest his soul, was always a friend of mine. Every Christmas he give me a double sawbuck, an' I always keep me eye cocked on that mansion of his. I knew he had enemies, lots of 'em, specially these here foreigners who come down here with their horses.

"Well, here I was walkin' along; I see the house dark, and I say, 'That's funny.' I thought he'd be celebratin' night before the Derby. Then I see a light to the left and kind of back of the mansion. I knew that was in his office—one-room brick house out in the yard. You seen it, Major?"

"Been in it many a time."

"Where he did business—talked with people he didn't want to let in the big house."

"You were one, m'lad," Shep Thomas whispered into Austen's ear.

"Go to thunder!" Austen grinned back.

"That office is kind of surrounded by bushes and shrub stuff. I been there many a night. In winter he use to—but nev' mind that. He's got a lot of his guns on the wall—pistols, rifles. Sort of a hobby.

"Well, sir, I was takin' a good look toward that office and thinkin' a bit, when I hear a shot—just like this." The patrolman slapped his hands together. "Then I knew there'd been some dirty work. I opened my coat, pulled my cannon out, threw off the safety, and started poundin' up that driveway what leads to the office."

"Did you hear a shout or a cry?" Austen asked.

"Nary sound. Just as I'm halfway up—you know, it's cloudy-dark tonight—well, just as I'm halfway up a man runs right smack by me. I sense him comin'. I throw out my arms. I make a flyin' tackle—"

"Did he bump into you in the dark, Tiny?"

"No sir-ree! I tell you, I sensed him passin'—couldn't see. He tried to fight—he slashed at me—and after a desp'rate struggle I give him a swift one right in the mug. And—"

"Your weight, Tiny?" Austen interposed softly.

"Two sixty-eight—every ounce muscle too. As I was sayin'—"

"I see." Austen nodded.

"I frisked him quick-like and took a gat outa his pocket. The gun that's there on the cap's table. I put my hand around his throat and I walk him back to that office, and what do I see?"

He paused, looked straight at Austen.

"I've no idea, Tiny. You tell us."

"I see poor Mr. Madison kind of halfway slidin' over a table, and there's a red place on his forehead. That's where this man—this kid—this jockey I caught—this Barton—shot him. Poor Madison was dead. I put in a call to the station from his own phone, holdin' Barton safe. And that's all. I got the kid that did the job."

Tiny sat back, wiped his forehead, though the room wasn't hot.

"Who else did you see running away from there, Tiny?" It was Shep Thomas' question.

"Who else?" Tiny walled his little eyes up at the gangling reporter. "Nobody—that's who else."

"Did you hear anybody running away?" Austen's question.

"Course not. If I had-a heard 'em I'd-a caught 'em."

"I know you would. Now that office—it has two doors to its one room: a front door, a back door. When you led Barton back to the office was the front door open or shut?"

"Shut, of course."

"Of course? Now that rear door—you are a keen observer, Tiny: you never miss a detail. That rear door, was it locked?"

"Well, now, I—"

"Was it shut—or just partly shut?"

The patrolman shuffled huge feet uncertainly. "Come to think of it, it was kind of open-like."

"Inch or so—or couple of feet?"

"Say! I don't tote a tape measure!"

"All right, Tiny. You didn't look out that back door, did you?"

"What would-a been the use? I caught my man, didn't I?"

"But he denied doing it, didn't he?" It was a shot in the dark.

"Course he did. They ain't never guilty till we break 'em down."

Shep Thomas looked sharply at Austen, then asked a question himself:

"Now, Tiny, Madison was shot with this pistol of Barton's, was he?"

Thomas pointed to the old-fashioned .32-caliber revolver on the captain's desk.

"Naw. Take a look. I'll tell you what happened."

Thomas lifted the revolver, broke it. There were six unfired cartridges in the chamber. "All right, let's have it."

"When I got there Madison's .38-caliber automatic was lyin' on the floor. Between him and his desk. That was the gun he always toted, and when he went into his office he always put it on the desk. Seen him do it a thousand times.

"What happen was this kid gets sore and grabs up Madison's gat and shoots him with it. There was a extry chair beside the desk where he would-a been sittin'. He just jumps up and kills him."

"Why?"

"Ain't he sore 'cause he can't ride Red Moon tomorrow? He kep' talkin' about it."

"Where's that .38, Tiny?" Thomas persisted.

The captain opened a desk drawer and took out the automatic. "First shell missin', see?" He opened the breech.

Austen asked quietly: "Fingerprints on this gun match Barton's?"

The captain scowled. The patrolman moved uneasily. "Say, you a lawyer?" the latter blurted.

"No, but I'm entitled to the facts, Tiny. You know me— and what I do. You didn't wrap up the gun in a handkerchief to shield the prints, did you? You just assumed the jockey did the killing. You shoved the gun in your pocket, didn't you?"

"Say, I know how to handle a guy when I catch him red-handed."

Austen turned aside. "Thank you, Tiny." The big fellow lumbered out of the room.

"Cap, your fathead bungled things nicely. We're going to have a tough time discovering the person who croaked Madison."

"Look here, Austen, we caught that jock red-handed. No need of fingerprints—"

"Why should this boy want to kill him?"

"You're smart, ain't you? The boy talked plenty—comin' back. Madison wouldn't let him ride Red Moon—"

"Good lud!" came from Shep Thomas. "You don't kill a man for that!"

"Don't, eh?" The captain turned on the reporter. "You smart alecks in Chicago don't know ever'thin', mister. This is racin'—in Kentucky. Funny things happen—and this is one of 'em."

From outside came the cry, "Extry! Extry! Madison killed by Jockey Barton! Extry!"

The captain lumbered out, leaving them by his desk.

"There's my story on the streets." Thomas grinned. "I'll say you Kentucky folk are fast. Couldn't done much better in Chicago."

The detective returned with a copy. "Confound it, how'd the papers learn all this so quick?" he muttered to himself. "H'm'm. This here paper says what Barton admitted: that Madison slapped him. Kid threatened him, too, a-fore witnesses." He turned on Austen: "Both of you know this. Why ask me?"

"Cap, you think they're slow in Chicago"—Austen grinned—"but that story you're reading—look at the head on it, *by Shepherd Thomas.* Here's the guy that did it." He stuck his thumb at Thomas.

"Well, I'll be—" The man's eyes grew large, then he said quickly: "The kid got hopped up with booze—you can chin yourself on his breath now—then he did it."

"Cap," Austen began softly, "two other men in my room this afternoon—Guy Slenk and Rock Doyle—were provoked by Madison. Either one had good reason to go gunning for him, according to Kentucky lights. And you know Madison had given a hundred others good reason to hate him. Any one of the hundred could have beaten Barton to the job."

"But we caught Barton runnin' away!"

"Let's speak with him."

"Now look here, Austen—"

"Cap"—Austen measured his man—"you don't want to be made a jackass, do you? You will if you try to shut off my investigation of this case. The Racing Commission will protest in a split second's time. I demand to see Jockey Barton. Bring him out!"

9

For a long moment the captain of detectives stared at Roderick Austen. Then he said:

"You wanta see him? Why not? We got nothin' to hide."

The captain went out of the room, called, "Bring out Barton."

"You're wise," Shep Thomas said in low tones to Austen.

"How?"

"Not mentioning the woman. I think she's the whole show in this case. Find her and we'll know who did the trick. But if you'd told of her telephone calls—well, this realist in charge of detectives would have laughed at us."

Footsteps were heard outside. "In you go, boy." A turn-key and the captain together shoved Danny Barton through the doorway. The boy had been drinking. He stumbled into the room. His eyes were blurry. His hands were shaking. There was a huge bruise on his jaw where Tiny's fist had crashed. He looked from Austen to Thomas and then to the captain of detectives. He was like a trapped young animal.

"Sit down, son," Austen said, leaning against the captain's desk. "You know me, and this is Mr. Thomas—friend of mine; going to be your friend, too, Danny."

"Is—is he a lawyer? I want a lawyer!"

"You'll get a lawyer, Danny. Now just tell us the truth. We're your friends, lad."

"I—I was sore because Madison took me off Red Moon."

"Sure. Go ahead."

"Wouldn't you be, if you lost a chance to make a fortune? You see, I'm the only jock who knows how to ride that horse. And I got my money up on him in the future book, and—well, I went out and got a few shots o' booze. And I start thinkin' it over, and I think maybe I can talk Mr. Madison into lettin' me ride. So I went to his house—"

"Where'd you get the gat?" the captain interrupted. "Tell that again."

"I—I bought it at a hock shop on Chestnut Street. They throw in six shells."

"Yeah, went gunnin' for Madison, didn't you? A man who'd never done you dirt—"

"Oh, he didn't?" Barton flared. "He took me off Red Moon. He hit me in the face—"

"So that's it!" the captain shouted. "You went out for revenge—to kill him because he hit you! Tell me you didn't do it, you lyin'—"

"Hush, Cap, hush!" Austen broke in. "This is no time for a third degree. Let the boy tell his story. Go on, Danny."

"I—I went out on the Shore Road. Got off the bus at the corner. Started up the driveway leadin' to Mr. Madison's office. I heard a shot in that office. I run toward it."

"You get that, Cap?" Austen demanded.

"Get what?"

"The boy didn't run away when he heard the shot—he ran up to see what happened."

"What of it? Let him talk."

"I certainly will, Cap—thanks to you. Go on, Danny."

"The front door was closed. There's a window by the door. I looked in the window. I saw Mr. Madison stumblin'—beginnin' to fall. He was throwin' his hands out as if to catch hisself. I see him fallin' over that table in the middle of the room.

"That ain't all I see, either. At the same time I catch it quick-like—same as you see three-four horses movin' at one time—I see out of the corner of my eye. I see a hand."

"Go ahead, lad." Shep Thomas spoke.

"I see a hand. It was about halfway up that back door. It was like somebody was tryin' to pull that door shut. Then the hand was pulled out, and the door—"

"Did the door close, Danny?"

"No sir," he answered Austen. "It was just swung shut a bit, but it was still open."

"Did you see any more of that hand?"

"No sir, I got there too late. Whoever killed Mr. Madison was just leavin'."

"The hand—was it wearing a glove, Danny?"

"Why—I—if it was it was a mighty light glove. I jus' catch a glimpse of it, you know."

Shep Thomas leaned over, asked casually:

"Was it a woman's hand, Danny—or a man's?"

"Why—why—it warn't big a-tall! Still, 'twarn't little."

"Wasn't the paw of a field hand?"

"No sir! It was—was—it sure warn't big."

"You didn't see the edge of a coat sleeve?" Thomas persisted.

"No sir, I did not!"

Thomas straightened, smiled, muttered something that sounded like *"Cherchez la femme."*

"What did you hear, Danny?" Austen wanted to know.

"I hear somebody stumblin' and runnin' through the bushes back there. You know the sound that makes. Like he was failin'—mebbe she!—over roots and vines."

"A man wouldn't make so much noise, I think," Thomas drawled. "A woman—her skirts catching on briars—"

He looked meaningly at Austen, then stopped speaking.

"Go on, Danny."

"I know those bushes. I used to ride for Mr. Madison. I went to his office a lot."

"What else happened?"

"Nothin', 'cept that I got scared and turned and started down the driveway. It was dark, and I run plump into somethin' big, and it was a cop. And he—"

"You wait!" That from the detective.

"Now *you* wait." Austen turned on him. "Go on, Danny."

"Well, sir, he—he cracked me on the jaw." The boy rubbed his bruised face. "Then he marched me back to the office."

"Front door still closed?"

"Yes sir."

"Back door still partly open?"

"Yes sir."

"All right. Then what?"

"He marched me inside and he said, 'Why, it's Mr. Madison, and you killed him.' First, though, before takin' me in he frisked me, found my gun. He stopped at the door and, holdin' his arms around me, he broke my gun. He saw it hadn't been fired—by the light from the window. He stuck it in his pocket.

"Then we went in. He saw a gun on the floor. It was an automatic. He picked it up. He said, 'This is the gun you killed him with,' and I said, 'I didn't do any such thing,' and I tried to tell him what I saw, but he told me to shut up. He called for the patrol wagon over Mr. Madison's phone, and they brought me here."

Thomas asked: "Was the window open that you looked through?"

"No sir."

Austen: "Did you tell all this, about seeing the hand, to the captain here?"

"Yes sir."

"Oh! That'll be all, Danny."

The rider stood up. He gulped once, twice. "Major Austen, I—I'm in trouble. I—I didn't kill Mr. Madison. I—I got to have help, to make 'em believe—"

"Don't worry too much, Danny," Austen said. "I'm here from the Racing Commission. We look after our own, son."

"Yes sir. Thank you, but am I—going to—?"

"You're goin' to burn!" The detective looked evilly at him.

"Cap!" Austen turned on the man. Then to the jockey, "We'll try to get you free, son."

The boy nodded. Again his hands were shaky. As the turnkey walked him out the detective growled, "Look here, Austen, I don't like—"

"You are going to like a lot before this is through. If you don't watch out Shep Thomas here will tell the world about you. And if you want to make a record while your superior is absent why don't you play ball with me?"

"Play? What do you think I'm a-doin'?"

"Fine! Now bring Tiny in again. I have an important question to ask him."

The big fellow shuffled in once more.

"Tiny, how are your ears?"

"Me ears? Perfect, like all the rest of me."

"That's good. As I understand it, the instant the shot was fired you started up the driveway."

"Sure did. I was in front of the driveway when Barton fired."

"How long is the driveway, from the Shore Road to the office?"

"Oh, fifty—mebbe sixty yards."

"Where did you catch Barton—at the gate?"

"I did not. Caught him halfway up the drive."

"I see." Austen smiled sardonically. "Allowing that the drive is even two hundred feet long, you were within—you

would hear a door slam shut on a quiet night, wouldn't
you?"

"That I would."

"The window was shut. So if Barton killed Madison he
must have shut the front door after him."

"How come?"

"It was shut when you got there, and since you were
not more than two hundred feet away when the shot was
fired— Well, that's all, Tiny."

"One minute!" Shep Thomas spoke up. "Did you see a
woman anywhere near the Madison place—parked in a car,
say, or walking on the road? Any time within an hour of
the murder?"

"Didn't see no woman. What would a woman be doin'
there?"

"That's all."

The man lumbered from the room, muttering.

Austen looked at the acting detective head. "Cap, do
you honestly think that if this boy killed Madison he'd
come out the front way and close the door carefully behind
him—so carefully that even Tiny's perfect ears couldn't
hear it—and go down the front driveway to meet the cop
on the beat, when he could have run out the back way? He
knew the grounds, remember. Men who kill in passion and
on the spur of the moment don't act that way." He shrugged
shoulders. "And don't forget the hand on the door—"

"That's what he says—got to say somethin'."

"Well, no chance of finding fingerprints on the gun.
It's got nothing but Tiny's prints on it now. What about
fingerprints on that rear door? Look, Cap, here's an idea,
the three of us working together: Let's take Barton out,
have him indicate just where he saw the hand, have your
experts look for prints—"

He stopped speaking. Someone in the outer room was
bawling:

"Look-a here, I pay a license to hack in this town. It's up to you cops to straighten this out."

The captain and Austen and Thomas went to the door. Standing at the desk sergeant's rail was a nondescript fellow in a dirty topcoat. To the topcoat was pinned a cab driver's license.

"Here I go and haul Guy Slenk to half the bars in town. He runs up four-twenty on my meter. Last bar, near the Shore Road, he leaves me standin' in front and chases out the back way, and I want you should make him pay my fare. You know him: he's that ex-jock what trains horses."

The captain stepped into the room, followed by Austen and Thomas. "What were you doin', haulin' Slenk around?"

"What was I doin'?" The driver was angry. "I was makin' a livin'—that's what. A honest livin'. Was, till that dirty skunk run out and didn't pay me."

"Say, buddy," Austen broke in, "did Slenk talk to you while you hauled him from bar to bar?"

"Did he? Talked all th' time—was goin' to kill a batch o' people."

"Who—for instance?"

"Was goin' to kill Henry Madison. I didn't pay no 'tention—long as he was just ridin' an' drinkin'. I heard people cuss Madison before this, and he ain't dead yet."

"No?" Thomas raised eyebrows.

The driver went cagey. "Look here—he ain't dead, is he?"

Three heads nodded.

"I knew it—knew it all the time!" he exclaimed. "Knew he was goin' to kill Mr. Madison—one of the finest guys—"

"Why didn't you do somethin' about it, then?" The detective seized the man's shoulder, shook him.

"Boss, I—I ain't seen no cop—no officer. Nobody I could turn him in to!"

"Why didn't you bring him here? I'll charge you with bein' accessory before the fact—"

"Listen, Cap'n, please—I ain't hidin' nothin'—not me. Everybody knows me. I'll tell you ever'thin' right now."

"Shoot!"

"Guy Slenk, he kep' takin' a gun outa his pocket, an' he'd say, 'Look at it. It's a .38-caliber automatic. And I'm goin' to kill Madison for stealin' my horse.'"

10

Austen stepped over to the man. "Look here, buddy, what time did you start out with Guy Slenk?"

"About seven."

"Where'd you pick him up?"

"He whistled me down at—" He named a street crossing within a block of Austen's apartment.

"Where'd he tell you to take him?"

"Told me to take him to Sam's for a drink. Told me to wait outside. And when he come out he says, 'I got it. Now we're all fixed.'"

"Got what?"

"That's what I asked him, boss." The taxi driver was talking fast to save himself and his license. "I says, 'What you got?'

"He says, 'I got a gat. We're goin' to get Madison because he stole my colt this afternoon.'

"And I says, 'We ain't goin' to get nobody. Leave me outa this.'

"He shows me the gun. I tells him he better think it over—tries to talk him outa it, see? I says, 'Mr. Slenk, let me drive you around—fresh air do you good. Then I take you straight to the Downs.' He says no, he wants another drink. So I decides, since I don't see no cop—officer—that

65

if I let him drink hisself stupid he won't do no harm. So we keep drivin' and stoppin' at bars—"

"And headin' straight for the Shore Road where Madison lives!" the captain accused.

"I didn't think about that, Cap'n. I was just tryin'—"

"Where'd Guy Slenk skip? Come clean or I'll throw you in the jug!"

"It—it was about two—two blocks in the—behind Mr. Madison's house, Cap'n."

"Swell guy you are! Drive him right up to the house so he can kill his man."

"Cap'n, he didn't look like he could do much harm then. He'd had so much to drink."

"That's what you say. It's the drunken fools who shoot, you louse."

"Look here, I ain't no—"

"Shut up! Tell us what happened at that last bar!"

"He kep' me waitin'. I go in when I see the meter goin' up, 'cause I didn't want to lose my fare. I says to the bartender, 'Where's Guy Slenk?' He says, 'Guy Slenk's gone.' I say, 'Where to?' He says, 'I don't know. Went out the back way and said he was goin' to kill somebody.'"

"What did you do?" Austen asked.

"Looked out the back way, boss. Saw it was a alley goin' to a cross street. Didn't see him nowhere. So I cruised around the neighborhood, thinkin' I'd see him. I went back to the next to last bar. He ain't back there. So I come on down here."

"Able to walk last time you saw him?"

"Well—yes sir."

"That's all from me." Austen looked at the detective captain with eyes hard and cold. "Well?" he said.

The wheel had turned for Cap'n. This was a new angle he hadn't figured on. He barked out an order:

"Send out a radio call—all cars. Search for Guy Slenk. Find him—bring him in, connection with Henry Madison's murder."

He turned to Austen. "That suit you?"

"So far."

"I want to ask a question," Shep Thomas drawled. "When you were cruising around did you pass Mr. Madison's home?"

"Why—er—yes, boss."

"Hear anything suspicious?"

"Not a thing."

"See a woman—alone? On the road or parked in a car—or did you see a woman—or a girl—with a man, either waiting or going in or coming out of Madison's place?"

"What's this woman stuff?" the captain demanded.

Thomas raised his hand. The driver's face looked blank. "Why, no sir, boss. Didn't see no woman—no girl, neither."

Thomas nodded. Austen spoke quickly to the detective:

"Call your fingerprint crew. We'll go to Madison's office. Take Barton along."

"Do what?"

Austen smiled. "We're playing ball, you and I. Call him out, Cap."

The detective grunted but ordered, "Bring Barton out."

"We better go through the back way—give the slip to reporters waitin' outside," the detective said. Then, looking at Shep Thomas, "Guess we'd better leave this friend o' yourn."

"Just as you say, Cap." Austen shrugged shoulders. "Of course, Shep knows a lot now, but as long as he's with us he can't write anything."

"H'm'm." The man rubbed his mouth with the back of his hand. "Then I—guess—we—we better take him along." He turned to meet the turnkey and Barton. Shep Thomas lowered his left eyelid just a trifle at Austen, then raised it.

The jockey, one shoulder in the grasp of the tall turn-key, said to the detective:

"What've I done now?"

"Keep quiet and stick 'em out." The man reached forward with his bracelets. The boy pushed back. "Please—"

"Not necessary, Cap." Austen spoke quickly and with disgust. "You're holding him merely on suspicion, aren't you? Not formally charged with murder?"

"Well, er—"

"Then put 'em away—the kid's got too much sense to run away. He just wants to be cleared. Besides, can't you keep a hand on him?"

"A'right." The man put the handcuffs back on his belt. He called to the desk sergeant: "Hold this here driver. Put him in protective custody till we check up on his yarn." He glared at the fellow. "And if we find you lied one little bit—into the jug you go, as accessory. Get me? Now just cool your heels on the settee till I come back."

As they went down the rear corridor Austen said:

"Swell idea of yours, Cap."

"What's swell?"

"To check up on the driver's yarn before we go to Madison's."

"That's the only way to detect, Austen," he answered. "I don't know nothin' about this book detectin', but if you follow every lead—say, you bound to come out on one of 'em. They ain't all blind alleys. And I'm takin' Tiny and an extra man in a second car too."

In the courtyard Austen said:

"Cap, you sit up with your chauffeur. Thomas and I will sit Barton between us, and you've got our word that he won't skip."

"He better not. Let's go."

As Shep Thomas stepped in first Austen whispered, "Nothing about the girl's phone calls."

"Okay—first time."

They drove by Sam's. The head bartender, a red-faced, bald-headed bruiser called Shanty, came to the curb, hands under his apron. Sure, he knew Guy Slenk. Bet on his horses. Sure, he was in tonight. Took two, three, mebbe four snifters. Yeah, plenty mad at somebody. Didn't say who.

The captain leaned head out of the car, demanded:

"Lend him your gat?"

"Naw. We keep that under the bar. Don't lend to nobody."

"Did he get a gat from anyone in there?"

"Well, now, I mind my own business."

"Yeah? Come clean, Shanty, or I'll jug you and let you think about it overnight."

"Sure, he got a gun."

"Who from?"

"Borrowed it from a guy at a corner table."

"Who was the fellow?"

"Honest, I don't know, Cap." The man's hands came out from beneath the apron.

"Is he there now?"

"Nope. Went out half-hour 'go. Kind of seedy—like a track hanger-on. He'd been sittin' there fifteen-twenty minutes, nursin' a dandelion highball, when Slenk come in. Slenk knew him. I think he's a tout. He been in two-three times before. Never got his name. Always paid in silver—no bills. Kep' to hisself."

"Know where he lives?"

"No, I don't. If I did I'd tell you."

"What did Slenk pay for the cannon?"

"Don't think he paid. Seems like he borrowed. He went to the table. I'm keepin' my eye on him—he owed for a brace of drinks, bonded stuff, too—and he sits down with the man at the corner table.

"They talk together four-five minutes. I'm keepin' my eye peeled—mebbe they'll order. But they don't order. The man reaches under his coat. I seen him passin' somethin' under the table. It's a cannon all right. I don't have trouble in my place. I jumped the bar; I put my hand on Slenk; I say:

"'Listen, pal, none of that stuff goes here. Pay up and clean out.'

"He wants to give me lip. I don't take lip from nobody.

"'Pay up and get out—take that toy with you, Slenk.'

"He sees I mean business. 'Oh, a'right,' he says, meek-like. He stands up. He sticks the artillery in a hip pocket and he pays. With a two-dollar bill. He asks:

"'How much change I got comin'?' 'Dollar-ten,' I says, bein' it was bonded stuff.

"'What does this frien' of mine owe?' he wants to know.

"'Thirty,' I tell him—he's drinkin' blended bourbon.

"Slenk says, 'Take out the thirty—give him another drink, buy cigars yourself with the rest,' and I did. But that stranger, he yells for the best bonded bourbon—I'll say he knows his likker—and I—"

"And you had to take three for a quarter 'stead of three for a half," the detective broke in.

"That's right."

"Anythin' else?"

"Fellow went out—didn't buy no more hisself. That's all I know. Honest."

"All right. Now listen, Shanty. If that other fellow comes in tonight or tomorrow or a year from now, you hold him—buy him a drink if you have to—and call headquarters. Get me?"

"Sure."

"That's all."

They drove on, leaving Shanty standing on the sidewalk, hands again under apron, scowling after the two police cars.

11

The police cars sped through the business section, which was aglow with Derby carnival spirit, despite a falling spring mist. Shopwindows gleamed with light; banners swung from poles; flags hung across streets. Doors of cafés were flung open, and shouting groups rushed out to cars, laughing, blowing horns at passers-by. . . . Austen craned forward, looked to the right as they passed one intersection.

Yes, there was the wagon diner. An ornate place of its kind. In passing Austen got a quick view through one window. He saw women in evening gowns lined against the counter with top-hatted escorts, munching hot dogs. It was the thing to do this season.

The diner was the place from which those last two mysterious phone calls had been made. Austen would come back here.

They stopped at the suburban bar where Slenk had disappeared. No, they hadn't seen hide or hair of him since he skipped through the back door. Owed for a double highball too. A detective was dropped with instructions to pick up the trainer's trail. Then they rode to the Madison home.

The place was dark. "What about the servants, Cap?" Austen asked as they stepped from the car. Instantly a detective from the rear car joined them, placed a hand on Barton's arm. "Just in case," he said.

"Servants?" the head detective answered. "Only two stay here—a n•••• cook and her husband who acts as house-boy. Tiny says they heard the rumpus and came runnin' out of the kitchen when he was puttin' in his telephone call. They didn't see nobody or know nothin' about it."

"Where are they now?"

"Fact is, Austen, they were scared to death."

"Don't they live on the place? Most servants do in this section."

"Think they live in a shack in the rear. I'll send a man to get 'em. See? There's a light—bet they're holdin' prayer meetin'."

"Get them here before we do anything."

The car had been stopped in front of the now-darkened office.

"Don't turn on the lights inside—yet," Austen suggested. "Place the servants in front of the car's headlights—question them there."

In a few moments two scared servants were led into the circle of light.

"Let me do the questioning. You've had your chance at them," Austen said. He stood in the shadows.

"What's your name—you, the butler?"

The gray-haired and portly old fellow, dark as the night itself, answered in deep bass:

"Samuel Henry Washington—that's my name, suh."

He drew himself up with importance.

"And yours?" to the woman, a thin and waspish crea-ture.

"Same as hisn, 'cept it be Susannah Clay Washington. We been married nigh onto thirt—"

"Never mind, just answer my questions. You, Sam, where were the two of you when Mr. Madison was shot?"

"In the kitchen, suh. Eatin' a late snack. The winder wuz open. We hear a pistol shot. It skeered me. Skeered Susannah, too, 'cause she starts prayin' to the Lord."

"What did you do?"

"He run and hid in the pantry—that's what that no-'count n••••• did," the wife spoke in squeaky tones.

"That right, Sam?"

"I—er—thought I'd better shet the pantry winder."

"Never mind. Did either of you go out to the office?"

"Naw suh!"

"We stays stuck," Susannah volunteered, "till Mr. Tiny comes and shouts for us. We knows his voice. Then we goes out to the office—and we sees pore Mr. Madison killed dead."

Her voice broke. She held her apron to her face, cried with sudden hysteria.

The butler's eyes grew saucer-large in the blinding headlights. His body began to shake.

"Then what happened?"

"Mr. Tiny—he say, 'Who is Mr. Madison's folks?' I say he ain't no close kin hereabouts; he got a half brother in New Awleans. 'Who's his frien's?' says Mr. Tiny. I says, 'Ain't no special frien'. He kinda likes Dr. Fellowes—up at the Pendennis Club.' Mr. Tiny telephones there—"

A voice behind Austen—that of Mr. Tiny himself—broke in:

"I got Fellowes on the phone. He rushed out, said last he had seen of Madison was when Madison dropped him at the club after being at your place, Major."

"I live only a block away from the club. Go on, Tiny."

"Medical examiner come out. Dr. Fellowes come. Examiner said instant death at short range—four or five feet. Powder burns on his head. Body shipped to morgue—they gonna take the bullet out. It'll fit the gun we found on the floor, all right!"

"Thank you, Tiny. Where's Dr. Fellowes?"

"Said he'd go back to the club—wanted to find that half brother's address, send him a telegram. He said, 'Guess I'll have to do it. He's got no relatives here.'"

"Thank you, Tiny, and now, Sam, did Mr. Madison say where he was going when he went out?"

"Naw suh. We thought he wuz goin' to a frien's. You know, he ain't got close frien's, but he knows ever'body. Visits a lot—specially the ladies."

"You shut up, n•••••!" his wife exclaimed.

"Well, he do!" Sam turned accusingly on her.

"Shame on you—and he ain't cold yet, pore man!"

"Instead of going to a friend's, he stopped in the office. Did he go to the office at night often?"

"Ever' now an' then, boss. He talk business there—the house be for—for—"

"N•••••!"

"I ain't said nothin', woman. Shet up! Let me talk. The house be for social things."

"Was he expecting anyone tonight?"

"Nary a soul."

"Who was the last man who threatened to kill him?"

"I don't ezactly remembers." The butler scratched his head. "Mr. Madison—he got hot under the collar some-times, suh. He allus sayin' he'd have to kill so-an'-so, if he didn't want so-an'-so to kill him fust. But we pays no 'tention to that—he jes' talk that way."

"How long was he in the house?"

"'Bout ten minutes—time to take a light snack standin' up at the sideboard."

"Anyone telephone for him during the day or evening?"

"Yes suh! Jes' one gent'man. 'Scuse me, suh, but his voice, hit sounded powerfully like yourn, suh."

"I did phone, Sam." Then, "Any questions, Cap?" The detective had none.

"That's all, Sam."

"Please, suh, we's got frien's in town. Could we, please, suh, go wid them tonight? We's a-skeered to stay here. We done lock the house up."

"Sure—beat it," the detective agreed, "but you better be back early tomorrow to watch the place."

"Yes suh, thank you, suh." They shuffled away in the blackness.

One of the detectives lighted the office. The group went in. Shep Thomas, seeing the racks of firearms on the walls, the pistols grouped above the mantel, remarked: "Madison had plenty of cannon for display, but he couldn't defend himself."

Austen said: "Now, Barton, we want you and Mr. Tiny— Come on in, Tiny," he called to the patrolman, standing in the doorway. "We want both of you to show us what happened here. You, first," he told the jockey, "point to where you saw that hand."

"It was right about here." The jockey pointed without hesitation to a place just above the doorknob, about one third of the way up the door. Austen turned on the chief detective.

"Cap, if you were leaving a place in a hurry and tried to slam a door behind you so you wouldn't be seen, would you stop to take the doorknob in your hand or would you grab the door at the nearest point and pull it after you?"

"H'm'm."

"Now let's get some prints. You've got your man with you. Let's see you find Barton's fingerprints anywhere here."

"Huh?"

"If he was talking with Madison he must have been nervous. He would have seized something—edge of the chair, the table, the doorknob—when he came in. Let's see if you can find a single print that will match those of the boy's you took at the station."

The fingerprint man went into action with his dusting powder and brushes. He dusted chair arms, table, desk, knobs, edge of the door.

Austen nodded to Shep Thomas to step outside with him.

"They've got no more on that boy, Shep, than they have on you and me."

"Nothing," Thomas drawled, "except the damning circumstance that he was caught at the scene of the crime with a loaded pistol after he had threatened Madison. That's all—and that's a lot."

Silence a minute. Through the opened window they saw Danny Barton standing against the far wall, a detective beside him, hand on the jockey's arm.

"He must be at least twenty-two," Thomas said. "Look at him! But I swear, he passes for sixteen or seventeen."

"Kid's kept straight. Shows in his face. But he's up against it, Shep. This is a clannish town." He turned, looked out where the lights of Louisville flared skyward.

"People stick together here. Madison was a leader in business, a big man in sports—stood out socially."

"More feared than loved, wasn't he?"

"He was never loved—still, he was one of them. Barton—he's a *foreigner,* boy from a hill pasture. He first rode at county fairs—the half-milers. Then he went into Maryland, and from there to the Big Apple; was a sensation at Saratoga and Belmont. Funny, he didn't ride in Louisville till he became famous in the East. So they regard him as a Northerner here, while he's really native Kentucky."

"Madison bought his contract, I know. What happened?"

"Early last year they split up. In New Orleans. Madison sent a tough-mouthed old hide to the post: one that had a habit of running out on the turns. Got the horse entered at one hundred and three pounds—Barton rides at one hundred and eight. The boy had to sweat off five pounds overnight—had to hit the road with the rubber shirt to do it.

"Race was a rich handicap. Barton was so weak from the reducing that he didn't have the strength to hold his mount against the rail. The old fellow was leading, coming around the turn; he suddenly shot to the outside rail. They lost the race, lost the purse, and the gold cup too."

"The public will bring that up," Thomas said, "will say Barton double-crossed Madison. They'll shout for blood. The papers will praise the cops for good work and quick work," he added cynically. "You've got the upper hand tonight, Major, because you've pointed out a lot of boners the cops have pulled, but you can't get the upper hand of the newspapers and public sentiment. You can't control the district attorney."

"He's a decent, square fellow."

"But what of the grand jury? Composed of Madison's type? Shucks, they'll railroad Barton. Your chance is—"

"Find the woman!"

"Exactly! Whoever she is, looks to me like her man did it. Unless Guy Slenk did it. Say, remember, Slenk was gunning for Madison and had a gun and a big-sized grouch."

"I haven't forgotten."

"But about the woman—say, any scandal about Madison?"

"Plenty. He was always poaching on somebody's beauties."

"There was the woman with Rock Doyle. You say she smiled knowingly at him."

"She did. And remember, I sent George Trigg out here to pick her up—if she was in the neighborhood. Well, we don't see Trigg, and he doesn't see us. Know what that means?"

"Sure! He's picked her up—is tailing her."

"The woman, Slenk— I've got an idea." He stepped to the front door of the office. "Cap, will you come here a minute?"

The detective lumbered out. Austen led the way around the office as a mass of clouds moved away from the sliver of moon. In the faint glow a hedge was revealed fifty yards behind the house, bordering a rear roadway. In one corner of the grounds stood the servants' quarters built above the garage.

Austen turned to both men. "The type of man who'd come to kill Madison—don't you see, he'd drive up the rear road— Come on, I'll show you." He led them to the hedge.

"He could park out there— Oh, darn!" He jerked a hand back from the hedge's top. "Briars," he muttered; then, "Servants wouldn't know he was on the place. He'd shoot, then take the shortest way out—the back way out."

"And tear himself up on that hedge?" the captain demanded. "I heard you cussin'—"

"Think this little hedge would stop a desperate man?" Deliberately Austen pushed through it. He called over the top. "Didn't stop me, did it? Now I'm coming back," and he did. "Just a matter of throwing your arms up in front of your face, and a man in a hurry probably wouldn't do that. His idea would be to get out of here."

"Humph!"

"Do you think if Barton killed Madison that he'd run out the back door—remember, Tiny didn't hear that front door close!—then circle around till he came to the front driveway? Bosh! A man running to save his skin goes in a straight line; zigzagging is done by convoys only!"

"We caught Barton with the goods," the captain said heavily. He flashed a light on the ground. "Grass here—no place for footprints. That what you want?"

"No! If there were footprints the servants would have tracked 'em up. I just want to show how the killer got away from you—"

"From me? He didn't. We got Barton—with the goods."

A shout from the house. "We got something!"

"Didn't I tell you?" the captain exulted. "They've found the kid's fingerprints. Come on now—you smart boys!"

He waved them around to the front entrance.

12

The jockey was sitting on a hard, straight chair in a far corner of the office, big Tiny standing in front of him, and a detective had hold of his shoulder. He didn't look up when the captain and Austen and Thomas came in. He just clasped and unclasped his hands; he seemed in a daze.

"Well, let's see 'em," the captain demanded. "I knew we had the kid dead to rights, but a few fingerprints won't do no harm."

He looked straight at his fingerprint man: a small, baldish chap with snaggleteeth.

"We found something—knew you'd want to know right away," the expert said. "So had one of the boys call you."

"All right, all right." The captain was impatient. "Let's see 'em. And where'd you find 'em?"

"The fact is, Captain, these are not fingerprints. But they're very important—highly important."

"Not fingerprints? Then what in thunder are they?"

The expert straightened. He had made a discovery and he was taking full credit for it.

"Some authorities say it can't be done, but I claim it can; I've proved it tonight, and we're going to take a picture of them in just a minute—soon as you see them, Captain."

"See what, man—see what?"

"On the door. Above the knob. Right here." The man crossed to the rear door, now almost closed. He opened it wide and, taking up a powered microscope, spoke with the air of a scientist, not a man hunter: "If you will look, sir—hold it about this far from the wood"—he demonstrated—"you will plainly see the marks."

"Marks of what?" The captain's back was now toward Austen and Thomas. They saw his neck turning red.

The fingerprint man announced his find:

"The mark of gloved fingers, sir. May prove what the prisoner said is true—about the hand on the door."

A moment of odd silence, in which Tiny shuffled his weight from foot to foot.

A sudden cry from Danny Barton: "I told you so! You tried to make me think they'd found my fingerprints."

He tried to get up.

"Shut up!" Tiny pushed him back in the chair. "And stay down!"

The captain said: "I be double-damned!"

Austen smiled cynically. "I knew the lad wasn't a liar," he said. "Let me see the marks, Sergeant."

The captain barred his way. "Look here," he barked at the man, "what's this you found? I tell you to find finger-prints—"

"No prints with whorls matching the jockey's," the man said shortly. "And on this door the powder doesn't pick up glove marks, for no oils from the hand penetrate through the gloves. However"—the man cleared his throat, spoke as though lecturing police recruits—"a microscopic exam-ination revealed that this door had not been dusted in some time. In fact, it had been touched only on the knob in some time, and evidently not used much in the past week, because its closing would have knocked off part of the dust. The—"

"Come on, man, get to it!"

"Yes sir. Now a microscopic examination reveals distinct marks of gloved fingers on the inside of the door—marks of the hand extending around the edge of the door, marks of a gloved thumb on the door's outside. Showing that the door was tightly grasped, as if the person was excited."

"Heh—heh!"

"Giving you the facts, sir. I—"

"A man or a woman's hand?" Austen shot the question at him. "Let him answer, Cap."

The man pursed lips over his snaggleteeth. Again he spoke as the fact finder:

"Wouldn't wish to commit myself. I'll say, if a woman's, a large hand. If a man, then a small hand, wearing a cadet-sized glove: that is, one with fingers shorter than ordinary. If a man, I'd say distinctly small—if a woman, one with broad fingers."

"Peasant fingers," Shep Thomas said in low tones. The captain frowned at him, started to say something, then stopped. "The platinum-haired angel would have such fingers," Thomas volunteered.

"Heh! Who're you talkin' about?" the captain demanded.

Austen looked blank.

The captain turned full around, stuck a spatulate finger at the racing man's chest. "Come clean! You're holdin' out while pretendin' to play ball. You better come clean!"

Austen's face was without expression.

"Heh, you!" The captain grabbed Austen's coat lapels, but before he could say anything Austen snapped:

"Take your hands off me."

The tone cut like a whiplash. The captain dropped hands.

"You can't shake me like you would a dog."

"Listen, Austen—"

"You listen to me! And keep your distance." Then Austen's voice grew almost friendly. "If I were you I'd forget joking remarks about peasant women—we don't have peasants in America, Cap. I'd find the woman, or the man, with a gloved hand who closed that door in an almighty hurry tonight. Your expert has found the glove marks."

"Yeah? And why don't he take a picture, then?"

The man answered for himself: "As there's no oil from the glove to leave whorl-marks, sir—or any other kind of marks which the lens can catch—we can't make a picture. But the microscope plainly shows marks in the dust."

"I told you to get fingerprints!"

"I can only get what's here. Thought it would be enough."

"Aw, thunder!" The captain moved aside with disgust.

Shep Thomas whispered to Austen: "Pretty fast, boy, the way you changed the focus of the captain's interest."

Austen, back to the crowd, lowered an eyelid, spoke from the side of his mouth: "Had a break when the captain grabbed my coat."

Now the captain was speaking to all:

"You smart boys forget we're looking for another man too: Guy Slenk. I haven't forgot it." He picked up Madison's phone, dialed police headquarters.

"The desk."

In a few seconds he was connected.

"'Lo there! . . . Yeah! . . . Swell. . . . Got him, did you? . . . One minute!" To the room, "My man's caught Guy Slenk—knew we'd get him."

Austen touched him on the shoulder. "Ask him if Guy Slenk's wearing gloves."

The captain frowned. "A'right." Into the phone, "Slenk got gloves on?" He listened a minute. "All right. Book him. We're comin' in."

Deliberately he put the phone down, picked up his hat, put it on his head. "You fellows, pack up! We're goin' in." He started toward the door. "Keep a mighty good hand on that jock."

As he went out the front door he said grudgingly over his shoulder:

"Yeah, Slenk is wearin' gloves—pair o' light gloves."

13

"So!" a smile shot across Roderick Austen's face. "Slenk has on light gloves—and glove marks were found on the rear doorway, where Danny Barton saw a hand for an instant." He turned to the captain, spoke judiciously:

"You've done good work, Captain. Slenk had a gun and was looking for Madison. He had threatened to kill Madison. Now you've got Slenk."

The captain nodded. His Adam's apple worked an instant. "Mebbe he—he and this jockey together—"

"Bosh! Let's go!"

On the way to the station Barton said: "Major Austen, I'm awful hungry. Ain't had a thing to eat since breakfast. I wonder if—if there's a chance—"

"You bet there's a chance. Wait till we get to the station house. You and Shep and I will have a good meal."

The city was putting on its nightcap as they rode downtown. A few roisterers were still on the streets; now and then a car, crowded to the foot guards with boys and girls, swept by. Once Austen caught the shout:

"Bet on Red Moon tomorrow!"

Here and there a café door swung open, disgorged a hilarious group in evening clothes. But lights were going out. Louisville, unlike Eastern centers, tucks in early.

They reached the station house; a turnkey came out, took Barton by the arm, and hustled him inside.

"Cap," Austen asked, "can Barton, Shep Thomas, and I have a bite to eat in the station—alone?"

The captain shuffled his feet on the sidewalk. "Now look here, Major, you're not the kid's mouthpiece."

"Come on, Cap, what harm can it do?"

"All right—all right. Hey!" he called to an idle detective. "Whistle for a waiter from down the street, will you?"

In the station they found the detective who had trailed and caught Guy Slenk. A wiry, red-haired fellow in his thirties, named Hunt. Austen liked him on sight.

"I got him," Hunt said laconically. "He's in the cooler now."

"Bring him in," the captain ordered.

"Take two of us to do that—plus a stretcher."

"How come? He resist? You had to beat 'im up?"

"They don't resist me—and I don't have to beat them up," Hunt explained with cool assurance. "He's cuckoo drunk."

"Let's see him."

The captain led the way to a tier of cells. In one, under a bright light, was the sportily clad trainer. He was lying on a steel cot. His mouth was open. Deep snores were resounding. On his hands—one across his breast, the other dangling toward the floor—were light doeskin gloves.

"Look, Cap, the gloves." Austen emphasized them.

Detective Hunt, who didn't know the meaning behind the remark, said: "Funny, we tried to make Slenk take those gloves off. Thought he might have a ring on that he'd lose, but he wanted to fight, so we just let them stay on. You know, Cap, I've seen him at the track; he considers those gloves the mark of a gentleman. I've even seen him wearing them before breakfast on a hot day."

"Wake him up!"

The turnkey opened the grilled door. Hunt stepped in, put hands under the fellow's shoulders:

"Come on, Guy—time for the Derby!" he urged.

Guy Slenk wasn't interested. He raised an arm, snored again. Hunt lifted him to a sitting position. The trainer's bloodshot eyes opened. He stared unseeingly. His tongue lolled aimlessly about in his head. He fell back against the steel wall. Hunt shook him, lifted him to his feet. It was like handling a sack of meal.

Hunt shook him again. "Come on, Guy—wake up and face the music. Snap out of it!"

But there was no snapping out of it. Guy Slenk was drunk and dead to the world. Hunt eased him back on the cot.

"Worst drunk I've seen this season," he said. "Water, light—nothing will bring him to. He'll be out for at least twelve hours."

The captain nodded. "I believe you're right, Hunt. Come on and make a report to us." The captain led the way back to his office. "Well?" he said, relaxing into a swivel chair.

"I went into the bar where you dropped me, Cap." Hunt ran hands thoughtfully through his red hair. "Barkeep said Slenk had been there about an hour and a half before. He was drunk but able to navigate. He drew out a gat while standing at the bar—said he was going for somebody."

"Automatic or old-fashioned gun?" Austen put the question.

Hunt smiled. "I asked that question too; it was an old-fashioned gun—.38, the barkeep said."

Shep Thomas said softly: "A .38—that type was found on the floor of Madison's office."

"Yeah, but that was Madison's gun. Tiny identified it," the captain spoke up. "There was the vacant spot above the mantel where it had been jerked from."

"Yes?" Thomas persisted. "But the bullet—"

"One chamber empty," the captain snapped.

"Report on that bullet—by your ballistics expert?" the reporter kept on.

"Here, now—" the captain began to protest, but Hunt interrupted, "We have heard, and here's our man. Oh, Sergeant Matthews!"

A lithe, bespectacled, gray-haired person came in soundlessly. He spoke without being asked:

"Bullet was sent over from the morgue more'n an hour ago. Another shot was fired from the gun found on Madison's floor. That bullet compared microscopically with the one taken from Madison's head." He stopped.

"Well?" the captain grunted.

"Each consistent with the other."

"That means—"

"They were fired from the same pistol. Similar riflings. I split the bullets horizontally: put the top half of one on the bottom half of the other. The riflings coincided microscopically."

"Humph! That's all, Matthews." The captain nodded to the man and then looked disdainfully at Austen. "Now all we got Guy Slenk for is public intoxication. Shucks! This trouble—"

"One minute!" Austen warned. "Did you ever figure, Cap, that Guy Slenk has a lot of animal cunning? I haven't heard the rest of Sergeant Hunt's report, but I'll bet Guy Slenk didn't have a gun when he was found. Guy Slenk would be smart enough— Say!"

"Say what?"

"How do you know that he didn't go into Madison's office, that Madison didn't point his pistol at him? How do you know that Slenk didn't jerk it out of his hand, shoot him with it, then run out, throw his own pistol away?" Austen turned swiftly on Hunt: "Find his gun?"

Hunt shook his head. "No trace of it."

"Told you so!" Austen snapped. "Remember, Cap, you talked about the briars maybe holding a man back, and I said he'd push through? Well, I noticed that Slenk's clothes were torn by briars. Come on, I'll show you!"

Again the group, at Austen's insistence, went back to Guy Slenk's cell. The turnkey opened the door.

"Look!" Austen lifted a gloved hand. "If there aren't scratches here—and here"—he lifted the other glove— "then I'm a Hottentot! And look—tears at the elbow!" He spoke with suppressed excitement. "Guy Slenk went through the briar hedge all right!"

"What if he did!" the captain snapped. "Mebbe he went through fifty hedges. That ain't the only hedge in Louisville. Behind that bar I bet—" He looked inquiringly at Hunt.

"Yes sir, out back there, where Slenk walked, there is a hedge. I know—look!" He held up his left sleeve. There was a slight tear on it.

"Now what you got to say?" The captain turned on Austen as he motioned for the turnkey to close the door again.

"Sergeant Hunt's telling us facts. That's all we want: facts," Austen said evenly. "From those facts we can deduce a lot."

"Deduce the devil!" The captain led them back to his office. "We got the kid runnin' away—and that's that! We're holdin' Guy Slenk for public intoxication—Barton for investigation into the murder of Madison. And that's that!"

"Suppose we let Sergeant Hunt finish his report," Austen insisted.

"Barkeep said he'd have taken the gun from Slenk's hands, but Slenk backed off, then ran out the back door."

"Ran?"

The sergeant grinned.

"I asked the same question. Barkeep said Guy came to life mighty quick, that he went out very spry. Now"—he sobered—"while there are thornbushes back behind that saloon, there's also a driveway that leads straight to the rear of Madison's place."

"What?" the captain exploded.

"Yes sir. I started down that roadway, looking for Slenk. The clouds were passing away from the moon. I saw a man coming up that roadway—leading from behind Madison's place. He was in a hurry, though walking a bit unsteady. You know, there are times when excitement will make a drunk keen—for a short space of time. Then he relapses again."

"Cut the medical lingo," the captain commanded. "What happened?"

"Yes sir." Hunt compressed his lips an instant, controlled himself, and went on: "This man, oddly, didn't seem to see me until I was within twenty yards of him—or else his mind was on something else. Then he stopped, and even in the slight moonlight I saw him jerk his head back. That's when he saw me. He turned, started running, jumped into a low ditch on the left of the road—no water in it. I jumped after him. He tried to run—"

"And you overpowered him?" the captain offered.

"Not quite. He slipped and I fell on top of him," Hunt said modestly. "I just sat on him. He gave two or three big gasps, then seemed to slip into a drunken stupor. I called. A man who had stepped outside the bar for a second heard me and came down. And that's all. We had to lift Slenk into the patrol. He was coming back from the direction of Madison's when we met."

14

The captain of detectives got to his feet, scowled down at the smaller Hunt. He stuck his finger against Hunt's chest.

"And where," he demanded, "was Guy Slenk's gat?"

"I frisked him. He didn't have one."

The captain snorted. "I see a waiter out there." He nodded to the outer room. "Guess you want to stoke up."

"Nice of you, Cap," Austen said easily.

"Humph! You-all can eat here in my office—shut the door, for all I care."

"That's fine, Cap. Now there's a real favor—"

The captain looked at Austen with cold and fishy eyes. "Oh yeah? Ain't I done enough for you?"

"This will be for yourself—as well as for me."

"How come?"

"I wish you'd turn Sergeant Hunt over to me."

"What?"

"As an assistant—just for two days. Want to work with me, Hunt?"

The detective smiled. "Yes sir—that is, if the captain wants me to."

"Cap, you've got other things on your mind. Let Hunt represent you. He and I will work together. And if we break anything—remember, it's just for two days—the police department will get the credit. Fair enough?"

The captain's jaws worked a moment. Then, "Sure, all right by me—if you want to pal up."

The desk sergeant poked his head around the door, called:

"Want that grub in there? Three steak dinners waiting."

"What about you, Sergeant—make it a fourth?"

"Give him a cup of black Java," the captain answered for him. "He's already et one porterhouse tonight. See you tomorrow, Sergeant, and don't take lip from this bunch." He pretended to smile at his own witticism, then went stomping out.

"While the table's being set," Austen spoke quickly, "want to tell you everything up to date, Sergeant. Might listen in, Shep, case I forgot to tell you everything."

Austen began at the beginning—from the moment the Racing Commission was asked to decide the ownership of Red Moon. He stressed the mysterious phone calls. "I've told you all, Sergeant, and you don't have to keep secrets from the captain, either."

Hunt nodded thoughtfully. Said: "The woman business—it turns everything upside down. I'll bet she has a hand in it—was the cause of Madison's death, directly or indirectly." He pondered a moment, then said: "Well, I'll tell the captain anything he asks for." He stressed the last three words knowingly.

"Good! The woman theory is a little hard for a practical man, such as the captain, to put much faith in," Austen agreed. "But let's eat. Here's Barton."

The boy had been brought in by the turnkey.

The four sat down together: Danny Barton, looking ill; the sharp-eyed, sharp-nosed, and sloppily dressed Shep Thomas; the alert Hunt, and Austen.

"Don't be afraid to eat, son." Austen spoke kindly, trying to make Barton feel at ease. "This won't put much

weight on you. Anyway, you've missed grub today. What's
your riding weight now?"

"Still one hundred and eight. I've held it there for two
years, sir."

"You'll hold it a few more years too. You've got small
hands and feet—signs that you won't spread out fast. You'll
be riding fifteen-twenty years from now, and in that time
you'll win four or five Derbies too. By the way, you've
never had a leg up in the Derby, have you?"

"No sir, but I win the Belmont Stakes last year."

"And how!" Austen exclaimed. "I was up in the clubhouse. You got away last—"

"That mount o' mine was a slow breaker—had to let
him get settled in his stride."

"But what a finish!"

"He's a game horse. He'll be a handicap champion this
year. Now Red Moon, he—" The rider's manner changed.

He looked confusedly about, as if he had spoken a name
that should not have been mentioned. He lowered his eyes,
and again he was back in a shell.

"Red Moon," Austen spoke easily, "he'll have to show
his stuff tomorrow. By the way, Danny—" The boy had
pushed his plate forward; he was through eating for that
night. Austen did the same, stirred his coffee. "Danny"—
he grinned at the jockey—"you have a girl, haven't you?"

"Why—er—er"—the boy's face flamed into red for a
long moment—"I—I—no sir!" he blurted out the words.

"Generally," Shep Thomas remarked, "you boys are surrounded by girls."

"I—er—don't specially like 'em." Again he blushed.

"No?" from Austen.

"Why not, Danny?" Thomas leaned forward. "Every
man has a reason. I'd like yours."

"Well, sir—it's this way: girls, they're nice—when
they're nice."

Austen bowed his head gravely. "Go on, son."

"But most girls—around tracks—they—they want somethin'."

"Oh!" from Austen, as if he didn't know.

"Yes sir." Barton was earnest. "They're always askin', 'Are you goin' to win tomorrer?' Not figgerin' that it's the horse that's got the answer. Best horse in the world—Sea-biscuit himself—any horse can lose against a bunch of skates if he runs when he don't feel right. Maybe he gets the bellyache before goin' to the post and he can't tell us."

"Sure!" Austen nodded. "And girls won't believe when you—"

"When I can't promise to win they get sore! They go and bet on me when—when I'm tryin' to win but haven't got much chance—and they fuss if I don't come in first."

"But you've met the other kind, too, Danny—the kind that are not trying to get something out of you?"

"Oh, yes sir. Lots of 'em." The jockey warmed up. "We saddle under the trees at Saratoga and Belmont—at Empire, now, too. There's always a lot o' people around when I go out for my mount. Generally the trainer or owner introduces me to his friends before giving me the leg up."

Austen broke in suddenly, "When was the last time you talked with Rock Doyle?"

"Why—" The boy leaned suddenly against his chair back.

Austen stretched forward, struck the table with an open palm:

"Come, Barton, when did you talk with Rock Doyle last? You know him. Don't say you don't."

"Why, I—I met him. He's a big lawyer."

"Sure, you met him. When did you see him last?"

"Why, he was at the track two-three mornin's ago—but lots of people come out to the track mornin's."

"I know, but I'm talking of you and Rock Doyle. Understand?"

"Ye-yes sir," Danny Barton gulped.

"What did he talk to you about?"

"No-nothing much. Guy Slenk introduced him."

"Don't tell me that—that he talked about nothing much. What did the two of you talk about?"

"I—I—Guy Slenk, he—he didn't seem to want to talk to Mr. Doyle. Acted like he wanted to get away—quick-like. Seem like he wanted to pass Mr. Doyle over to me. He did it too. Said he'd be back in a minute."

"And the minute never came, did it?"

"No sir. He—he disappeared."

"What did Doyle talk about. Answer that, lad."

"He asked the same question everybody'd been askin': What was the chance of Red Moon winnin' the Derby. I told him I thought—everythin' bein' equal—that he was goin' to be the winner. He'd already been Derby distance, private workout, in 2:03 4/5—that's faster'n some Derbies been won in."

"What else did he say?"

"He asked me to come downtown and eat with him. I—I explained I was in trainin'—didn't want to go out till after the Derby."

"Wise boy!" Austen commended him warmly. The jockey relaxed, mopped his face with a handkerchief.

"By the way," Austen asked casually, "what was the name of the girl that was with Rock Doyle?"

Again the boy's shoulders struck the back of the chair. Once more he colored. His hands clenched and unclenched. For a minute he didn't meet Austen's direct gaze.

"I—I—I—"

"What was her name, Barton? Let's have it!"

15

Austen straightened. His manner became cold, impersonal. He looked calmly at the confused jockey sitting opposite him, said:

"You don't have to answer that question. I was merely trying to help you—I, and Mr. Thomas here, and Sergeant Hunt. But I see you are holding out. So I guess you'd better be taken back to your cell." Austen pushed away from the table. "Hire yourself a lawyer and get out of this mess the best way you can."

"Wait, Major!" The boy jumped to his feet, knocked over his chair. "I—I ain't purposely hidin' anythin'."

"No? Then why aren't you telling the facts?"

"I—I didn't want to drag a nice girl into somethin' that—that she warn't mixed up in."

"So she's a nice girl! Fine! The one who was with him today—the platinum-haired one?"

"Y-yes sir!"

"Her name?"

"It was—was Miss Maxwell. Mr. Doyle, he called her Marge, and she said to me, 'I'm goin' to call you Danny, and you call me Marge.'"

"Sit down, lad." Austen motioned to the chair Barton had been sitting in and took the chair opposite again. Thomas and Hunt had not moved.

"Have many talks with her, Danny?"

"She was out just that once, sir—with Mr. Doyle. Mr. Doyle, he walked off—talkin' to one of the guineas in the stable—and Ma—Miss Maxwell, she cottoned up to me."

"I see! Cottoned up to you!"

"Yes sir. Got friendly-like—you know." He grinned.

"Maybe I do. Go on. What did she want—or was she one of the nice kind who didn't want something?"

"Funny—she knew I'd told Mr. Doyle I thought Red Moon would win, but she—she—a girl—was tellin' me how to ride!"

"Telling you how to ride?"

"Yes sir!"

"What did she say?"

"She said she loved to see a horse come from behind and win. That she wanted me to rate Red Moon off the pace till I got to the far turn—and then to take command and come on and win."

"She did, eh? Tell you why she wanted you to ride that way?"

"Yes sir, 'cause I asked her. She said she wanted to see me bowl over tenpins. That was her words—to bowl over tenpins."

"Meaning?"

"I asked her. She said: 'Danny, it gives me a kick, a thrill, to see you come chargin' down from the head of the stretch, passin' horse after horse—like seein' tenpins knocked over in a bowlin' alley.' She added, 'Please, won't you ride him that way for me in the Derby?'"

"So she wanted you to give her a thrill. What did you say?"

"Told her that might be the way to ride a slow-breaking horse, but if you had a fast breaker you ought to get him out front, free of interference, then steady him down and

save something for that last spurt down the home stretch.
I told her Red Moon was awfully fast."

Suddenly the boy became silent.

"And a fast breaker—fast on the start?"

Barton nodded. For some reason he was becoming
secretive again.

"What else did you tell her about Red Moon?"

"Nothin', sir."

"You sure?"

A look of fright came into Barton's eyes. "Yes sir—yes
sir! I—I wasn't goin' to give 'way my ridin' secrets. You
see, I was the boy who made a winner out o' Red Moon.
Because I know how to ride him—but that's my secret!"

"Don't worry, Danny. I'm not asking for your riding
secrets. Did you tell her how you were going to ride Red
Moon?"

"No sir, I did not!" He was emphatic on that. "I just
asked her why she wanted me to come from behind and
I told her about the two ways of ridin'. But I didn't say
which way I was usin'—tomorrow. You know, sometimes
you change styles—to throw 'em off."

Austen nodded.

"There was that match race at Pimlico between Seabiscuit and War Admiral. Ever'body—includin' War Admiral's
people—thought Seabiscuit was a slow breaker. So they'd
outrun him in the first mile. But Seabiscuit—and Georgie
Woolf on him—fooled ever'body by takin' the lead at the
start an' beatin' the livin' daylights—"

"Yes, yes," Austen broke in, "but let's get back to Marge
Maxwell. What did you finally say to her?"

"Told her I was goin' to ride the winnin' way—and that
would be decided on in the paddock—just before we went
to the post."

"What did she say then?"

"She—why, it was kinda funny, Major. She come up close to me, and she sort of half whispered, so nobody'd hear: 'Think it over, Danny, because I want you to win.'"

"And what did you think of that?"

Again the rider looked confused. "I—I sorta didn't know what to think," he admitted. "You see, she was sweet and nice—not like some of the hard ones. I thought maybe she was tippin' me off to somethin'—I—I don't know, sir."

"You are an experienced jockey. Were you a little bit suspicious?"

"Yes sir, I was."

"Tell anybody?"

"No sir. Nothin' to tell—just a hunch that ever'thin' wasn't exactly jake."

"If you were on Red Moon tomorrow how would you ride?"

"Why—I—I—that's my secret, sir! Just give me a chance—I'll show you!"

Austen smiled. "Good lad! Keep your winning secrets to yourself. Now, Sergeant, suppose you call the turnkey. Let Danny get a good night's sleep."

The jockey was led away. The three men looked knowingly at one another for a moment.

Austen spoke: "Doyle represents gamblers. You said it first, Shep. Those Chicago gamblers took thousands of dollars on Red Moon in the Derby—"

Thomas broke in: "And they planned to tie up Red Moon—win every nickel of that coin! They were going to get control of the colt through Sam Bosun, then scratch him out of the race. Every penny bet on him in the future book would be forfeited then."

"If they couldn't do that," Austen added, "they were going to try to control the jockey."

"The old stunt," Thomas said with a wry smile, "always good—of sending a pretty girl out to snare him."

Sergeant Hunt chimed in: "I don't know Doyle. I do know his type. Don't think he would kill himself—if it was merely a matter of money. But he'd egg on another person to do it, and he's got the brains to plant the suggestion in somebody's mind."

"Huh, you Southerners are psychological man hunters." Shep Thomas grinned.

Hunt grinned back. "Guy Slenk lost his horse today, didn't he? Didn't feel any too good about it, did he?" Austen and Thomas shook their heads. "Rock Doyle lost control of the colt—and maybe some thousands." Hunt was silent a moment. Then, "We got Slenk back there now."

The desk sergeant called around the doorjamb:

"Maje, phone for you! Take it in there?"

"Yes. Thanks, Sarge." Austen took up the captain's phone.

George Trigg's voice came over the wire.

"That you, Major?"

"Yes, where've you been? Did you find 'em?"

"I know, Major, I been away a mighty long time."

"Did you find the woman and Doyle?"

"Yes, Major, I found 'em. I got 'em both."

"Where are you, Trigg?"

"First, lemme tell you—we crossed the state line. I'm way 'cross in Indianny."

"In heaven's name, come to the point! Where are you now?"

"Major, I got 'em both: Doyle and the woman. I followed 'em way over the state line. They were beatin' it. She'd been out to Madison's. Their car skidded, climbed a telegraph pole. I got 'em both, and they're guilty as hell!"

16

George Trigg's voice came over the wire in exultant tones: "I got 'em, Major—Rock Doyle and the girl—and they're guilty, I tell you!"

"One minute! Where are you, Trigg?"

"Callin' from the hospital."

"What hospital?"

"Over here." The little man named a community far across the Ohio River. He said: "I followed instructions, boss. I tailed 'em. They were headin' full speed for Chicago. I'm behind 'em. They skid—climb a telegraph pole. Smash the car. Somethin' awful. I stop and pull 'em out. Awful job it was, Major."

"Yes, yes. Go on."

"Then I brung 'em here to the hospital—my car. They're still out—dead to the world. Want me to stay here?"

"Right where you are, Trigg. We'll be there." Austen put down the phone, repeated the facts to Thomas and Hunt. The detective was on his feet. "Let's get going," he said.

Shep Thomas snapped his fingers. "You fellows go on. Now's when I beat it to the newspaper office, and do I scoop the world on this yarn!"

"Better go slow," Hunt cautioned.

"Huh?"

105

Hunt grinned, said, "There may be another girl, you know."

"I know, but we got one girl, and I'm going to town with her. If you fellows tell anybody else what Danny Barton told us—"

"Sure, you'll cut our gizzards out," Austen said. "We're too busy to talk to anyone. Let's go, Sergeant." But Shep Thomas passed through the door first, rushing to a typewriter.

Forty-five minutes later Roderick Austen and Sergeant Hunt were within the white walls of a small-town hospital. George Trigg, looking tired but happy, was telling his story.

"I got there, waited across the road from the drive leadin' to Madison's house. I see a big snappy roadster lookin' like the one Doyle rode off in comin' up. It slowed down awful quick when it got near—then idled along. Clouds made a spot in the sky for two-three minutes—piece of a moon gimme light. I see a woman—a girl—drivin'. The one what was at the door with Rock Doyle."

"Was she alone—could you see?" Austen asked.

"Yes sir, boss, she was. She started to turn in the driveway. Then she thinks better of it. She stops, then she drives on slow-like, about two hundred yards past the place—you know, no houses near Madison's on either side. Well, sir, she drove up there and she stopped. She—"

"Switch her lights off?" Hunt asked.

"Yeah. From where I was standin' you couldn't see that roadster, hardly; she'd pulled off the road under a heavy tree—"

"What time was this?" Austen broke in.

"Eight o'clock. She got out the car—come walkin' down the road. I walk toward her. I passed mighty close, wanted to be sure it was her. It was. She just went right on by me."

"Did you follow her?" Austen demanded.

"Well, now, Major, I—"

"Did you follow her?"

"I understand you to say I was to cover—that is, wait outside, and then when she come back to follow her."

"All right. Go on."

"I got an idea. I'd went out in a taxi but had let the taxi go. But I had to cover her, didn't I?"

"Sure."

"Well, I didn't know which way she'd go and I couldn't follow her on my dogs—she might see me—" He hesitated and grinned.

"Yes, yes," Austen prodded him. "What did you do then?"

"I climb into the rumble seat of her car. Yes sir! I did." The head on the misshapen shoulders nodded vigorously. "You see, rumble seat was open—had a couple tall packages there that pried up the top. I get in, drop down on the floor. Suddenly I hear somethin'. A backfire. Or—"

"No, it wasn't backfire," Austen snapped. "It was a shot, and you know it. Cut the drama."

"Yes sir. Sounded like it was in Madison's office."

Austen's face was getting red. "And what did you do— just lie there?"

"No sir, I didn't. I stood up. Then I see somethin' sort of white-like comin' across the grass, comin' cater-cornered from the house. The girl was dressed in white. I figgered it was her. Look like she was sneakin' out, so I drop back to the floor. I hear her footsteps—soft, light-like. She jumps into the car, pantin', and I hear her say to herself, 'Of all the doggoned luck!'

"She was mad about somethin'. Then she steps on the gas, and she sho did step. We come straight to town."

"You know Madison was killed, don't you? What you thought was a backfire—"

"Sure, I figgered that. Didn't the girl on the telephone tell you he was goin' to be bumped off? I can put two and

two together—same as you!" Trigg sounded aggrieved. He
went on after glaring for an instant at his boss:

"She stopped square in front of the Brown Hotel. She
got out. I heard the car door slam. I—"

"You stood up and let the world know you were in the
rumble seat?"

"Sure, I stood up." Trigg was truculent. "Had to watch
her, didn't I? I see her goin' through the revolvin' door of
the Brown. Then I step out on the sidewalk."

Sergeant Hunt leaned forward: "Didn't think about calling the police station, telling about that shot, did you?"

Trigg looked at Hunt, frowned, said: "My orders was to
follow her. If I went to a telephone she might-a got away.
But she didn't get away, 'cause I carried out orders!"

He turned back to Austen, continued:

"I guessed she'd be out soon and would drive off. So I
hired a taxi now, told him to keep that car in sight. In fifteen—well, make it twenty—minutes she come out again.
And, Major"—the man ignored Sergeant Hunt—"Rock
Doyle was with her! And behind come two boys carryin'
suitcases. They pile them cases into where I'd been, and if
I hadn't contracted for the cab—"

"Yes, yes—you did right, Trigg. Please, just keep to the
story," Austen urged.

"They drove off. I followed."

"May I ask another question, Major?" Hunt asked.

"Sure—and answer it, Trigg."

"You got a good look at her, Trigg. Did you see her
hands?"

"Why—er—yes. Yes, I sure did."

"What color gloves was she wearing?"

"Color—gloves? Why, lemme think. They—I remember—pinkish—no, sort of white."

"Then she did wear gloves when at Madison's?" the sergeant persisted.

"Why, yes. I seen her hand pushin' against the glass door to the hotel."

"That's all. Go ahead, Major."

"Trigg, what happened when you got on this side of the river?"

"Nothin' much. They shot through this town hell bent, then hit the Chicago road. Their car's makin' better time than our taxi, but we hang on, like a distance runner behind a sprinter."

"Speed it up, Trigg," Austen begged.

"Yes sir! They disappear over a hill. We hear a crash-bang! We get to the top. Moon out a little. We see down the hill, Major—"

"All right, Trigg. Keep going."

"There's a curve at the foot of that hill, and a telegraph pole, other side. They jump the road, hit the pole, tried to climb it—they crack all up! I bring 'em back—and here we are!"

Trigg beamed with success.

"Good work, boy." Austen spoke warmly to the mis-shapen, middle-aged fellow who once won great races.

"Thanks, boss. And here's the superintendent." Trigg turned importantly to a white-coated official who came into the room. Trigg introduced them.

"And I'm from the Louisville Police Headquarters." Sergeant Hunt showed his badge an instant.

The physician raised his eyebrows, asked: "Why are you here?"

"To arrest—"

"Maybe—and maybe you won't," the official said brusquely. "I'm afraid somebody else got here ahead of you."

17

Austen looked quickly at the hospital physician. He was young and dignified, inclined to be unimpressed by signs of worldly authority. He spoke as one in touch with the invisible forces that rule humanity.

"Who got here ahead of us—death?" Austen asked suddenly.

The physician removed his rimless glasses, cleaned them without speaking, replaced them on his face, and said:

"Death's outside the door of one now—door of the man. In layman's language he's unconscious, not expected to live through the night. Has a skull fracture, brain concussion, two ribs fractured, compound fracture of the right leg—"

"And the woman?" Austen broke in.

The physician shrugged shoulders. "Who knows?" He shook his head, looked from Austen to Trigg to Hunt and back to Austen. "The resistance of woman is much greater—at times. She has no fractures, but contusions and abrasions. She was unconscious when brought in, was revived and given a draught to allay pain. Sleeping restlessly now."

Austen looked at Trigg, said again; "Good work, son. Suppose you hop a bus, go home and get some sleep. Meet me at ten sharp in the morning."

"Yes sir. Sure you don't need me?"

"Sure—you've done two men's work, Trigg. Good night." As the ungainly fellow shambled out the physician said: "Your—ah—associate was quite—ah—officious. Almost ordered me around."

Austen smiled. "You understand, Doctor—just his zeal. Did he tell you anything about them?"

"Your man is closemouthed. I gathered they were criminals."

"Maybe—maybe not," Austen said.

Hunt broke in: "Mind if I take charge, Major?"

Austen nodded. Hunt went on:

"I ask that those two be held in protective custody. Suspicion of connection with the murder of Henry Madison in Louisville tonight."

"Ah!" Then the physician caught himself, maintained his impersonal calm. "The turfman?"

"Right," said Hunt. "Will the man regain consciousness?"

"I do not think so."

"The woman . . . ?"

"Doubt if she will be rational for some hours. Would you like to see for yourself—since you are a detective?"

"Both of us would," Hunt said.

They were led first into the men's ward. There lay what was left of the living Rock Doyle, seemingly a mass of bandages. One bandaged and strapped leg was elevated on a pulley. Nothing of his face showed save his blade-like lips, partially opened, and the end of the scar on his cheek. The man was moaning.

"Seen a good many in that fix," Hunt spoke softly to Austen. "Doubt if we'll ever get his story." Then to the physician, "Now the woman?"

"This way."

They were led across the hall. Austen asked:

"You found their names in bags or billfolds?"

"The name on the chart of the man, I noticed, was marked 'Rock Doyle.' An attendant had marked 'Margaret Maxwell' on the woman's chart. So"—he smiled slightly—"I presume their names were found. Now—in here."

The physician led the way into the women's ward. They passed a cot on which lay a silent, still figure, curled up like a gnome.

"No—not that one." The official scowled as Hunt paused an instant. "Here." He had stopped at the foot of the second cot.

Austen stepped up beside him, Hunt on the other side.

In front of them lay a woman—not the glamorous girl of the afternoon or the seductive creature who had tried to tell the great little Barton how to ride a race. Instead here was a common and coarse piece of flesh and blood, breathing in jerks which caused the plain white sheet to rise and fall with her full breasts. The make-up had been wiped from her face. The platinum hair was pulled straight back. Now and then she gasped; again she moaned.

"She'll come out all right," Hunt said.

"You think so?" the doctor asked pointedly.

"You said so, didn't you?" The detective smiled as he asked the question.

The physician shrugged shoulders, as though it were a matter not to be discussed further.

"May I see one of her hands, Doctor?" Austen asked.

The physician looked at him curiously. Austen's expression was blank.

"Why—ah—certainly."

The physician himself lifted the cover, raised her right arm.

Austen took one quick look, so did Hunt. The investigator and the detective glanced quickly at each other.

"Short, thick peasant fingers," Austen murmured. "You'll talk to me tomorrow, old girl."

"I beg pardon?" The official frowned at Austen after drawing the coverlet up again.

"Nothing of interest, Doctor," Austen said easily. "But this is important: May Sergeant Hunt sit in a chair by her bed during the night? A lot of truth—sometimes—comes out before a person is fully conscious, but I don't have to tell you that."

"He may. We always co-operate."

"And will you keep reporters out?"

"We always do."

"Thank you, Doctor. And let me speak to you, Hunt."

In the hallway Austen said:

"You know what to do?"

"Sure!"

"You know we are in a tough spot," Austen went on. "We've got two people wearing gloves—a man and a woman. One had threatened to kill Madison—the other was there when he was killed. Now both of them are *blotto*. Question: Which one did it?"

Hunt's face was thoughtful. "You forget a third person—the jockey, Barton. He was caught there and he'd threatened to kill the big fellow too."

"You really think he did it?"

The sergeant was silent for a long moment. At last he said :

"In the department we can't overlook bets."

"You're right." Austen nodded. "But the next time a murder's done I hope somebody's caught doing it—instead of a whole convention found running away from the crime. Good night. I'm going to bed."

But Austen spoke too quickly. His night had only begun.

He had driven slowly across the bridge and back into Louisville's business section, when he saw something. Something that caused his eyebrows to arch upward.

He slowed down at the curb, looked out again, whistled softly, then said aloud:

"I would forget that. And right before my eyes too."

18

One of the city's nighthawks jumped in front of Austen as he stepped to the sidewalk, shoved something toward him.

"Extry! Read about Jockey Barton killin' Red Moon's owner."

Austen took the paper, said: "Here's a quarter." He held it in his hand. "If it says that, man, I'll give you the quarter."

The man's dirty face crinkled in the street's light. "It makes 'em buy the paper, boss. It does say—look!" The eight-column streamer proclaimed:

JOCKEY BARTON HELD AFTER
RED MOON'S OWNER SLAIN!

"Do you think Barton killed that man?"

"Me? *Naw!*" The syllable came out with explosive force. "I've seen him—he's a decent kid, boss. You know them flatfoots—they grab the first guy they see. Gotta catch somebody."

Austen gave him the coin. "Keep the quarter—and good luck!"

"Thanks, boss!" He turned, ran across the street, accosted a group of girls and men: "Extry! Extry! All about Jockey Barton killin' Red Moon's owner!"

"I'm darned," Austen muttered to himself, then grinned. Business was business with the newsdealer.

Austen shrugged his shoulders, turned around. Before him stood the *something* which had caused him to stop his car.

It was the wagon diner, from where the last mysterious phone calls had been traced, a structure built to resemble a railroad car and extending from the street back to an alleyway.

Austen walked up three steps, pulled a weighted door back, stepped into the corridorlike eating wagon, with its long counter and row of stools. The door slammed shut behind him. One glance, and Austen saw a phone booth—empty—near the alley entrance.

Even at this hour—past midnight—the place was half filled. Women, men—quite a few in tails and white ties—were munching hot dogs and discussing the Derby between bites.

"Red Moon's a standout." . . . "Shame Barton killed Madison." . . . "Don't believe he did it." . . . "There's a long shot to look out for."

Austen took a place near the cash register. He guessed the owner was on duty tonight—the small-eyed, sullen-faced fat man standing behind the register.

He ordered chili and buttermilk from a counterman, then spoke to the sullen-faced one. "You doing good business here."

"Me? I'd make money if there was a Derby onct a week. Half the time fellers come in just want free water or to telephone. No dice in that."

"I'll say there isn't," Austen agreed, ladling a spoonful of chili. "Course you can't refuse a man a glass of water. But I bet you make money having a telephone here."

"Yeah? What I figgered I'd do. Phone feller said to put it back there—everybody'd have to walk by the grub to get to it—make 'em hungry. But now they come in that back door—don't have to pass the counter."

"How's that?" Austen asked innocently. "I thought that's an alleyway back there."

"So 'tis." The proprietor moved a toothpick from the left to the right side of his pudgy lips. "But a good many people park cars back there when they're goin' to the theaytre."

"You mean the playhouse—"

Austen paused, to let the man finish the sentence for him.

"Yeah. They opened it up for the Derby season, brought a—a stock company down from New York. Been runnin' a coupla weeks." The man chewed on his toothpick, frowned, went on:

"Seems like ever'body that parks back in the alley forgets to empty the ice pan or let the cat out. So they come in here before they go to the show—telephone home—they see that Bell sign hangin'. Had a line—five-six people—people with dough, too—waitin' to use it tonight. Not one of 'em bought a hamburger, much less a nickel hot dog."

"That's too bad! Can you remember any of them?"

"Say! I got troubles enough without tryin' to remember people who don't spend dough here. Why you want to know?"

"Oh, nothing." Austen sipped his buttermilk. "Friend of mine tried to play a joke on me. Think he put in a couple of calls from this place tonight."

"Did, eh?" The man's jaw set solidly. He looked straight at Austen. At last he said: "I don't remember a soul that was here—not a one. I got troubles o' my own." He turned his shoulder toward Austen, nibbled again on his toothpick.

"Sure, we've all got them," Austen agreed. He finished his chili, called for another buttermilk, then changed his mind.

"Coffee," he said.

"Black or white?"

"Straight black!"

"Java from the coalbin!"

A moment later a cup of weak, steaming coffee was put in front of Austen. "Sugar, sir?" The tall, blond waiter suddenly became servile, as if he wanted something. Austen shook his head. The man took a napkin from the box, opened it partially, placed it at Austen's right hand.

"Got a sure winner for tomorrow, Cap?" He leaned over, asked the question in low tones.

"No." Austen looked up. "Have you?"

"Well, now, I—"

Austen took one, two gulps of the coffee, pushed it away. He placed a dime under the saucer, took up his check, laid it and two coins by the side of the cash register. The money was rung up. The waiter still stood leaning over the counter.

"I—I got a sure thing up my sleeve, boss," he said out of the corner of his mouth. "Friend o' mine who rubs horses for Monahan, he says he knows a dark horse—been kept under cover."

"Yes?" Austen looked innocently at the man.

"For about five bucks I might tell a pal," he was saying, when Austen cut him short:

"You mean you are willing to divulge such priceless information for a measley five bucks? Why, man alive"— Austen was on his feet—"you've got a fortune in your grasp if you positively know the winner! Don't dare tell it to a soul! You go out to Churchill Downs—win all the money yourself! I wouldn't think of depriving you of your secret for as little as a five-spot."

Austen turned aside to keep a straight face. He heard the man mutter: "What the heck! Who does he think he is, anyway?"

The man moved off as someone at the far end called: "Waiter—service—a tall waiter for a tall glass!"

There was sudden laughter, shouts, from the diner's far end. Austen turned around. One man, silk hat in front of him on the counter, was playing the drum with knife and fork beating on the hat. Others were pounding the counter with glasses, silverware; one even smashed a plate down on the floor.

"Heh! Dollar for the plate—four bits for the waiter!"

Austen heard the man at the cash register curse and call out: "Buddy, that plate costs you two dollars!"

"What do I care? Here goes 'nother—and keep the change!"

Another plate was smashed to the tile floor. The man's crowd laughed and chortled. Someone tossed a five-dollar bill on the counter. "Take it out of that!"

Now there was a movement down the line. Someone was pushing through and against protests:

"Heh—you can't leave us this soon. Night's just begun! Lis-listen! Let's stay up till Derby's run!"

Not one, but two persons broke loose from the group, started for the center door of the diner. One was a girl. She was the most gorgeous creature Roderick Austen had ever seen. For an instant he stood still, actually staring at her beauty. Then he noticed the man with her—it was Shep Thomas!

His hand half outstretched, Austen went toward them, just as Shep reached the center door.

"Why, hello, Shep!" Austen smiled at the newspaper-man. Shep Thomas looked around, saw Austen, stared at him an instant. There wasn't a flicker of recognition in his eyes. Then he spoke to his companion:

"Come, my dear," he said in drawling tones. "Shall we go?"

The girl nodded without speaking, glanced at Austen, turned her head away quickly, drew a silver fox around her shapely shoulders. Shep Thomas flung back the door. He placed the other hand on the girl's arm; she smiled up at him.

Together the girl and Shep Thomas passed out into the night.

"What the hell!" Austen exclaimed. He saw them wave a cab and step within; ten seconds later they were out of sight.

Austen muttered something under his breath, then went through the door himself.

"Heh, buddy!" the tall, blond counterman was calling. "I'll give you that winner for a two-spot!"

19

Roderick Austen let the door of the wagon diner slam behind him. He went down the three steps to the pavement. A news hawk came out of the shadows, calling:

"Extry! All about Jockey Barton killin' Red Moon's owner. Extry, mister?"

Austen stopped on the sidewalk. He asked, "Do you ever look at the face of your customer?"

"I got my eyes peeled for coin, boss." The man glanced up. Recognition showed in his words. "Oh, gee!" He backed off.

Austen smiled wryly, went to his car, got behind the wheel, and closed the door. He sat motionless for a moment. Once, twice, three times his fist struck the horn button. Three spaced blasts sounded in the night. The news hawk shuffled over diffidently, peered into the car, and asked:

"You want somethin', boss?"

Austen turned his head. "Thanks, no." He slammed his foot on the self-starter, threw the car into gear. Ten minutes later he stopped in front of the old-fashioned house where he had holed in for the Derby season. The outlines of a familiar figure showed on the stoop.

It was George Trigg.

The ex-jockey rose, rubbed his lantern jaw, said:

"Major, there's a question I'd like to ask; mebbe you'd like to ask it too."

"Come inside—these stones are hard. Something I want to tell you too."

"You seen another girl?" Trigg asked quickly.

Austen stopped inside the doorway. "Now what put that thought in your mind?"

"Well . . ." Again the ex-jockey stroked his chin.

"Come on." Austen led him to his apartment, opened the door, flashed on the light. "Come in." He closed the door quietly, threw off his hat, sprawled in the table chair. George Trigg was sitting opposite him, sitting on the edge of his chair.

"Yes, I've seen a girl, Trigg. A—a beautiful girl." He added thoughtfully, "One of the most gorgeous girls I've ever seen."

Trigg looked at him curiously. "Who was she, boss?"

"Her name? Oh, I—I didn't meet her."

"How come?"

Austen gave a laugh. "Mr. Thomas—Mr. Shep Thomas —saw to it that I didn't meet her. He was her escort."

"You mean he—he—"

"Yes, he cut me dead tonight, Trigg. Wouldn't speak when I did. Oh, he recognized me all right! And it was Shep Thomas. I heard his voice!"

Austen told the incident. "What do you make of it?" He watched Trigg sharply.

"Listen, boss," Trigg said, "that Mr. Thomas—he warn't no jealous pup with a pretty bone. He—he must-a had good reason for not wantin' to speak. Them calls—two of 'em—come from that wagon diner. And you see Mr. Thomas and a beaut of a girl together in that diner—" He broke off, stroked his chin reflectively an instant. He finished: "He'd-a given you a meetin' to her if—if she was jus' a girl friend or somebody he'd jus' met himself. But she—she might-a be the girl, Major. She's pretty—you say. That's the kind men shoot over. Mebbe he wanted to sound her out—first."

"Maybe."

Both men were silent a moment. Austen looked up. "She's the dashing, mistress-of-herself type that would appeal to Madison. But, Trigg—"

"Yes, boss?"

"She looked as if she didn't have a care in the world! Now if she'd been mixed in a murder—"

Trigg broke in with a grin, "I'd say she's happy 'cause she ain't mixed in it; the cops are sayin' Danny Barton did it—not her sweetie."

Silence again.

Austen bit his lips. "You're right."

"Women—they fool you. When you think they are— they ain't. I knew a girl once, back in the days when I was ridin' at Tanforan—"

"Yes, Trigg. I remember that story," Austen interrupted. "But—well, I'll corner Shep Thomas first thing in the morning. Now what was that question you wanted to ask?"

"Well, sir, I sorta wonder if anybody talked with Guy Slenk a-fore he got in that taxicab? Did anybody put idees in his head?"

Instantly Austen reached for the phone.

"Somebody might-a egged him on to Madison."

Austen was dialing police headquarters. He said over the transmitter:

"You earn your month's pay, asking that question, Trigg. Answer may tell a lot."

"Slenk might have a silent partner," Trigg said, warming up. "Like a lot of owners. He might be a plunger. Mebbe he bet heavy on Red Moon in the future books. Slenk tells him he's losin' the horse, that Jockey Barton won't ride. Shucks! Can't you see a desp'rate gamblin' partner sendin' him out to Madison?"

The phone clicked. Austen heard, "Police headquarters!"

An instant later Austen had the desk sergeant:

". . . and, Sarge, you've got your hands on that driver who drove Slenk around? . . . Good! Coming right down—want to ask him something. . . . No, Sergeant Hunt's across the river on another angle. . . . Be right down."

He shut off the phone. "Go home, Trigg. You've done your work today."

Trigg grinned with embarrassment. "If it's all the same to you, Major, I'm goin' to the station house with you."

"Suppose you come, then—for luck."

Twenty minutes later the taxi driver, protesting, was brought into the station house's front room. He rubbed his eyes and squawked:

"You flatfeet got nothin' on me. You—"

"Shut up!" a turnkey commanded. "You got no kick. You're just in protective custody. We lettin' you sleep on a detective's cot."

"I want my own bed!"

Austen nodded to the turnkey. "Thanks—and close the door as you go out, will you?" To the driver, "Now, buddy, if you answer all our questions—well, you'll be out just that much quicker. When you picked Guy Slenk up tonight—seven o'clock, wasn't it?—who was talking to him?"

"Say, what's this?" The chauffeur drew a threadbare and oversized topcoat tightly about him. "You tryin' to put me on the pan? I ain't done nothin'. And I want my four bucks and extry change Guy Slenk owes me."

The desk sergeant had stepped into the room a moment. "Shut up, Haney! We got nothin' against you now, but we'll have plenty if you don't answer Major Austen's questions. If you don't want to talk we'll hold you as accessory before the tact—five-thousand-dollar bail. Speak up or shut up."

The driver did neither. His mouth widened. He howled.

"You dumb clucks can't do nothin' to me! I'm good as you! Guy Slenk owes me four-twenty on my meter. You gotta get it for me. I pay a hacking license. You gotta make Slenk pay."

"Wait, wait!" Austen raised a hand, then the fingers of that hand went into a vest pocket where he kept money for emergencies. The fingers drew out a five-dollar bill.

"Guy Slenk owes you four-twenty; here's five, and keep the change, buddy. And I'm sure the captain will let you go your way tomorrow—after you get some sleep."

A dirty hand took the bill. A none-too-clean face expanded into a big-mouth grin. "Now that's somethin' like it. What you want to know, mister?"

Austen asked his leading question casually: "You remember the man Slenk was talking to just before you picked Slenk up?"

"Remember him? Jees, I should! A perfect gent—like you, mister! I pick him up at the Muhlbach Hotel—'bout seven; he tells me to drive, slow-like, to the Saddle Rock Café—"

Austen made a gesture to stop the torrent of words. "You knew him, of course?"

"Sure, mister. Didn't he give me a buck tip? And yestiddy when I hauled him to the Downs he says:

"'Wait here for me—never mind the meter. I'll make it square.'

"I wait twenty minutes—mebbe it was a half-hour—and when I take him back to the Muhlbach he slips me a five-spot."

"You had never hauled him before yesterday, had you?"

"Never seen him before yestiddy, but when I drop him back at the Muhlbach the starter, he says:

"'Jees, you had a swell fare. What'd he slip you?'

"'Oh, a buck,' I says, knowin' if I say more he'll want a split. You know how those clucks are—always wantin' a cut from a honest guy, specially if it's more'n a buck.'"

Austen grinned, shot a quick glance at Trigg, who answered it. He'd let the driver ramble on until he revealed what Austen wanted to know.

"And the starter says:

"'Jees, gen'rally he slips a two-spot or better.'

"And I says:

"'Well, I didn't haul him far,' and he says:

"'If you'll do the hotsy-totsy I'll steer him to you every time he comes out—if you're in line. He's gravy-rich.'

"I says:

"'Okay by me—who is the bird?'

"He looks at me like I'm ign'rant an' says:

"'Don't you know him?'

"I says, 'I ain't been here but four months from Noo Yawk.' He tells me:

"'That's a perfect gent. He's Colonel James Pigler—got a big place back o' Henry Madison's but comes here every day.'

"That cluck, I figger, I can do business with him, so I do the hotsy-totsy—slips him a half buck—and he thanks me."

George Trigg, rubbing his jaw in excitement, leaned forward, broke in:

"That's Jim Pigler! He's owned some big horses."

"So, Haney, you reached the Saddle Rock Café," Austen said. "And what did Colonel Pigler say when he stepped out?"

"He steps out, hands me a buck, says, 'Keep the change, son,' and as he starts off I hollers, 'Don't you want me to wait, Col'nel?' He says I can hang round if I want to—that he's got to meet a feller.

"So I hang round. Col'nel Pigler, he goes into the Saddle Rock. Through the winder I see him takin' a snifter. Pretty soon he comes to the door, looks at his watch, then goes back in. In a minute—mebbe two—Guy Slenk comes up and goes in the joint. I know Slenk—seen him at Empire City lots."

"Play the ponies, Haney?" Austen broke in.

"Well, mister, when I get a sure thing."

"Sure!" Again Austen grinned. "Go on."

"In five, mebbe ten minutes, Slenk and Col'nel Pigler come out together. I raises my hand, but they pay no 'tention, go walkin' down the street. Lot o' street light there, and I see the Col'nel is mad-like. He hits the pavement hard with his cane. I follow along the curb, then stop at the corner. I draw 'longside. I hear Slenk say:

"'He stole my horse,' and the Col'nel breaks in, 'Your fault, you fool! Now do as I say,' and Slenk says back, 'You leave this to me—I know my business.' He turns and, seein' my cab, starts in. The Col'nel says after him:

"'You messed this up enough. My advice to you is to steer clear of that girl. Girls are poison!'"

20

The taxi driver, Haney, drew a long breath. He again pulled his too-big coat tightly around him. He looked at George Trigg, then at Roderick Austen.

"If they'd let me out of this here station house—so's I could get back to work—" he said meaningly.

"You may be out in the morning—if you keep on answering questions straight," Austen advised.

Haney grinned. "Okay by me, mister. I'm tryin' to help. You been square—"

"What happened," Austen cut in, "after the Colonel shouted that advice to Slenk?"

"Col'nel Pigler stomped off, mad-like. Slenk tells me to take him to Sam's for a drink. That's where he got the gun."

Austen stopped him. "I know. Now what'd he tell you about the girl?"

"What girl?"

"You know—the girl."

"No, I don't, mister."

"The girl the Colonel spoke of."

"Honest, I don't know her, mister."

"Didn't you hear her name? Didn't Slenk repeat it to himself?"

"No sir! All I hear is what Col'nel Pigler say, 'My advice to you is to steer clear of that girl. Girls are poison.'"

"But while riding in your cab Slenk named the girl—"

"No sir-ree! Hope to die he didn't! He never mentioned no dame. Guy Slenk's mind was on somethin' else, mister. It was on a horse—his horse he says was stole. That's all he talked about—never mentioned a dame a-tall."

"That's all. Thanks, Haney. Trigg, call the turnkey."

Haney stood up, once more drew the huge overcoat around his small body. "Any time you want me, mister—"

"Thank you, Haney," Austen said as the turnkey put a hand on Haney's shoulder.

When the room was cleared Austen turned to Trigg.

"A good question, son. Now—for Pigler." He thought a moment, said aloud: "Peculiar gambler—Pigler: sometimes he's a bookmaker on a big scale, taking bets others shy away from; then—"

"Then he plays the fool"—Trigg spoke with a chuckle —"and plays the ponies hisself. Bet he laid some long bets on Red Moon in the future books—mebbe with Rock Doyle's gang."

"Maybe. Of course he knows the woman—or girl—who seems to have messed things up for them all. Think that's Marge Maxwell?"

"I"—Trigg grinned—"I kinda like that beauty you been ravin' about, boss, specially since Mr. Thomas seems to be playin' safe with her."

"Thing to do is to see Pigler, but first we're overlooking a man who may be able to tell us a lot: Dr. Ralph Fellowes. Did he—?"

"I believe he got in the car with Madison." Trigg anticipated the question. "Remember, I say I seen him walkin' around it. Course he could-a gone across the street—lot o' people—heavy traffic."

"I'll call him."

Three minutes later:

"Major Austen?" The voice at the other end of the wire was firm, wide awake. "You won't disturb me at all! I've been searching for the address of Madison's half brother —just found it. If you'll come by the club I'll be in the secretary's office. . . . Glad to see you."

Austen put the phone down. "One man we don't have to badger into talking. Let's go."

A man, his back to the door, was standing at the desk as they entered the club. A man in black coat, light trousers. He turned; it was Fellowes. The physician smiled.

"Glad you got here. I've just found that address, and now I'm sending off the wire telling of Madison's death— beastly job, nobody else to do it."

"You his closest friend?"

Fellowes shook his head. "He had no close friends—to my knowledge. Guess I was as near as—as he'd let anyone be. Peculiar man—you know that yourself. But come, let's go into the lounge."

He led them across the hallway and into a heavily furnished room which was deserted now.

"The crowd's downstairs—hear them?"

Austen and Trigg could catch the muffled sounds of merriment below.

"Night before the Derby, y'know."

Fellowes waved them to a lounge, drew up a chair facing them, and sprawled in it. Though crisp in manner, he had none of the marks of the physician. He was distinctly man-about-townish, a man of the fleshpots.

He smiled. "Now—shoot!"

"As you might guess, we're checking every angle," Austen explained. Fellowes nodded. "What you tell us may throw a light on something else."

"Certainly, I understand. After we left your place Madison dropped me off here at the club."

"Just what happened after you left my place?"

"Shall I tell you in chronological order?"

"Yes—please." Austen apparently had relaxed into a corner of the blue overstuffed divan, but from that position he could catch every shade of expression upon Fellowes' face.

"When we left Madison remarked that the Doyle person represented a Chicago gambling syndicate—that Sam Bosun was merely a *front*, he called it, for the gamblers.

"Now Rock Doyle was desperate; his people must have taken many a wager on Red Moon, for he was fighting to get his hands on the colt, Henry said, to scratch him out of the race so his people could win all that future money. I—"

"Did Doyle speak to the two of you?"

"Coming to that. As I walked around Madison's car to get in on the right side this Doyle came up. He said:

"'Madison, I'll give you forty thousand, spot cash, for that colt.'

"Madison sneered at him. Doyle said:

"'I'll make it fifty thousand—and one third of what he might win tomorrow.'

"Madison leaned out, cursed him—"

"What did he say?" Austen asked.

"That Doyle was a shyster and a bastard. Then Madison stepped on the gas, and our car roared off. Madison was furious. He swore again.

"'Those blankety-blank gamblers want to get Red Moon,' he said, 'to scratch him—to make thousands of people lose money they bet on him. I'm keeping him in the race and I'm winning with him. They can't have the colt for a million dollars.'

"And, gentlemen"—Fellowes nodded his head—"I'm fully convinced that Madison would have spurned the million if it had been offered."

"Any women in Madison's life?" Austen asked.

"I'd imagine there were many," Fellowes answered quickly, "but I wouldn't know them. Our interests ran on diverse lines." He added, "'Fraid I'm a bit more bookish than Henry Madison was—not that I'm a saint under glass, y'know."

Austen looked straight at Fellowes, said quietly, "When you were in my place I overheard Madison say to you, 'Ralph, think I'll throw a party for her tonight. Celebrate getting Red Moon.' Who was the girl, Dr. Fellowes?"

"His latest flame," Fellowes answered promptly, "and if I knew her name I wouldn't tell you—but I don't know it." He smiled. "Some girl he had just met—someone here for the Derby season. There are thousands of visitors in town, y'know—in fact, I've taken a house myself for entertaining. He'd mentioned her name; it went out of my ear—and memory.

"You must understand," he said matter-of-factly, "that Madison was talking women most of the time. Generally I was saying yes, yes, and letting it go at that. We had a strong mutual ground—our love of horses. Madison knew breeding, bloodlines, and that's a hobby of mine. So at times I had to listen to his babblings about women."

"What was the woman's last name?" Austen persisted.

"My word of honor"—the physician spoke quietly—"I know neither the first nor the last name."

"Was it Maxwell—Marge Maxwell?"

"No! And it wasn't Barbara or Jane or Marylyn. Really, I don't know. I'm not lying."

"Thank you, Doctor. You last saw Madison—"

"When he dropped me here."

George Trigg spoke quickly: "What time was it, Doc?"

"Shortly after seven, I'd say."

"One minute," Austen broke in. "Could you be a little more exact?"

"I shall be." Fellowes pressed a button on a taboret. "I'll be scientific—exact." There was amusement in his tone, assurance in his manner. A green-coated attendant came softly in. "Philip, you were on the door when I came in, I believe."

"Yes sah."

"What time was it?"

"I—er—don't exactly remember, sah."

"Get my last 'in' card, Philip. Bring it here."

The attendant went out. Austen raised eyebrows at the ex-jockey. The latter spoke out: "I asked 'cause I just remembered Haney said he picked the Colonel up at seven o'clock at the Muhlbach."

Austen nodded. Nothing more was said till the boy shuffled back hesitantly. "I's sorry, sah, but I just didn't stamp yo' card, Dr. Fellowes. Didn't stamp two-three mo', neither. So many you comin' in about then, and we never has to use cards—I knows who's in—but it was about seven-thirty"—the boy was speaking fast and earnestly—"or if it warn't, then it was about seven—and if it ain't seven, then mebbe eight—"

Fellowes dismissed him with an impatient wave of the hand. "There you have it!" he exclaimed. "Nobody knows when I got here—not even myself. But I'm here."

Austen grinned. "Forget it. You are here, Doctor." Then his manner sobered. "Now tell us, who do you think killed Henry Madison?"

"Oh lord!" Fellowes threw up his hands. "How can I say? The man was no diplomat—made enemies, had a primitive streak, y'know. Went for what he wanted—took it. But now, about the colt—he was in the right in exercising his option."

"Yes, he was," Austen agreed. "Do you think Rock Doyle had provocation—"

"Rock Doyle was mad enough, desperate enough to do it—or have it done," Fellowes added slowly.

"Did you know that woman with him?"

"Never saw her before. Madison said he knew her. Strangely, he spoke well of her, said she was straight. Yes"—he grew thoughtful—"Doyle had provocation to kill. Danny Barton certainly did, yet I can't believe he's the killer type. Boy has a clean reputation; between us, I think Henry was too hard on the boy, but it was Henry's horse and not mine. Of course he never should have touched the lad."

Austen spoke: "Tell you a bit of news." He told of Trigg shadowing Doyle and Marge Maxwell.

"Splendid!" Fellowes nodded cordially to Trigg. "I know that must be hard to do—successfully. Now Doyle could have sent her out to talk with Madison. She might have lost her head, seized his pistol, but it's not probable. Possible, yes. But Guy Slenk had a better reason than the girl."

"We've got Slenk in jail now," Austen said, "but he's drunk to the world."

Fellowes nodded his head thoughtfully. "When he comes to," he remarked, "you may have something. Yet"—his brow furrowed—"people seldom kill over money down in this section, Austen—that is, money alone. Usually a woman is at the bottom of our murders—" He stopped, smiled philosophically.

Austen was sitting forward on the edge of the couch, the muscles of his face tight. His keen eyes gleamed through narrowed lids.

"Exactly an hour before Madison was killed," he said slowly, "Slenk was warned to steer clear of a certain girl."

"Slenk mixed up with a girl!" Dr. Fellowes was amusedly curious.

Austen's face relaxed. "You know who killed Madison, Fellowes," he said quietly; then in a sharp, accusing tone, "And you know the woman!"

"For heaven's sake, Austen, what are you saying?" Fellowes was more overcome with incredulity than anger. "What are you talking about?"

"You have a strong suspicion," Austen snapped back.

Fellowes met Austen's gaze soberly. "Suspicion is not enough to justify the charge of murder," he said quietly.

"No?" Austen squared his shoulders. "We may be better judges of that. You know my questioning you—this isn't an official investigation, so let's have names and facts. I give you my word, if they don't stand up I'll forget it."

Fellowes measured the detective, said nothing.

Austen remarked in slow and measured tone, "Usually I don't pass the salt or give advice till asked. Still—" He looked straight at the clubman.

"Yes?" Fellowes was studying Austen.

"Be pretty tough if you were called to headquarters—questioned, booked for withholding information—" He broke off, his face hard and set.

Blood rushed into Fellowes' lean cheeks. "This threatening, Austen, is hardly in order."

Austen repeated, "The matter dies here—if the facts you give don't justify investigation."

Silence again, broken only by sounds of a masculine chorus winging up from the taproom below.

Fellowes looked at Austen searchingly. "All right," he said after a moment's pause. "I don't volunteer this information, and I—I dislike very much to give it out."

"I understand," Austen agreed quickly, "but you've got to do it to help the law. Go on, Doctor."

Fellowes cleared his throat, looked from Trigg to Austen, drew in a deep breath, and released it.

"There's one person," he said, "who—according to his lights—had real cause to kill Madison. And murder wouldn't stop him! That man's Colonel James Pigler. Know him?"

21

Trigg fidgeted on his stool; looked, openmouthed, at Austen. The investigator nodded his head ever so slightly.

"Either of you know Colonel James Pigler?" Fellowes asked again.

"Known him for years," Trigg answered quickly. "A tough 'un too."

"I know him—casually"—Austen spoke with understatement—"as I know scores of men on the turf."

"Then you know how proud he is. Madison—" Fellowes hesitated. "Madison barged into Pigler's preserve and stole his girl."

"How do you know that?" Austen demanded.

"Last night Madison dined with me. He had drunk too much. Suddenly he laughed and asked:

"'Seen old Jim Pigler lately?'

"I hadn't. Henry said:

"'Old Jim Pigler is dragging his tail between his legs.'

"I asked him why. He took another drink, said:

"'Ralph, I've struck Achilles in the heel—wounded his pride.'

"Naturally I asked how. He winked, took one more drink, explained:

"'I've stolen Jim Pigler's girl—made a good job of it too.'"

Austen leaned forward. "But Pigler is a woman hater," he protested. "I've known the man, to speak to him, for years. He's old-fashioned toward nice women. The others he leaves severely alone." He turned to Trigg: "Remember, the taxi driver told us he heard Pigler warn Slenk, 'Girls are poison'?"

"Yes sir, he sure did."

Fellowes spoke quickly:

"I know his reputation too. I told Henry to hush his chatter, that he was drunk and talking nonsense, that Pigler didn't play with girls. Henry said:

"'Sure, he don't play with girls. But he met a girl a few months ago—the kind they used to call a nice girl. The old bozo lost his head—after all these years. Wants to marry her—honestly does. Well, Ralph'—here he drained his glass —'I've met the girl, a nice girl, Ralph, and she rather fancies me—'"

Fellowes broke off; his face colored again. "You understand, Austen," he said uncomfortably, "I don't like this tattletale business. I didn't intend to talk—"

"I know it"—Austen spoke soothingly—"but it's the only way we can get at the truth of this mess. It's tough—seeing an innocent man put to death for what somebody else did."

"I know. Well"—Fellowes shrugged his shoulders—"Henry went on talking. He said:

"'Three years ago, Ralph, Jim Pigler did me a dirty trick at Belmont Park. I kept it to myself, but I swore I'd get even with Pigler where it would hurt him the most—in his pride.'"

"What did Pigler do to Madison?" Austen asked.

"I asked the same question. Madison wouldn't say; you know how closemouthed he could be."

Austen nodded. Madison had the reputation of playing his business cards close to the vest.

"Sometime during that talk Henry mentioned her name. I was standing at the sideboard, paid no attention. You know"—a half-smile crossed his face—"Madison has bragged about a thousand girls in his time—this was just another one. I went on mixing the salad."

The man's face sobered. "Now I come to what makes me think Pigler killed Madison. Henry said:

"'I'm going to have her as guest in my box, Derby day, Ralph. That will slay old Pigler! He wanted her in his box.'

"You gentlemen know the custom, Derby day, for some girl to be not only a bachelor's guest but also his hostess for the afternoon, greeting all who come by the box to pay respects. Madison had stolen Pigler's girl and was going to flaunt his prize before the world."

Fellowes stopped, looked sharply at Austen. "That's the girl he was referring to when he spoke in your house this afternoon. I told the truth when I said I didn't know her name. If I did know her name I wouldn't tell it."

Austen and Trigg exchanged nodding glances. "Pity you don't know her," Austen said. "I'm afraid she's very much mixed in this."

"How?"

Austen shrugged his shoulders, shook his head. "I'll tell you—maybe. When I find her." He looked keenly at the physician.

"What was the last thing Madison said to you," he asked, "just as you got from his car?"

"He said he thought Pigler was looking for trouble and that he'd give him plenty."

"Did you ask what kind of trouble?"

"Yes. Henry said:

"'Jim Pigler phoned at noon—said he had to see me. I put him off. Insisted he had to see me before Derby day—'"

"One minute! Did you know Pigler and Slenk are close—have had horse dealings together?"

"No, but wouldn't be surprised."

"I happen to know," Austen told him, "that they were concerned together over Red Moon and that Guy Slenk was mixed up with a girl, too—a girl that Pigler warned him against."

The physician nodded. "I'm not surprised."

"Go on, Doctor."

"Henry, he—ah, where was I?—he said, and these were his exact words, just as he stopped in front of the club:

"'Pigler will be by tonight—says it's business, but I expect it'll be personal business.'"

"What did you say?"

"I was exasperated—Henry always flying after a new girl and falling in the soup. I warned him not to see Pigler alone, suggested he have a couple of witnesses present. He said, 'Oh, bosh!' So I got out of the car, and he drove off."

Austen was on his feet. "I'm going to see Pigler now," he said. "Come on, Trigg. Thanks, Fellowes." Then, as an afterthought, he turned to the clubman.

"Like to go along—as a friend of Madison's?"

"Why—" Fellowes hesitated, then stood up. "Yes, I would! I'm in this, now, in a manner of speaking. I'd like to be there when you quiz Pigler."

"Good!"

"I'll get my hat—be back in a minute."

Trigg looked at his boss as Fellowes went out the door. "Say! If the doc just remembered the gal's name—"

"If everybody remembered everything, Trigg," Austen interrupted, "this would be an open-and-shut case."

"Yeah—guess so. But look here, Pigler's house is on a lane, sorta back of Madison's."

"I know it," Austen said.

"He could-a—yes, he could-a—" Then Trigg abruptly changed tack. "Look, boss, you know everythin'. Who lives there with Pigler?"

"He lives alone, except for a black manservant who's stone deaf—and mute. The only other person in the house. He can't talk and tell."

Fellowes came through the doorway, hat in hand. "Couldn't help overhear that last. Wish you'd tell us all about Pigler as we drive out, Austen. Man's been a mystery, though I've known him, to speak to, for some time."

"How'd you label him?"

Fellowes fingered his hat. "Why—ah—a slender, quietly dressed, tight-lipped chap who keeps his word—if you can get it."

Austen dropped his voice. "Ever do any writing, Fellowes?"

"No." The clubman smiled. "I read."

"I suspected it," Austen said, grinning. Then, soberly, "Ever been in Pigler's house?"

"Never. Precious few have, I'll wager. Lives like a hermit. But come on." He led them into the hall. "We'll go out the back way, get my car. It's in the club lot." He started around a turn in the hall, which shut off the rear from the front entrance.

"Why not use my car?" Austen suggested. "Save taking yours out of the lot."

"All right. Thanks."

Austen revealed high lights of Pigler's career—"some facts he's conveniently forgot"—as they drove toward the city's edge. First he asked:

"How do you regard Pigler?"

"Why—ah—he's on the governor's staff," Fellowes answered slowly. "Gives a lot to charity, has owned some fine horses, though his stable wasn't so hot last year. I'd say—"

"A gentleman?"

"Why—ah—of course!"

"Where'd he get his money?"

"Why—ah—out West, I believe."

"Uh-huh! They generally do."

Fellowes' tone showed he was puzzled. "That's our understanding. Do you—?"

"Out West is a swell place to get it," Austen went on. "But how do you place him: financier, businessman, promoter—"

"Oh! Retired businessman. One who settled here, did the usual thing: established a racing stable."

"Know who he really is?"

"Why, I—I don't get you, Austen."

"Listen, Fellowes, Pigler's one of the biggest gamblers in America. I mean big."

"Pigler?"

"Yep—Pigler."

"I'd heard he bet a bit—"

"You bet he bets! But he never bets on an even chance—always makes the odds in his favor."

Austen slowed down, tooled around a stalled truck.

"There's an office," he said, "behind a plain glass door in a certain side street off Broadway. Telephones and teletypes behind that door—and men in eyeshades and open vests, working over figures. Racing figures. That's Nick the Dago's place—run by a squat, baldish man with a harelip. It's—"

"I've heard of Nick."

"He's well known among the heavy players. Runs a clearinghouse for race bets—bets wired in from half the cities of America. Bets on big races and little races. Well, Nick the Dago is the front for James Pigler, Esq., of Kentucky."

"You mean—" Fellowes broke off, astonishment in his tone.

"Sure, I mean Pigler owns the joint."

Silence in the car as they turned onto the Shore Road. Then, "By jingo, I understand it now!"

"Understand what?" Austen demanded.

"Jim Pigler going off the dead end for a girl of class. He wants somebody—in his home—somebody to—to put the stamp of dignity on his money. He found a girl, impressed her, but Madison butts in; he steals the girl— Say! Sounds like old-fashioned fiction, doesn't it? Funny, tragic," he went on. "Now one man's dead, and—"

"And here we are!" George Trigg spoke up from the back seat.

"Yes, we are!" Fellowes snapped with irritated tone.

They turned into a lane, kept on it for a hundred yards, then moved onto a curving driveway which gleamed white in the faint rays of the new moon.

The drive led to a square stucco house of the colonial type: rectangular pillars reaching from veranda to second-story roof, a house James Pigler had acquired to match his title.

No light showed as Austen's car stopped at the front steps; the wide doorway was hidden in porch shadows— shadows that stretched across the porch itself. "H'm'm. Asleep," Austen muttered. "Got your flash, Trigg?"

"Here 'tis!" The light flashed, showed them the way to the dark vestibule. "Here's the bell," Trigg said, finding it on the right side. Trigg pressed the bell button, released the flashlight. Now they were in darkness.

"Better push that bell hard," Austen suggested.

Trigg leaned his small, lean body against it. A sudden blast of sound echoed in the rear.

"That oughta wake 'em up," Trigg muttered. Again he pressed the button. Again the house reverberated with the ringing of a giant bell.

Trigg stepped away from the button. They waited. No stirring within. No light. Outside, and beyond them, the wind soughed through the boughs of maple trees, then died off. The place seemed completely desolate.

22

For what seemed a long while those three men—Major Roderick Austen, Dr. Ralph Fellowes, and George Trigg—stood waiting in the deep shadows on James Pigler's porch.

"I'm tryin' once more," Trigg finally muttered and again leaned against the bell button.

Once more the house resounded with deafening clangor and was followed by deep silence. "Nobody home," Trigg muttered. "Wait a minute," Austen said. "Try the bell again." Trigg did. Resounding ringing—then the place was utterly silent. Austen started to say something, but suddenly lights flooded the porch. The three men turned toward the door. Someone behind that door had switched on the porch's overhead lights.

The door itself was swinging back—slowly, soundlessly. Inch by inch that whitened portal opened into blackness. The listening men heard a sound from across the threshold, as if something heavy and cumbersome were being dragged across polished wood.

The dragging sound ceased. The eyes of the men, now accustomed to the heavy gloom, could make out a bulky form moving within.

Lights flashed on inside the hallway.

Fellowes, standing slightly to the front and on the left of Austen, threw his head back. "God!" he exclaimed. Then, again:

"Great God! Look!"

Framed in the doorway stood two figures: that of
Colonel James Pigler and his black deaf-mute bodyguard,
Brutus.

The giant black—he was more than six feet tall, with
enormous shoulders—was dressed in black-and-white liv-
ery. He stood erect, but one arm was stretched around the
immaculately dressed Colonel James Pigler, tightly clutch-
ing him about the waist, as if to support him, holding him
as a husky girl would a large doll.

The gambler's body inclined forward slightly. His outside arm dangled with hand opened—a hand wearing a
light doeskin glove! The head drooped to the right. The
face, usually cold and expressionless, had a grimace on it;
the mouth was half opened, as if the Colonel was about
to protest something. The eyes had an odd glaze in them,
eyes set in vivid red rims. The grayish hair, usually so
neatly parted on the side, was rumpled, as if the Colonel
had rubbed it against an unyielding surface.

Brutus took one step forward.

Colonel Pigler's feet did not move. The left arm dropped
from Brutus' shoulder—this hand, too, encased in a light
glove.

With a sudden jerk—as if overbalanced—Colonel James
Pigler's body leaned to the right. Gently the giant deaf-
mute lowered his master to the floor, at right angles to the
threshold. As the figure neared the carpet the face turned
downward, exposing the rear of the head.

"Great God!" the clubman repeated.

The back of the gambler's head was smashed open. A
blob of brain tissue dangled on the edge of the crushed
skull.

"Murdered!"

Austen and Trigg and Fellowes uttered the word together.

23

Brutus, the towering deaf-mute, stepped back and folded his arms. His face was blank.

For an instant the three visitors stood frozen. Then each went into action, according to his trade.

Dr. Fellowes stepped swiftly to the body and knelt beside it. Austen, striding about the wide hall which divided the lower floor, glanced around for signs of struggle. The room, with its thick rugs, its stiff reception chairs by either side wall, the heavy crystal chandelier aglow with light, its pier glass extending from floor to ceiling, the ancient suit of armor standing at the foot of the curving stairway, seemed entirely in order.

"Hands up!"

Austen whirled around at the command. George Trigg—a self-important Trigg—was pointing an automatic at Brutus' heart. Brutus, arms still folded, gazed impassively at the small ex-jockey.

"Put that up, you fool!" Austen snapped.

"But, Major—"

"Do as I say!"

Trigg obeyed. Still the black stood immobile.

Austen went to the physician's side. With trained eyes and hands Dr. Fellowes was making quick examination. He said without looking up: "Funny—how it all comes back—

you never forget." Then he stood up, rubbed his fingers carefully with a linen handkerchief.

"Putting it in non-technical language," he said, "Pigler was killed by blows struck at the base of the skull by a sharp instrument which penetrated to the brain—looks like what the newspaper boys call an ax murder."

"How long has he been dead?" Austen asked.

Fellowes shrugged his shoulders. "You know, Austen, I've never actually practiced."

"You just said it all comes back."

"I don't wish to pose as an authority," Fellowes said crisply. "Medical examiner is the one to say, but I'd guess less than six hours—more than two hours. No *rigor mortis*—that sets in at about the sixth hour after life departs. But body heat is absent. Dead at least two hours."

"We've got to call the police. Let me get to a phone." Austen looked around him. No phone in the hall. But wide doors opened on either side.

"Should be one here—somewhere," Fellowes said. "I'd guess that room." He nodded to the one on their right.

Austen started toward the door. Quick as a panther the black leaped forward and threw a great arm across Austen's chest. For the first time sounds came from him—a horrible and guttural gasping.

"Back—get back!" Trigg again had his gun out and was jamming it against the deaf-mute's side. Brutus looked at Austen, and Austen nodded his head. Brutus dropped his arm, stepped back.

"I'll keep him covered, Major."

"No, don't!" Austen warned.

Fellowes went with Austen into the half-darkened room. "Should be a light switch on the wall—somewhere," the physician said. "Here it is!" Austen answered. Overhead lights flashed on in a room richly, even tastefully, decorated:

one which could boast of being a study by virtue of a patinaed secretary in the corner, of high shelves filled with old calfbound books.

A phone stood on a side table. Austen dialed police headquarters. ". . . and dig up a sign-language expert and bring him along. Only live man we found in the house is Pigler's deaf-mute—want to examine him tonight."

He put the instrument down. "They'll be here in eighteen minutes," he said to Fellowes. "Homicide squad. No medical examiner—at this hour; they'll bring an intern from the City Hospital."

"He'll do." Dr. Fellowes spoke with professional tones. "This is no strange poisoning case. Any blacksmith can see it's ax murder."

Austen glanced around the room. It was in immaculate order. It looked, judging by the correct placing of the chairs, as if it had not been entered that evening. Even the wood piled in the fireplace had not been touched by a match, though the weather was coolish.

Fellowes frowned. "Wonder why that black man wanted to keep you out of this room," he said. "No signs of a struggle—no torn papers—no overturned bottle spilling a mysterious, colorless liquid."

Austen managed a grin. "Read detective stories, Fellowes?"

"Hundreds of 'em!" Fellowes grinned back. "But I do wonder why that black—"

"Interfered with me? That's easy. We are not uniformed officials. We are strangers coming at an ungodly hour—after his master's been killed. I start through Brutus' domain—quite naturally he stops me."

"Yes, I guess you're right. But the murder—"

"Was not done by that black. Again it's too obvious," Austen explained. "Probably by some intruder—unknown to Brutus."

"Or by a caller during an argument, while the black man was in the back of the house?" Fellowes asked with amusement.

"Perhaps." Austen ignored Fellowes' manner. His mind was on something else. "I'd say the black stumbled over the body as he came to answer the bell—lifted it in his big arms, and then, when Trigg rang again, switched on the porch lights, opened the door, switched on the hall light. Melodramatic as hell—but it works out. Trigg!"

"Yes, boss?" Trigg answered from the hall.

"Both of you keeping away from the body?"

"Yes sir. This—this Brutus feller is standin' against the wall, easy-like. I'm here by the front door."

"Good! Don't either of you touch a thing. We don't want a squawk from the cops when they come." Then to Fellowes: "As I was saying, loving his master as he did, Brutus probably didn't want to drop the body merely to answer a door call."

"You say *loving* him?" Fellowes emphasized the "loving".

Austen nodded. "I know a good deal about Pigler—my business to know everything I can about the men on the fringes of racing. Ever see the sword cane Pigler carries?"

"Sword cane? Didn't know it was a weapon."

"Was—and is. Eleven years ago Pigler was passing a bar on Royale Street. Know the French Quarter, New Orleans?"

"Slightly."

"Then you know how tough it can get—late at night. Brutus was thrown out by not one, but three, lugs. Brutus got up fighting. More men came running out of the bar— ganged up on him. One was lifting a beer bottle to bring down on his skull. At that split second the Colonel, who was passing, stopped, jerked out his sword, pinked the bottle man. Scared the others. They backed off. Pigler put the black in a car, rode off with him, and discovered the fellow was a deaf-mute!"

"I'm darned!"

"From that minute Brutus adopted Pigler as his master—been with him ever since. Man's no fool. Had been trained in the sign language, so Pigler learned it. Made an ideal servant for Pigler. You know Pigler's tight-lipped; wouldn't let the men around him talk—and Brutus can't talk! Probably was Pigler's best friend."

"Best friend?" Fellowes looked doubtful. "Remember, the man's a primitive. In a fit of jealous rage—well, y'know what elemental creatures will do. Besides, we found him here."

"Oh lord, you and the captain!"

"What's that?"

"Nothing. Let's take another look at the dead man. I've an idea this murder is linked to Madison's. Come on."

The body was lying, untouched, in the hallway. Brutus stood impassive against the opposite side wall. Trigg had his back to the closed front door.

"Dead six hours?" Austen looked at Fellowes.

"I didn't say that," Fellowes corrected. "I said less than six hours."

"Could be five and a half hours?"

"Oh, perhaps."

Austen glanced at his watch. "Not quite 2 a.m., Derby day. He wasn't killed before eight o'clock—"

"Hardly, or *rigor mortis*—stiffening of the joints in death—might have set in. But bodily heat has definitely departed. He wasn't killed any thirty minutes ago."

"I was just thinking . . ." Austen walked five paces down the thick carpet and back again. "Madison was killed a few minutes after eight o'clock, Fellowes—not quite six hours ago—"

"Look at those light gloves, Major," Trigg interrupted.

"I saw them." Austen dropped to his knees. Over his shoulder he called out to Fellowes:

"Barton told us that just as he got to Madison's office he heard a shot fired inside—remember? That he looked through a window, saw Madison slumping over, and a hand in a light-colored glove pulling the rear door shut."

"Ah! That backs up my Pigler surmise, doesn't it?" Fellowes said with noticeable pride. "What are you finding, Austen?"

"These gloves—scratches on them—but—" He stopped speaking as he began to examine the body's clothing.

"Briar scratches, eh?" Fellowes said. "He might have gone through the briar hedge in the rear of Madison's."

"Yes, he might," Austen admitted. "His clothes—but there are no briar pricks on the front, where they should be. That's odd." Austen got to his feet. "Question: Who killed Pigler? We've got a second murder with a racing background."

"Question is, who would use an ax?" Fellowes said. "The skull wasn't crushed by a blunt instrument; it was hacked in—using non-technical language—by a sharp and heavy weapon in the hands of a powerful person—"

"Say! Look here!" George Trigg broke in excitedly. "Look what I found!"

Trigg had lifted an object from the brass umbrella holder which stood to the left of a tall mahogany hat rack that backed against the left wall. Trigg now was holding up the object: a mace, or battle-ax, slightly larger than a kitchen hatchet and with a pointed head and a sweeping scimitarlike edge. The handle—of gnarled and worm-eaten wood—was twice the length of a hatchet's and curved at the end. The metal was browned with rust.

The edge of the ax blade and the haft where it entered the ax were both smeared with blood, and a few hairs stuck to the weapon.

"Battle-ax murder!" the physician exclaimed with a whistle. "Say, that ax—"

"Heh, don't touch it!" Austen stopped him. Trigg, who had been holding the end of the handle with a handker-chief, carefully placed it against the wall.

"Sorry—forgot." Fellowes stepped back. "I'm no detec-tive, Austen, but look here, that ax—looks antique, doesn't it? I'll bet it goes with the suit of armor. Someone seized the ax and killed the Colonel as he started up the stairs."

Fellowes paused, looked from Austen to Brutus. The black was standing as if in a trance—a far-off gaze in his dark eyes.

"Battle-axes," Fellowes continued, "are hard to handle, and here's a powerful man." He nodded toward Brutus. The black was looking at Fellowes with no understanding in his eyes.

"Oh hell, Fellowes!" Austen turned and walked toward the study. "If Brutus is that elemental he'd be running through the next county this minute. Think up something original, won't you?"

Fellowes looked like a small boy who had been called down for acting up. His man-of-the-world manner dropped away as he followed Austen into the study.

A siren wailed outside.

"Here come the cops," Austen said and grinned. "Here's a tip, Fellowes: this is reality—not one of your detective yarns. Don't be so thin-skinned. If you think I'm rough"—his eye-brows went up for a second—"wait until you face old Cap."

Fellowes' face reddened. "Really, Austen, I—didn't mean it that way—" He looked chastened, but he did not go on, for someone had begun to bang heavily on the front door. Then the house bell pealed loudly.

From the hallway came weird sounds—gurgles and gasps, a shuffling of feet, a sharp smack, then a resound-ing crash.

24

In four strides Austen was at the door to the hall, Fellowes at his heels.

"I'm darned!" Austen said.

The ceiling-high pier glass was shattering to the floor; Trigg's automatic lay at the foot of the frame. Brutus had a half nelson around Trigg's neck, and now Brutus was dragging the squirming Trigg to the door!

Austen and Fellowes could construct the preceding moment from that visual evidence: though deaf, the black no doubt was sensitive to vibrations put in motion by that tremendously loud doorbell; perhaps that was why Pigler installed it. Brutus must have felt the ringing of it, started toward the door; Trigg pulled his gat, and . . .

Now Trigg was gasping words as Brutus fumbled for the door's latch with his free hand: "He knocked—gun outa my hand. It hit the glass—broke it. He—he—grabbed me—"

Austen was forced to smile even in that sorry setting: the master of the house lay sprawled on the floor, his head chopped open, and the huge Negro was calmly performing his appointed task of opening the door, despite a gun having been aimed at his midriff.

The door swung back. Brutus released the gasping Trigg.

The acting chief of detectives pushed into the hall, followed by members of his homicide squad.

Cap was grouchy from interrupted slumber. "Lucky all of us who worked the Madison case decided to bunk at headquarters," he barked. "Now, I guess this"—sarcasm was in his tone as he pointed a foot at the dead gambler—"this is the man who killed Madison, eh?"

He looked sharply at Austen. Austen raised his shoulders, said nothing.

"It's quite possible he did—even probable, sir," Dr. Fellowes said, putting the captain in his place.

"Who're— Oh, good evenin', Dr. Fellowes!" The detective's manner was immediately deferential. "Didn't recognize you."

"You know Major Austen, officer. I'll let him tell you what we found. Then you can make your own deductions." Fellowes turned to Austen. "Suppose you tell him, Major."

"I was pumping Haney, the taxi driver, at the station."

"Puttin' over somethin'?" Cap growled.

"Nobody could put anything over on you, Cap." Austen grinned. "Then I wanted to ask Dr. Fellowes a few questions. He was with Madison at my place, you know."

The detective grunted. "What did Dr. Fellowes tell you?"

Austen repeated the conversation in detail. "Right, Fellowes?"

The physician nodded.

The intern stooped over the dead man. The captain looked at Brutus. "Handcuffs on the n•••••," he snapped. Brutus made no objection.

"Now what do you find, Doc?" the captain asked the intern.

The youngster looked up. "Murder," he said.

"I could-a told myself that," the captain snapped. "Go on. What killed him? How long's he been dead? Make it snappy."

The intern stood up. For an instant he fingered the stethoscope hanging from his neck. Then he answered quietly:

"Death resulted—on superficial examination—from a blow with a heavy, sharp-edged instrument to the base of the skull. That's putting it in language you will understand."

"How long's he been dead?"

"Hard to say, but I would judge not more than six hours. Certainly two or three. Am I right, Dr. Fellowes?" he deferred to his senior.

"Quite, Doctor."

The battle-ax was indicated. Trigg told of discovering it. Dr. Fellowes pointed to the suit of armor. He said:

"Someone—evidently a person capable of wielding it— picked it up in a jealous rage and killed Pigler. As Pigler turned his back, say. Probably turned his back in dismissal—after an argument—"

"I'll bet that n•••••," the captain interrupted. "You say the house don't look like nobody broke in? Get to work, men."

The command was to his fingerprint and homicide experts. The men began examining every foot of the room. "You—May," the captain called to a slim, keen-faced youngster whose hair kept falling down in his eyes. "May here—he was with us at Madison's—he acts as court interpreter sometimes for deaf-and-dumb witnesses. Let's put the n••••• on the pan."

"First I suggest," Austen said, "that you order an autopsy held on Pigler's remains."

"What?" the captain expostulated. "Didn't my doc say how he was killed? Didn't Fel—Dr. Fellowes," he corrected himself quickly, "agree with him? And can't you see for yourself? Why that autopsy business? Do you think this guy was bumped off with some new poison from Africy?"

Austen's eyes closed to mere slits—a mannerism he had when forcing a point. "I demand an autopsy," he said. "Complete. Examination of heart, lungs, stomach, brain, pancreas—everything. And if you want to know why, Cap, it's because—" He paused, and his eyelids opened, and he grinned at the irritated detective. "It's just that I have a hunch, and I won't tell you what it is, either. But I demand the autopsy."

"What do I care?" the captain blustered. "Sure, Doc, we want an autopsy. Now let's get to the n•••••. We'll get out of the way of these boys." He nodded to the experts with their powders and brushes, searching for prints. The captain took the black by the arm and piloted him into the study, placed him in the middle of the floor, manacled, while he and May stood on either side of him.

Austen, Fellowes, and Trigg found chairs and faced the standing trio.

"Suggestion to make, Cap," Austen drawled.

"Suggest what?"

"Before you begin grilling why not take the cuffs off Brutus? He talks with his fingers, you know."

The captain grunted, ordered the links taken off. Then, "Say, Austen, you hook up this murder with Madison's, don't you?"

"I certainly do."

"Then you shoot the questions. May will thumb 'em to him."

The captain sat heavily in the nearest overstuffed chair, stuck his broad-soled shoes in front of him—blunt toes to the ceiling. He unbuttoned the lower part of his vest, patted his paunch. "Shoot, Austen. I'm listenin', even if I do shut a lid."

"Tell him, May," Austen said, "that we want to ask a few questions. First explain who we are, but let him know we are friendly toward him."

"Friendly—huh!" the captain grunted. He closed both eyes, put his head against the back of his chair. His hands rested on his paunch.

May turned to the black; his fingers fluttered. Instantly the black came to life; his face was animated; he raised his right hand, and his fingers waved deftly.

Austen gazed keenly at Brutus for the first time. The man's skin was black—so black it was almost blue—but he lacked true Negroid features. His cheekbones were high, the nose thin, and the lips neither thick nor thin. The jaw was strong and the forehead high, eyes set well apart. But there was no trace of an eyebrow—that's what made the man look sinister at first glance—and the head was shaven cleanly.

Fellowes leaned over, said in a half whisper:

"Just what is that fellow, Austen?"

"Must be a maroon," Austen said, not taking his eyes from the flashing fingers.

"Maroon?"

Austen nodded. "Yes, maroon. They're descendants of early slaves who skipped their Spanish masters and mated with Indians. You find them in Jamaica—and some by the bayous below New Orleans."

"I see. Odd chap. Primitive. Elemental."

May looked at Austen, interpreted: "The man says his name is Brutus, that he has been Colonel Pigler's body servant—he calls it—for years, and that he'll answer anything you want to ask. He's horrified at the death of his master."

"Did he use that word?" The captain asked the question, his eyes still closed.

"Yes sir. His word. Horrified."

"Huh. Educated n•••••. Go on."

"Ask him"—Austen glanced up at May—"to tell us what happened here tonight, beginning at six o'clock."

May held up his hands, nudged Brutus, who didn't need it, and May's fingers began moving. The black didn't look at the young detective's face but at his hands. His face was set in a poker calm.

May's fingers stopped; he dropped his hands. Without hesitation the black went into action. Austen shot a glance at the acting chief. The old fox was wide awake! His eyes, under heavy lids, were watching every finger movement, watching intently, as if he knew the sign language.

25

The detective, May, threw up a hand as sign that the black was to cease finger talking a moment. Brutus dropped his hands, and at the same instant all animation left his face; again he was impassive.

"Fastest finger talker I've run into," May began.

The captain grunted. "Huh?" Now his eyes were closed.

"He says," May interrupted, "that Colonel Pigler went into town late in the afternoon—"

"Did he say where?" Austen interposed.

"I asked that," May answered quickly. "Said the Colonel didn't say—generally he didn't name his destination. The Colonel said he would dine in town, that he frequently did that. Ate usually at the Muhlbach. He told Brutus not to stay up for him, that he might come in late."

"He was to go to bed—that is, Brutus was?" Austen asked.

May's fingers fluttered—and Brutus, flashing into life, responded in his sign language.

"Yes. Says his room is on the second floor rear—next to the Colonel's. That he cooked and ate his own dinner."

"Did he say dinner?" The captain asked the question. His eyes now were closed.

"Why—er—he said supper," May amended.

"Southern n•••••," the captain murmured. "Go on."

163

"After eating he went upstairs," May continued. "He played solitaire. At eight-thirty he—"

"How does he keep track of time?" Austen broke in.

"I asked that. He says he has a clock on the table, facing him. At eight-thirty he went out of his room for a glass of water. Said he saw a reflection of the hall light—the hall out there"—May nodded his head—"so he knew Pigler had come in."

"Why Pigler?" Austen demanded.

"Only Pigler would turn on the light. That he, himself, never burned house lights in the Colonel's absence. Pigler believed in saving—"

"Gosh, that's true," the captain said with a grunt. "Jim Pigler was tighter than a tick on a horse."

"Go on," said Austen.

"Brutus says he started down those curved front steps to see if he was wanted—that Pigler was standing in the doorway of this room, facing out; that a medium-sized man was standing in the hall—his back to Brutus—talking with the Colonel."

"Did he see his face?"

"He did not."

"How was that man dressed?"

"Said he barely noticed him—a dark-looking coat, and remembers he had some kind of dark slouch hat on."

"Go on."

"Brutus says the Colonel noticed him coming down the steps; that he waved his hand"—May indicated—"for Brutus to go on back up the steps; that he was not wanted. Brutus says he must have seen him coming down the stairs before Brutus saw the Colonel; that the Colonel was very quick to wave him back."

"Ask him if he hesitated on the stairs."

Another fluttering of the fingers. "He says no. That he had been taught to turn and go back instantly; that many times Pigler had men here on business and didn't want to be disturbed."

"Ah!" said Austen.

"Huh?" said the captain, turning his massive head and gazing at the younger man. "What's up?"

Austen raised his shoulders, made no answer. To May he said:

"Ask him if the Colonel waved him back casually."

"Easy or mean-like," the captain said sharply.

"Easy or mean-like," Austen repeated.

May asked the question. "He says the Colonel was angry—showed it by the sharp way he moved his arm. Look!"

The black, his face alight, swerved his right arm out, as if waving a crowd of people back. The fingers on his other hand moved.

"He says that's how Pigler did it. That he was mad. He adds that's why he paid no attention to the caller. His eyes were on Pigler the few seconds he was on the stairs, looking down."

"Now ask if he recognized the caller."

Another quick fluttering of fingers. "He says no; he didn't see the man's face, but that his back seemed familiar."

The captain grunted. Austen grinned. "Whose back was it?"

"He doesn't know, but the back of someone he saw once—somewhere—he doesn't recall."

Another grunt from the captain. "This is gettin' us nowheres, Major. We got a rogues' gallery of mugs—not of backs."

Austen ignored the interruption. "Ever see that back in this house before?"

A moment's linger fluttering. Then:

"He's not certain."

The captain slapped his thigh angrily. "Get on with the questions, Austen. He didn't see the man—just the back, and there's half a million backs hereabouts, and most of 'em look alike to me."

"All right, Cap. Now ask him what he did when the Colonel waved dismissal."

"Says he went back upstairs; wasn't sleepy. Took out his cards, played more solitaire. Once or twice he shut off his own light to see if there was light in the Colonel's room— he'd see it under an adjoining door—would show if Pigler had come upstairs. He didn't see it."

May stopped. The deaf-mute was nudging him. May smiled and heeded the man's flying fingers. For one minute, then two, then three May watched the fingers. Suddenly the man stopped.

"Gosh! Fastest I've ever known!" May swore. "He says for me to tell that much—he's got more coming. So:

"He didn't see the light. Says that though Pigler would tell him not to stay up, he made a practice of keeping his clothes on till the Colonel went to bed, that he might be needed for something.

"So he sat over his cards, thinking the Colonel was arguing downstairs. Says he must have fallen asleep, that sometimes he did over his cards. Suddenly he felt a tingling in his head—a feeling he always had when the front-door bell rang. He jumped up. Went out and to the stair landing. The house was dark. The Colonel must have gone out, turned the lights off, and maybe had misplaced his house key. Was ringing to get in. Brutus went down the stairs." May faced Brutus again. "Go ahead, pardner," he said aloud, then fluttered his fingers.

Once more Brutus went swiftly into action.

"As Brutus approached the front door—in the dark hallway—he stumbled over something, then felt that tingling in his head again. He stooped; his hand touched another hand, one with an odd-shaped ring on it, like his master wore.

"His hands felt up the arm to the shoulder—the head—felt for the small ears, close to the head. His fingers touched where the head was broken in. He knew the man—whoever it was—had been murdered. Then he felt again for the ears; they were the small ones of his master.

"He lifted his master up, dragged him to the door; again that tingling in his head. He found the vestibule light switch—"

"He say vestibule?" the captain asked, arousing himself.

"He did, sir."

"I said he was educated. Go on. Educated a n••••• and spoiled a good field hand." Again his eyelids drooped.

"Brutus opened the door, holding up the Colonel, then switched on the hall lights and lowered the Colonel's body to the floor again. He says you know what happened after that, and that he tried to keep you, Major, from entering this room because he didn't know you. He says he was standing against the wall with arms folded when you, Trigg, pointed a gat at his belly—just when he felt that tingling in his head again; says it always feels like a shock. That's why he tries to get to the door quickly—to stop the tingling in his head. That he tried to indicate the door to you, Trigg—"

"I ain't no mind reader!" the ex-jockey protested.

"—that you didn't understand, so he knocked the gat out of your hand against the pier glass—"

"Stop it!" Austen said with annoyance. "We're going into too much detail—nothing to do with the murder. And I'll say Brutus didn't do it! He—"

"You're right!" The exclamation came from the captain, now fully aroused. "The c••• tells too straight a tale—didn't hedge once. I know when a man's lying." He lifted a hand at Brutus in approval. Brutus, intelligence showing in his eyes, bowed slightly to Austen, then to the captain.

"At first I thought Brutus had done it," Fellowes said, glancing at Austen, "but I changed my mind. It's evident that a visitor—angry at the Colonel—seized the battle-ax, struck the gambler, then fled."

"But who put the lights out?" Austen asked quickly.

"Yes. Who?" The captain turned on the physician.

"I'd say it was a man who knew the Colonel's penuriousness," Fellowes offered. "Probably switched them off as he went out, hoping any chance visitor would drive away, thinking the Colonel was not in. Then the murder might not be discovered till morning. He—"

"He had on light gloves." Austen spoke quickly as Fellowes hesitated. "Pigler did, I mean. Gloves that could have been scratched on briars, and there's a briar patch back of Madison's. He—"

"Hold your horses!" the captain commanded. "Madison was killed a little after eight—Pigler killed mebbe a half-hour later, after the c••• went back upstairs. Men don't argue for hours and kill; they argue a minute, then *blooey!* Right, Major?"

Austen nodded. Usually it was that way.

"So"—the captain drew in a heavy breath—"we'll say Pigler was bumped off right after he waved the c••• back upstairs. Now there's plenty had it in for Pigler—but say, what about that dame?" He looked at Fellowes. "Let's hear that again."

Fellowes repeated the story he had told to Austen.

The captain nodded his head. "So they scrapped over a skirt, eh? Pigler could-a gone to Madison's, could-a shot him, but who in thunder bumped Pigler?"

"How about one of Pigler's gambling associates, Austen?" Fellowes asked.

Austen shook his head with impatience. "Don't think so; nothing points that way."

"What I want to know is, who is the woman? Always find the dame," the captain said heavily.

"We've got one woman now—rather your man Hunt has." Austen told of Trigg following Marge Maxwell and Rock Doyle.

"Huh? Why ain't I been told that?"

"No chance," Austen said. "Anyway, Hunt is sitting beside her cot now. But say, Cap, I'd like to know what your men found in the hall."

"All right." The captain put two thick fingers in his mouth and whistled sharply. The door to the hall opened almost instantly, and like bird dogs called off the scent, four fingerprint and homicide experts trooped in.

They had found nothing—not a fingerprint, not even on the battle-ax. There were no match stubs and nothing to indicate an alien presence.

"Huh!" The captain raised and lowered his shoulders. "That's not funny. Hall's used only to walk in."

The print man volunteered, "I'd like to say, Captain, that the person who used the ax did one of two things:

"He wore gloves, or else he wiped the handle of the ax after he used it."

The man spoke with the same calm he had used earlier in the evening, when he explained finding traces of a gloved hand on Madison's office door.

"The person who killed Pigler," said Austen in slow, thoughtful tones, "was neither a thug nor a gambler; such would have used a pistol, and an amateur at crime wouldn't think to rub fingerprints off the handle of an ax. So"—he glanced up a moment, then looked at the captain—"the person who killed Pigler must have been an average sort of person—wearing gloves."

"Godamighty!" the detective exclaimed. "We're back where we started—with Madison."

"No, we're much further. Send your experts home, Cap. All except May. I want to ask Brutus about a woman."

The captain dismissed his men. Dr. Fellowes leaned toward Austen:

"May I remain, Major?" he said. "I might be able to help."

"Certainly! And speak up—if I overlook a point." Then to May, "Bring your man up to us again."

Brutus seemed to know that he was wanted again. He stepped forward before May could do more than raise his hand.

"Ask Brutus to name Colonel Pigler's girl," Austen directed.

26

For the first time that night Brutus, the black deaf-mute, showed signs of annoyance. Furrows creased his forehead —a forehead devoid of eyebrows. Then his own fingers fluttered—almost angrily.

"I'll be hanged," May, the police interpreter, exclaimed.

"What's up?" Austen demanded.

May didn't answer instantly; he was looking at Brutus till the latter's fingers stopped. Then he said to the room, where Austen and the captain, Dr. Fellowes and Trigg were waiting for Brutus' answer:

"He sort of got sore—wanted me to repeat my question. I did repeat it. He flashed his answer: 'Everybody knows he had no girl.'"

"Huh!" said the captain. "Now we're gettin' somewheres. Go on, Austen, put him on the pan."

"Ask him that question again—as if you didn't get his answer, May," Austen directed.

The same answer was given, "Everybody knows he had no girl."

"Again—but in a different way," Austen suggested.

A dozen times the huge black—now showing no peevishness—denied that his master had a girl or had been in love.

"Ask him when the Colonel saw Miss Marge Maxwell last—ask it easy-like," Austen directed.

The question was fluttered to Brutus. Instantly the servant's fingers moved. "He says that several days ago the Colonel said he had talked—at Churchill Downs—with Rock Doyle and his secretary, Miss Marge Maxwell."

"How did the Colonel happen to make that remark to Brutus?"

May stated the question. Brutus turned slowly, looked at Austen, as if to say, "Did you ask that question?" Then he drew himself up, faced May again, raised his hand, spoke the language he knew, moved his fingers not fast nor with impatience.

"Brutus says the Colonel had a habit of talking with him after dinner, when coffee was served by Brutus in this room. He says the Colonel always drank three small cups and that between the cups frequently he told what he had done that day."

"Ask him if he bragged," Austen said quickly.

That question, too, irritated the black. Again his fingers moved impressively.

"He says the Colonel was a gentleman—"

"Huh! Glad to know it," the captain broke in.

"—and talked as he would to a friend."

"Cagey n•••••," the captain said with a snort. "He didn't tell nothin' then."

"What did Miss Marge Maxwell say to the Colonel?"

"Brutus says the Colonel only remarked that she was with Doyle—and seemed to be a clever girl."

"When was the woman out here—and did Doyle bring her, or did she come alone?"

"He says neither she nor Doyle were ever out here, that the Colonel carried on his business downtown or at the race track. That this was his home."

Austen got to his feet. "That's all, May. I'd suggest, Cap, that you leave Brutus here—in charge of the place for the time being."

"All right," agreed the captain.

"And say something nice, May, to Brutus for the police department. How he's helped, and so on."

May's fingers did so. For the first time a slight smile played across the black's face. He bowed, and again his fingers fluttered.

"He says he will shut up the house till the police or the Colonel's lawyers give him further orders."

"H'm'm! Knows his way about." The captain got to his feet. "That's about all."

Austen stepped in front of Brutus and said something the others didn't fathom and Brutus couldn't hear. It was:

"You are a loyal chap, old fellow, and the Colonel did save your life once."

He reached for his hat on the library table.

"Heh, what you mean by that loyal stuff?" the captain demanded.

Austen started toward the door. "Sometimes I wonder, myself, what I mean, Cap." He grinned at the detective. "Dr. Fellowes, Trigg—let's go. Oh, Cap!" He stopped again. "I'd like to get at Barton again tomorrow afternoon."

"You think the kid hasn't spilled everythin', eh? Now you see why I'm holdin' him!"

"I don't know. I'm going to talk with Marge Maxwell in the morning—with Danny Barton in the afternoon— about the time the Derby is run," he said, "and with Guy Slenk when he's sober. And, Cap! Don't forget the autopsy on Pigler's body; it's going to tell a lot."

As they were driving into the city Fellowes asked:

"That autopsy—what do you think it will prove?"

"I'm not sure," said Austen. "Just a hunch. May prove nothing, but I don't want to leave anything to chance. Where do I drop you?"

"At the club—next block." And as Fellowes was getting out of the car, "Thanks for letting me sit in, Austen. If there's anything else I can do—

"If there is I'll call. Thanks, and good night."

Austen dropped Trigg at his house and then drove to his own apartment. Notice of a Western Union telegram was on his door. Once inside, he phoned the telegraph office. A clerk read the message:

"BE SURE TO SAVE TOMORROW NIGHT FOR ME
WANT YOU TO MEET A PEACH OF A GIRL
                              SHEPHERD THOMAS"

Austen put the receiver down.
"Well, I'm darned!" he said.

27

"Rock Doyle croaked twenty minutes ago."

That was Detective Sergeant Hunt's report to Roderick Austen next morning—early. Austen had driven to the hospital across the river shortly after dawn. He found Hunt in the superintendent's office, red-eyed from his night's vigil, but still alert.

"I came down while they are changing dressings on the Maxwell girl," he explained. "Doyle—he never returned to consciousness—never muttered anything."

"Well, that's that," Austen said. "What of Marge Maxwell?"

"She came up for air about an hour ago. She was groggy. But the docs gave her something, and she's pretty steady now."

"Wait—I want her put in a private room." Austen spoke to the clerk behind the grille, made the arrangements, was told, "We'll have her put in a private room at once."

Austen went back to Hunt, told him of the night's developments.

"I knew about Pigler's murder," Hunt said. "Funny thing, but the radio got it last night; you know, there are earphones up in that ward, and I listened while Maxwell was out. Radio had it before the papers did."

Austen laughed. "Shep Thomas missed a scoop—for once," he said. "Serves him right. But go ahead: tell me about Maxwell."

"When she came to I put on my act: told her she was under arrest. She wanted to know what for. I said for killing Henry Madison."

"What did she say?"

"She said, 'God, I didn't do it; I didn't do it.' Then I sort of used the third degree on her."

"What kind of third degree?"

"Good old silence. I told her to hush up, that I didn't want to hear anything she had to say. That gets 'em sometimes, when you say you won't let 'em talk.

"She's been begging for the last fifteen minutes for me to listen. Wants to explain something. I just said, over and over again, 'Keep quiet, sister. You're under arrest for killing Madison.' She's going to talk now, and I believe she'll talk straight. She knows a lot."

"Good work. By the way, while she was unconscious did you ask to look at her things?"

"I did—and she had gloves on when brought in! Light-colored suede gloves. And her hand's big, you know."

Austen nodded. "Let's go and see her." And to the clerk, "Miss Maxwell in a private room now?"

The clerk phoned to a floor superintendent and reported: "She's just been changed."

"Thanks." To Hunt, "Come on—which way?"

A tall, bushy-haired young intern met them at the door of the girl's room. Austen identified himself. "She should recover," the intern answered Austen's question. "She's young, healthy, got the strength of a peasant."

"No objection to my asking her one or two questions, Doctor?"

"None at all, sir. But you may have to talk fast." The intern smiled.

"Why—the sedative?"

"Yes. It'll take effect soon. Wait here a moment; I want to give a last checkup."

The physician re-entered the room, glanced at the chart hanging from the foot of the bed, then stepped around and took Marge Maxwell's wrist in his hand.

"Question I'd like to ask, Major." Hunt was his alert self.

"Shoot!"

"You think Brutus is holding something back? You told me you said to him, 'You are a loyal chap, old fellow—and the Colonel did save your life once.'"

"What do you think?" Austen countered.

"He's part Indian—and all loyalty," Hunt said, furrows creasing his forehead. "He didn't see Pigler's visitor's face, but he recognized the man's back. Sure, he knows the man.

"You think, Major, he'll lay for the man himself—kill him in revenge?"

Austen grinned. "What do you think?"

Hunt raised his shoulders, grinned back. "I'm not working that end of the case. I'm just thinking. And here's the girl who may have caused the whole mess." He stopped as the intern came out.

"You may go in, Major Austen." He smiled. "Better work fast," he suggested.

"Thanks, Doctor." Austen and Hunt went into the room.

Marge Maxwell, her face haggard in the bright sunlight, looked up at Austen. She was different from the suave-looking girl who had stood on Austen's threshold at twilight yesterday. Then she had the beauty of a poster girl. Platinum hair, large sea-blue eyes, bright cheeks, and a figure of soft undulating curves, sheathed in something of soft and filmy blue. She had been twenty in the soft light.

Now she was—maybe thirty-five. The coverlet drawn up to her neck—one large, broad-fingered hand grasping it under the chin—she was merely another woman. A woman whose hair had been pulled back and at one point cut away to permit application of a bandage. The cheeks had been scoured of their artful make-up.

"You're Marge Maxwell—from Chicago?" Austen asked briskly.

The exposed hand went to her head for a moment. She stared at him blankly. Then her eyes focused. Austen sat in the chair by her pillow, leaned forward to catch her tones.

"Yes. Who'd you think?"

The answer came in a hoarse whisper. It told Austen nothing of her usual speaking voice.

He smiled at her with disarming manner. "Won't you talk a little louder, please, Miss Maxwell?"

Slowly the hand was withdrawn from her head, again grasped the coverlet.

"I—I can't," she whispered. "I'm—hurt."

"I know. Now don't worry. I'm only from the Racing Commission."

"I know you," she said.

"Sure you do. You phoned me several times yesterday afternoon—remember?"

For a moment she didn't answer. Her eyelids flickered.

"I did not," she said at last.

"Oh no! Don't you recall you retained me—as an investigator—to look out for the man who was going to kill Henry Madison?"

Her eyelids closed. She spoke in hoarse whispers, "Go 'way—you've got the wrong girl."

"No, I haven't! If I were you I'd talk to a friend."

She forced a smile on her face. "You—a friend!"

"All right! You don't want to talk, but you're going to tell about your relations with Colonel James Pigler."

"I just met him!" she protested. "He's a friend of—of my employer."

"And your friendship with Madison—another business friend?"

"That's my business!"

"Sure, and it's going to be mine. And what about Guy Slenk?"

"Any harm in knowing a horse trainer?"

"None. But you were a friend of Pigler's. He was in love with you."

"That's a lie!" she answered with fire.

"You tossed him over for Henry Madison."

"Another lie!"

"And Pigler told you he was going to kill Madison—or have him killed. You knew he was spurring Guy Slenk on to do it; you knew Slenk might do it because he was sore over losing Red Moon. No, you weren't in love with Pigler but with his coin. You didn't want Pigler caught; you telephoned me—"

"A lie—a lie!"

"When you phoned the last time I told you Danny Barton had been caught. You said, 'Oh, thank God!' Glad it wasn't your lover—you were willing for an innocent man to suffer."

He stopped speaking. She glared at him, said nothing.

"I know why you won't talk. Afraid you'll tangle yourself up." He leaned forward, within a foot of her face. "It was you who killed Madison. You went out to warn him against Pigler; you had a scrap yourself with Madison; you shot him!"

Austen straightened up as the girl gasped. Then she protested in throaty whispers:

"I never killed him—I didn't."

"Don't tell me that! I had you shadowed yesterday. You went out to Madison's, parked your roadster under a tree, went in, just a minute or so after eight o'clock. You found Madison alone; the two of you argued. You were out to buy Red Moon from him, and he wouldn't sell! You seized his pistol and you shot him. Wait! You came out of the place on the run. The new moon wasn't out; you didn't think anyone would see you! But they did. You scrambled back in your car, and, Marge Maxwell—" Austen stopped,

then smiled down on her. "These were your exact words as you started to drive off:

"'Of all the doggone luck!'"

He looked steadily at her. The look of a trapped animal came into her eyes. Her hand grasped the coverlet tightly. Her breath came in short gasps.

"Then you drove back to the Brown Hotel, went inside, picked up Doyle, and the two of you lammed for Chicago.

"If you didn't kill Madison, why the rush to get out of the state? I thought you came here to see the Derby."

Another silence.

"Hunt—the cuffs!" Austen demanded.

"Yes sir." Detective Sergeant Hunt came to the head of the bed, held out a pair of shining handcuffs.

"Think we'd better cuff her to the bed, Major?"

"Stop—stop!" the girl protested. "You can't do that to me!"

"Well, we are doing it, sister," Hunt said as he reached for her wrist.

The free hand was pulled under the sheet. "No—no!"

"Then you going to talk and tell the truth?" Austen asked. "Take your choice."

For a moment she stared at him, panting. Then, "You win, you big flatfoot," she whispered. "I—I didn't kill Madison, but I—I did see him shot."

28

Sergeant Hunt stepped back from the white iron hospital bed, jangled the handcuffs as he clipped them to his belt again. "I'll put them on if she doesn't come clean, Major."

Austen nodded. Then to Marge Maxwell: "You saw Pigler—Colonel James Pigler—kill Madison, didn't you?"

"I'm not saying. No, it wasn't! It wasn't him!" The harsh whispers came emphatically.

"You sure?"

She nodded.

"Then who was it?"

"I—I don't know."

"Gray-haired man?"

"I—didn't see—his hair. Just saw—his back."

"I'm darned!" Austen looked up at Hunt. The detective gave a short laugh; this was the second *back* to appear in the case.

"Was he a tall, powerfully built man?"

She looked straight at Austen. "I—don't know," she whispered. "I—was scared. Just saw two men fussing—"

"What did they say to each other?"

"I—heard nothing. Window was closed."

"H'm'm. You don't keep your word. Shielding Slenk—or Barton—or Pigler?" No answer. "Then I'll tell you something:

"Jim Pigler was killed last night too—his head cut open with a battle-ax!"

Marge Maxwell tried to sit upright; she fell back on the pillows.

"Oh, my God!" came in husky whispers.

"Did you go to Madison to warn him against Pigler and Slenk?"

"Mr. Doyle—sent me—to buy Red Moon," she whispered excitedly. "A man was—ahead of me. In the office. I saw him—through a window—side window. I waited— wanted—to talk to Madison—alone. The man—"

"Did he have a hat on?"

"Why—yes. Sort of—dark felt. His back to me—facing Madison—they arguing. I couldn't hear—but Madison was—pointing to—the door."

"What did the man do?"

"Madison did it—first. Reached for a gat—on his desk— by his right side. This man—reached too. His hand—got there first. He snatched up the gat."

"See that clearly?"

"I—I swear it!"

"See the man's hands?"

Her head nodded ever so slightly.

"What color gloves was he wearing?"

She looked up in thought. "Light—lighter than mocha. Maybe—doeskin."

"Go on. What happened?"

"The stranger—raised the pistol. Madison jumped him. Pistol went off. Madison—he stumbled, turned sideways. Fell over—a table."

"What did you do?"

"I—was scared. Tried to scream—couldn't. Then I knew—Madison was killed. I—got there too late—to get the horse. I—turned around. Started running."

"Well?"

"I know the stranger—came out."

"How do you know that if you were running away?"

"I saw—a flash of light in the rear. He had—opened the back door. Then—he must have closed it—dark again."

"Two of you run off together?"

Her head rolled from one side to the other, slowly. "He came out—I guess—that back door. I—I was looking in the side window. He—didn't see me—I guess."

"Why were you looking in the side window? Why, not the front window?"

"I had—cut cater-cornered—across the grass. I was—walking toward—the side. So—just walked straight to it."

"Did you see anybody looking in the front window?" Again her head moved. She added in her hoarse whisper, "It was awfully dark—then. Didn't get light—till later."

"When you were running away did you hear anyone else running away from the front—from that front window?"

Once more her head moved from side to side. The diffused blue eyes regarded Austen wearily.

"I—I was too scared to notice," she explained.

"That man who grabbed Madison's gun—did he wear a mustache?" Austen asked quickly.

The trick question failed. "I—I told you—I—never saw—his—face."

"Well dressed?"

"I"—a slight smile played across her face—"I didn't—make notes."

"About how old?"

Her eyelids closed.

"You—tell 'em," she murmured.

"Look here, Marge, don't you want your money back? The money you sent me?"

Her eyelids opened. She said in a drowsy whisper:

"Giving away—wooden nickels? Leave me—alone."

"What did Rock Doyle say when he learned you loved Pigler?"

She tried to straighten up but failed. The question had angered her.

"You—ask Doyle. He—he'll call you—a liar too."

"Never mind Doyle. He'll answer before a judge—before the fairest Judge of all."

"Fair! Huh! You can—buy 'em—three for—a dime."

"Not this One."

"Who—who is he?"

"You'll know someday—even as Rock Doyle knows now."

"I—" An odd look came into her sleepy eyes. "What—you mean? How long I—been here? Is he—Mr. Doyle—in court?"

"Never mind that! Why did you run if you didn't kill Madison—if you were not hooked up with the man who did shoot him?"

Momentary strength came to her. Her head raised; she grasped the coverlet tightly. Her words emerged in whispered gasps:

"None of your business—you damn flatfoot! You get Madison's real girl—she knows—all 'bout it! Make her talk!"

Austen touched her shoulders gently. "Come on, Marge, play the game, won't you? What's the girl's name? Tell me and I'll square everything for you!"

A trace of a laugh came through parted lips. She managed to say:

"Think—I'd tell? I'm—no snitch."

Strength left her. She gasped, then sighed, and her head would have dropped back, but Austen lowered her shoulders to the pillow. Her eyelids were shutting with heavy drowsiness.

Now she relaxed against the pillow. Her hand lay loose on the chilly whiteness of the sheet.

Marge Maxwell was again dead to the world.

29

Austen stood by the cot, looking down at the sleeping Marge Maxwell. "I can't get her natural voice, Hunt," he said. "She has only spoken in hoarse whispers."

"Is she the girl who telephoned you?"

Austen shrugged his shoulders. "It's hard to tell about women," he said. "They're deucedly clever actresses—all of 'em."

He walked a few steps down the room and back again. "The girl who phoned me," he said, "spoke the language of the cocktail lounge. A minute ago Marge Maxwell was talking in the lingo of the street. But that doesn't prove it couldn't be the same person."

"This one," Hunt spoke cynically, "she was dodging and hedging—"

"Yes, and holding back too," Austen broke in. "Nearly everyone holds back something—and she held back plenty. She didn't give a hint as to who the man was in Madison's office."

"Except that he was wearing light-colored gloves," Hunt offered.

"Yes, but nearly every man wears gloves on Derby day; you figure out why."

"I know—it's the dressy thing to do." He thought a moment, said, "If we'd had three hours to grill her—instead of seven minutes—she'd have broken down."

"Well, come on," Austen said. "She won't run away in a nightgown."

As they went out the door an orderly stepped up.

"Police headquarters calling from across the river, Major Austen," he said. "They say it's important. You can take the call in the office."

Austen and Hunt followed the orderly downstairs. The day desk sergeant was on the phone. "You better come over here right away. Guy Slenk's comin' up for air."

"Thanks, Sergeant. We'll be right over."

But the return trip took hours—not minutes. The North and West were converging by automobile toward the Ohio bridge; it made a bottleneck to Louisville. Once in the traffic stream there was nothing to do but stop, start, stop, and edge on by inches at times.

Everyone was Derby-bound.

"Be a hundred thousand there today!" Hunt exclaimed.

Austen made no answer. After a long while Hunt said:

"Say, Major"—excitement crept into his voice—"do you figure that maybe Brutus—"

"I'm working that side of the street already," Austen interrupted with a grin. "Sure! It's possible that Pigler was killed first. Possible that Madison drove out to Pigler's home—had a row and killed Pigler himself.

"Brutus may have seen it; Madison may have warned him off with his gat, and Brutus—being primitive, as Doc Fellowes says—may have decided on revenge himself. May have gone over and shot Madison. You recall Marge Maxwell wouldn't hint at the man's size—the man she saw."

"I got the idea—of Brutus—when she dodged your question about the man's size."

"Yes, but—" Austen spoke thoughtfully; he didn't finish the sentence; traffic gave a spurt, and they were on the bridge at last; now were rolling over it.

"You had an idea," Hunt prompted. Austen nodded, said nothing.

They were met by a blast of Derby-day celebration as they drove off the bridge into Louisville's business area. This was Mardi Gras time on Canal Street, Election Day on State and Madison, New Year's Eve on Times Square—all rolled into one.

Planes roared overhead, rushing visitors to the Derby; a stern-wheeler whistled at the city wharf below and behind them; locomotive bells clanged as de luxe specials switched into station yards; busses, crammed with small-town folk, edged along in a swarm of motorcars bearing licenses from far states; now the cars were moving forward four abreast.

Police whistles sounded; motorists shouted to one another; crowds surged on the sidewalks, waving pennants. Through it all ran the cry of newsboys, "Extry—extry—the Derby starters!" mingled with hoarse cries of pavement tipsters, offering folded tip sheets:

". . . the Derby winner for four bits. . . . A long shot wins today—an' we got 'im!"

At last Austen tooled out of the traffic stream. "You were saying," Hunt persisted.

"I was—but I'm not." Austen smiled wryly at him. "Here we are," he said, stopping in front of police head-quarters.

Inside, the desk sergeant greeted them with a broad grin. "Nothin' second-class about this dump, Major," he said. "We got a first-class trainer with a first-class case of heebie-jeebies waitin' for you in the jug."

"That's good, Sarge," Austen said. "Have him brought into the reception room. We'll chat with him awhile."

"Okay." The order was given to the turnkey. Then, "Here's a message from the cap. He dictated it before goin' out. He's at the Downs—it's Derby day, if nobody knows it."

Austen read:

"You and Hunt might sweat Guy Slenk. I'm not letting Barton go, and I'm showing you why.

"Pigler, mad because Madison stole his girl, egged Slenk on, knowing Slenk was sore because he lost his horse. Slenk goes to have it out with Madison—gets there too late. Barton had already shot Madison, being sore himself at losing a Derby mount.

"So Slenk chases over to Pigler's. Remember—Slenk was drinking. He has an argument with Pigler—maybe wants money right then.

"Pigler refuses him money—this is just when Brutus comes down the stairs and is waved back—so Slenk gets mad. He grabs that ax; Pigler turns to run into the other room; Slenk chops his head open. Then Slenk went out and got pie-eyed.

"If nothing new in the next twelve hours I'm going to book Barton for Madison's murder and Slenk for Pigler's."

Austen looked up. Trigg was standing in front of him. "I told the sarge where to reach you, so I came here myself." He grinned.

"Good boy!" Austen nodded. "Take a look at this." Trigg read it, muttered, "Aw, shucks!" returned it to Austen. "Take a look, Hunt," Austen said, giving the note to the detective. The detective read it, scowled, and passed it back. He made no comment.

"Well?" said Austen as they went into the front room and waited for Slenk to be brought in. Austen sat in a swivel chair. Trigg took a straight one.

Before saying anything Hunt pulled up curtains which would obscure the lower half of the windows. "An open-and-shut case for the jury—both Barton and Slenk," he replied tonelessly. "The police work is about done—both men are in the jug."

"Sure!" Heavy sarcasm in Austen's tone.

Hunt's face flushed.

"Neither Barton nor Slenk has influence or standing in this man's town," Austen went on. "Either *may* be guilty"— he emphasized the *may*, "but I want facts to prove it." He was silent an instant. Then, "I see something in front of each man's cell—now."

"Yes, what's that?" asked Hunt, who was leaning against a desk.

"A railroad car," Austen answered meaningly. "And the man who did both murders getting off scot-free—" He stopped as Hunt straightened up, interrupted him:

"Look here, Major, I'm a copper and I'm loyal to my captain. But I haven't been called off this case yet. I'm working with you"—he was earnest—"till I am."

Austen nodded. "Slenk knows a girl—and here's Slenk!"

The trainer was shoved into the room, the door closed behind him.

There he stood—a caricature of a man. His scraggly brown hair, grayish in spots, looked as if it had not been combed for days. A stubble of whiskers spotted his sallow cheeks. His eyes, bloodshot, blinked constantly. Gloved hands, which he swung up and down, trembled. His body shook.

Guy Slenk, once the idol of the turf world—when he rode great horses to great victories—was coming out of the worst hang-over of his career. The man had been on a drunken bust across the river. The drinks he'd put under his belt last night had completed the job.

"What you got me here for?" he blurted between hiccups. Seeing Trigg smirking at him, the trainer snarled, "You're respons'ble! Yet I ain't done you no dirt! What you got me here for?"

"Sit in that chair, Slenk!" Austen pointed to a stiff-backed chair facing them. "I want nothing but silence from you—and little of that." He turned to Trigg. "You got the gun, didn't you, the one Slenk used last night?"

"Yes sir. Found it in a vacant lot, Major, where Slenk threw it after he killed Madison and bumped off Colonel Pigler. We also got the battle-ax he used on the Colonel."

"Gun—ax?" Slenk repeated dazedly. "And Madison killed? Pigler—"

"Shut up, Slenk!" Trigg commanded.

The trainer did no such thing. He became wildly vocal. "Hey! Who's killed?" He started to rise. Trigg forced him back in the chair. "Listen, I don't know nothin'—and for Gawd's sake, gimme a drink—a drink; you hear me? My tongue—it sticks—to my mouth! I want—want a drink! I don't know nothin'," he screamed.

"Shut up!" Austen commanded. "Now, Hunt, you picked up this man's trail after he left Sam's bar last night?"

"I did. Slenk got the gun from a tout in Sam's place, but he didn't use it when he went to Madison's office."

"What did he use?"

"He had an argument with Madison—about losing Red Moon. He grabbed a gun from Madison's desk; he shot Madison with it. He—"

"Hey! I ain't killed nobody."

"Shut up! Go on, Hunt."

"Slenk then went to Colonel Pigler's house—it's back of Madison's—had a row with the Colonel, picked up a battle-ax in the hall, and slashed Pigler's head open with it. He then—"

"Hey! What're you—?"

"Shut up!" He was thrown back in the chair by Trigg.

"Slenk then ran outside, threw his gun into some bushes down the roadway, and I caught him."

For the first time Guy Slenk didn't protest. He was so dazed by the statements that he looked from Austen to Hunt to Trigg, his eyes widened.

Austen was silent. Hunt was silent. Trigg said nothing. The three leaned forward, glared at him.

At last the trainer spoke with a growl at Hunt: "You're a damn lie—"

Smack!

The palm of Hunt's hand struck him in the face.

The trainer threw up his gloved hands and shouted: "You're 'nother damn lie!"

Smack—smack!

Guy Slenk gasped. Drops of red trickled from his nostrils.

Trigg shouted at him: "You told me, when I caught you across the river, that you'd kill Madison if he took Red Moon from you. Didn't you?"

"You threatened to kill Madison in my room yesterday, didn't you?" Austen demanded.

"Colonel Pigler—you met him in the Saddle Rock Café. He egged you on, said you ought to kill Madison, didn't he?" Hunt threw the question at him.

Guy Slenk looked dazed. He gasped, wiped his face with the back of a gloved hand. "I—I want water—want to—to get out!"

"You'll never get out!" Hunt threatened. "It's the chair for you!"

Slenk swayed in his chair. He stumbled to his feet. This time no one stopped him. Slenk spoke hoarsely: "He was a thief! A—" Hunt slapped him back into the chair.

Slenk's breath came in short puffs. He shook his head; his eyes glared angrily. His dirty jaw stuck out. He was like a mangy coyote at bay. Suddenly he screamed:

"Madison oughta be killed! And if that woman had-a kep' hands off—"

He stopped, as if he had given something away. His eyes walled to the ceiling; his mouth gaped off. Then he slumped in his chair, whimpered, "Gawd! Gimme water!"

At last Austen spoke, and in casual manner: "Things look pretty tough for you, Slenk. Of course, if the woman—" He stopped, waited. Slenk said nothing, stared with a vacant look in his eyes.

"That Pigler's woman?" Austen suggested. "The woman Madison stole from him?" Still Slenk said nothing.

"You'd better come clean, fellow." Austen's tone was quiet. "That's good advice—and costs you nothing."

Slenk straightened with a jerk. "I—I want water!"

Austen ignored the interruption. "Remember talking with Colonel Pigler outside the Saddle Rock Café?" he said. "He told you, Slenk, 'You've messed this up enough. My advice to you is to steer clear of that girl. Girls are poison!' Who was that girl, Slenk?"

30

Guy Slenk didn't answer Roderick Austen's question. He shuffled his feet, clasped and unclasped his hands. Then his body swayed from side to side.

"I—I want water! Madison—he—he oughta—be killed! Stole my colt—" His voice died out in curses. The trainer seemed only half aware that he was being questioned in police headquarters.

"Slenk," Austen said, "you're so shot with booze that you can't even lie straight." Austen turned to Trigg. "I saw the city prison physician outside—ask him to step in."

The physician took one look at the trainer, said in bored manner, "Case for psychopathic ward. You'll have to finish sweating him tomorrow. He's gone loco."

"Thanks," Austen said, getting to his feet. "But just a minute." He motioned to Trigg and Hunt, stepped toward the door, as Slenk muttered to himself. Austen said something. Both men nodded. Hunt went out with the doctor. Austen stepped to his chair. Trigg moved to Slenk, seized his arm. "Come on—you!"

Trigg pulled the trainer to his feet, led him to a door opening into an adjoining room. "Come on—come through this door!" Trigg commanded. Slenk swayed with him.

Austen heard Trigg say, on the other side of the door, now partially closed: "Do as I tell you if you want a drink.

195

Put your hand up here." A protest was heard. "Shut up! Do as I say."

Sound of footsteps in the corridor—steps approaching the other door. Austen opened that corridor door, stood behind it.

Two persons came into the room: Danny Barton and Detective Hunt. A moment of silence. Then Barton's staccato voice:

"Look! The hand on the door. I saw it that way when I looked in Madison's office."

Austen stepped from behind his door. The hand fell from the other door, and that other door opened. There stood Guy Slenk, swaying against Trigg.

The trainer saw the jockey, straightened up. His jaw dropped.

"You did it, didn't you!" Barton exclaimed. "You killed Madison!"

Austen spoke quickly: "Take Slenk back to his cell. Give him a bucket of water—give him two buckets." A turnkey came in from the corridor, led Slenk out.

Austen turned to the jockey. "Danny," he said with confidential manner, "I believe you told me the truth about seeing a hand pulling the back door shut at Madison's office. But I want more truth."

"Yes sir."

Austen looked at the lad sharply. "You heard Guy Slenk threaten to kill Madison, didn't you?"

"Yes sir, I did. A week ago."

"Tell us about it."

"I had just worked Red Moon—a mile at a fast gallop. Slenk tied the colt to the stable rail, began rubbin' Red hisself. I heard him mutterin':

"'I'll kill Madison before he gets you, Red. I'll kill that bastard!'

"I didn't pay no attention to him. You know how it is on a race track, Major: somebody's always talkin' about killin' somebody else—and never doin' it."

"This time it was done, Danny."

"I know, sir. And that hand, with the glove on—that's the way it looked when I heard that shot and peeped in Madison's window."

"That's all, Danny. You'll have to go back for a little while."

"Can't I get a lawyer, Major? And am I—I charged with killin' Mr. Madison?"

"Rest easy for the time being."

"But, Major, can't I get out? The Derby's bein' run this afternoon. It'll soon be time—"

"Would you like to hear it—on the radio?" Austen asked.

"I—I—yes sir."

Austen turned to Hunt. He lowered an eyelid, said: "I see the cap has a radio on the table here. Any objection if—"

"If we brought Barton in to hear the race? No sir."

"Good! Then you'll hear the race, lad."

When the jockey was taken out Austen said to Trigg and Hunt:

"Everybody holds back something, and Barton's holding back a lot. We'll let him hear the Derby; he won't know it, but it'll be a new kind of third degree." He looked at his watch.

"The Derby will be run at about four forty-five. I've got to run to the Commission office, handle a few matters. Trigg, you help Sergeant Hunt."

"Yes sir! Anythin'! But I sorta wish I was at the Downs." He rubbed his chin.

Austen grinned. "So do I—and Hunt too. But can't be helped. The two of you make Barton at ease here. Have the radio on when I come. I'll wait till the horses are ready to go to the post, then step in, casual-like."

Austen went out. From the Commission's office he put in calls for Shepherd Thomas, knowing that they were forlorn hopes. Thomas, at this hour, wouldn't be at the club or a hotel—not even in the working press box at the Downs. He'd be eating late Derby breakfast in the cook-shack of some owner. He'd be talking to a trainer in the paddock, would have his long nose stuck in the jockey room, or he'd be moving down through the crowds, getting local color for a unique Derby story.

An hour later the Commission's phone operator reported:

"I've called every place; I've sent out messengers; I've heard from them all—Mr. Shepherd Thomas seems to have disappeared."

"Thanks." The girl had made no complaint at working overtime Derby day. Austen asked:

"You and the boy friend going to the Derby?"

She was a pretty brunette, and she blushed charmingly.

"Yes sir. He's—he's in the waiting room now."

"Got your tickets, of course?"

"Yes sir."

"Give 'em to somebody." Austen opened his wallet. "Use mine instead."

She took two tickets from him, looked at them. Her eyes widened. "Box seats—o-oh! But it's a shame—you not going—"

"Never mind about me—scram! And enjoy yourself."

Exactly at four forty-four Austen strolled into police headquarters, nodded to the desk sergeant, and walked into the front room.

An extra swivel chair had been brought in, and Danny Barton was seated in it. Trigg was on one side of him,

Hunt behind him. The radio was on a table to their right, and all three were listening—so intently that they barely nodded to Austen, who took the other swivel chair.

"We are now broadcasting the running of the Kentucky Derby from historic Churchill Downs. . . . Nearly a hundred thousand persons here, jamming the stands, the rail, the lawns, even the roofs of the stables behind the backstretch. . . . Now they're escorting a Cabinet officer into the stewards' stand. There's 'The Star-Spangled Banner'—hear it?"

Over the air came the martial notes.

"It's slightly misty—generally it is on Derby day. But the track is fast. The sun's behind clouds, but everything is bright here.

"Flags of a hundred nations—and countries that once were nations!—fly from the Maypole in the center field. And, folks, I wish you could see the crowds—from the top of the stretch down past the clubhouse turn—almost three eighths of a mile—just people! Tens of thousands of 'em— people who came from the four corners of America to see this one race—a race that's been looked forward to for months, that will last only two minutes—the greatest race for three-year-olds in the Western Hemisphere! The Derby, which has been run in the Bluegrass for three quarters of a century—a clash of East and West and North and South for turf supremacy.

"The horse that wins the Derby must have stamina— he's got to run a mile and a quarter—and he must have supreme speed. Today the winner will have to outlast and outrun nineteen others, for twenty are going to the post, and wait— Hear it? They're coming from the paddock, going to the post—and there!—'My Old Kentucky Home'!"

The strains of America's folk song came clearly; the last note died away. One could almost feel the sudden hush that fell over the gigantic crowd—a hush so still that one could hear, almost, the *clump-clump* of hoofs on the tan-bark as the entries were led from the paddock to the track.

"Ah, the sun, folks! It cuts through the clouds, strikes the flags whipping in the breeze, plays on the vari-hued silks of the jocks—what a parade!

"Twenty great thoroughbreds going to race for gold and glory! Marching up the track single file behind a red-coated outrider. One or two owners have won this classic before; others have tried for a lifetime and are trying again today."

Austen watched Danny Barton. The boy was hunched forward, his fingers slightly closed, as if riding to the post.

"How would you ride Red Moon, lad?" Austen asked as the announcer's voice dropped an instant.

"Get out in front and die there!" the rider exclaimed. "I tell you, Major, Jockey Tracey has got to break fast with that colt. Twenty in the field, and he's drawn number fifteen. That means he's three quarters across the track.

"The jock's got to break fast, get over on the rail. And a sweet chance he's goin' to have! Tracey is a lot slower-thinkin' than he oughta be.

"Eve Lovelace is on the rail. She's a bullet from the barrier."

He stopped. The announcer still was describing the scene. At a nod from Austen, Hunt lowered the sound.

"Now I'll tell you a secret—since I'm not riding," Barton went on. "Red Moon can run that race faster than any horse in the field if he gets free of interference. He's not chickenhearted, but he is a sulker. He's sort of awkward—long-legged. And if he gets bumped around in a big field—well, it's hard to get him goin' again."

"Will he come from behind and win?" Austen asked.

"Yes, if the right boy knows how to keep him clear from the other horses. But it's best to break fast and get away from 'em."

"How's this boy Tracey?"

"Tracey?" Barton spat in the cuspidor. "He ought to be ridin' trottin' horses—that's about his speed."

Hunt raised a finger. "Horses at the post." Austen nodded. Hunt twisted the dial slightly.

"They are all in the stalls. Red Moon, the favorite, is standing pretty. Trumpet Call is plunging to go. Now Master Charles is raring up; now he's down! Silver Sword is trying to back out; now he's stopped. Now they're almost in line. They're ready to start the run for the roses—and *there they go!*"

31

Utter silence for an instant in that police-headquarters room, save for a slight crackle from the radio. At the words, *"There they go!"* Barton threw his torso forward—automatically; he clenched his hands in front of him, as if he were lifting Red Moon free of interference, breaking toward the rail.

Then came the roar of massed thousands and a mighty shout, "They're off!" Then the crowd was shut out, and the announcer's voice (the expert was atop the grandstand) came in thrilling tones:

"There they go—the run for the roses! Eve Lovelace breaks first, off like a flash! Followed by Blue Flag and Star Gazer, neck and neck, then Trumpet Call, Silver Sword alongside—the rest jumbled together."

Danny Barton jumped to his feet, swore loudly. "All I got—eighteen hundred dollars—is ridin' on Red Moon's nose! I got five to one in the future book—stands to win nine thousand—and Tracey—damn him!—he don't get off smart-like." Again he cursed and leaned over the radio, as if to conjure Red Moon.

"Come on, feller, come on!" he pleaded. "Get through that pack o' nags!"

He stopped, straightened, as the announcer called:

". . . passing the stands first time around, Eve Love-lace a length and a half in the lead! Silver Sword second, Trumpet Call at the Sword's throat latch, Blue Flag a neck behind. Then comes the field, all massed together—the riders jockeying for position as they go into the clubhouse turn. Red Moon, the favorite—he's pocketed—"

"I knew it—I knew it!" Danny Barton cried.

"Red Moon between Navajo Kid—and Blue Flag on his right. Red Moon is running nicely, but he can't get through those horses in front; he can't take around; Blue Flag won't give way. Now they're shooting around the clubhouse turn, Eve Lovelace setting a sizzling pace!

"Now they're straightening out for the long run down the backstretch. Eve Lovelace opens more daylight between herself and the field. The first quarter in twenty-two seconds flat—that's fast, folks!

"Navajo Kid's dropping back. Red Moon's now on the rail. Eve Lovelace in the lead, Silver Sword and Trumpet Call—and now Star Gazer's going up—is fourth. Tracey's trying to run around 'em, but Blue Flag on his right won't give him room. Red Moon—he's pinned in—he can't get ahead, unless he can squeeze through."

"Shut that thing down!" Barton commanded. He seemed suddenly indifferent to the others in the room.

Hunt lowered the volume, looked at the jockey curiously.

"Tired horses, or horses that's been runnin' awful fast" —Barton's phrases came in staccato tones—"goin' into that far turn, generally they spread out a little. If Tracey—if he's got the guts"—he moaned frantically—"he'll shove Red Moon's nose between two of them front runners. There's where jockeyship counts. It takes nerve to jam through. I got nerve—aw, gawd!"

The jockey threw himself into the chair, then leaned forward tensely again as Hunt raised the radio volume.

". . . at the half! Eve Lovelace is dropping back. She's tiring; she was only a sprinter! Now come the routers. Silver Sword is moving up; Star Gazer is second; Blue Flag is third, Trumpet Call a close fourth. Red Moon, the favorite, is fifth—and behind pounds the field of flashing horses.

"Now into the far turn! Eve Lovelace is second—no, she's in third place! Silver Sword's taken the lead. Trumpet Call's passed her, then comes the filly—no, Star Gazer passes her. She's dropping out of contention. Blue Flag swerves by her and now Red Moon! Red Moon passes her and takes fifth place as they strike the head of the stretch, but Red Moon lost ground going around the turn—"

"That fool!" Barton's fist pounded the table at his side. "Tracey oughta jammed through. He didn't have the guts! Tried to circle the field on the turn—the fool—he oughta laid close to the rail. Aw, gawd!"

". . . a horse we haven't heard from before—red jacket, gold sleeves, black sash and cap! That's Master Charles— Master Charles from the Volunteer stable. Master Charles breaks loose from the pack in the rear; he's coming like a house afire!"

Tense excitement filled the announcer's tones as he went on:

"Here's a thrilling Derby moment! Master Charles, an outsider, at fifty to one—"

"That colt's better than anybody thought." Barton spoke quickly.

". . . Master Charles was rated off that sizzling early pace. He's got something left for the run home. Now he's alongside Red Moon, looking the favorite in the eye. Tracey's lashing out with his bat—"

"Stop it!" Barton yelled. "Hit him just once—or he'll sulk! Hit him just once to wake 'im up!"

". . . Tracey's arm rises and falls like a flail."

"Tracey's lost his head; he oughta be cool!" Barton shouted, looking from man to man, a wild light in his eyes. "He oughta hand-ride now."

". . . Red Moon spurts ahead, but Master Charles comes alongside again. Master Charles forges ahead. Master Charles is coming fast; he's passing Red Moon, passing the favorite!"

"No! No!" Beads of sweat stood out on Barton's forehead.

". . . Master Charles is about to steal the show! Master Charles passes Blue Flag; now the long shot comes to Star Gazer's saddle blanket. He's looking Star Gazer in the eye—a great horse, being given a great ride—"

"That's Jim Clay on Master Charles—took the mount at the last minute," Barton muttered, wiping his forehead with his shirt sleeve.

". . . Red Moon's coming again; at last the favorite's showing his stuff. . . ."

"That's the fellow. Show 'em, fellow!" Barton cried, holding onto the edge of his chair.

". . . Jockey Tracey's got the favorite making a great stretch charge. Red Moon passes Star Gazer. Red Moon shoots alongside Blue Flag, and they're running the last hundred yards—Trumpet Call's in front. Master Charles passes Silver Sword—Silver Sword and Red Moon. Red Moon's coming like a wild horse—fifty yards to go—"

The voice broke off, then came the words, "It's almost a blanket finish—four horses shooting alongside—"

An instant of breathless silence. Then:

"The finish!"

Another silence, then the staccato phrases, "In the last ten yards they separate—the winner, *Trumpet Call*, by a length. Master Charles second! Silver Sword a neck behind, then Red Moon—fourth. Behind, Blue Flag, Star Gazer, Navajo Kid, and a field of tired contenders. Eve

Lovelace, who led for the first half mile, comes in last. Red Moon, the favorite—he had a rough trip and he didn't make his bid till it was too late!"

Barton, white-faced, bit his lip and swore. "A nine-thousand-dollar win that fool jock cost me," he said hoarsely.

Now the announcer was excited again:

"They're breaking over on the track; five thousand people in the infield are breaking over the inner rail. The horses are stopping, are coming back. Mounted police with whips are driving the infield crowd back."

Austen signaled for Hunt to shut off the radio. Barton sprang to his feet.

"I would-a won with Red Moon!" he cried to Austen. "I would-a broke fast—got a contendin' position early. I'd-a kept my head, started my stretch run sooner. I'd-a won—and I'd-a had the leg up on Red Moon if—if—if it hadn't been for that damn girl!"

Austen seized the jockey by the shoulders.

"What girl?" he demanded in savage tones. "Come through, Barton. You've held out on me!" He shook the jockey, demanded again, "What girl?"

Barton's blue eyes blazed defiance. "Polly Day—that's who! She's the cause of everything—Polly Day."

32

Austen released his hold on the jockey's shoulders.

"Sit down, Barton."

The jockey sat down.

"You've made a fool of me, boy." Austen took a chair opposite while Hunt and Trigg looked on.

"No sir, I didn't mean to do that, Major." Barton crouched back in the chair, his face filled with fear.

"You've held back from me—something important for me to know. Do you realize I'm no lawyer? I'm an investigator for the Racing Commission, and I'm here just to see that you get a square deal; nothing more."

Austen ran a hand through his dark hair and frowned. "If you don't talk I'm going to walk out, Barton. And when the detective captain comes back from the Downs he'll put a sweet charge of murder against you. Take your choice—spill the truth or keep quiet. I don't much care what you do. I'm tired."

He reached for his hat.

"Wait a minute, Major Austen."

"Well?" Austen's hand stopped in mid-air.

"I'll—I'll tell you everythin'."

Austen's hand dropped. "It's time, boy. You've had us running around in circles, trying to save your hide. And you've been holding back stuff that might clear you. Where does Polly Day come in? Spill it—and spill it quick."

Barton dropped his eyes, then raised them and looked straight at Austen. "Polly Day, the actress, she was Madison's new sweetheart. You knew that, didn't you?"

"Go on, start at the beginning."

"I used to ride for Madison." Austen frowned impatiently. "I mean I know his ways," Barton added hastily, "always chasin' girls."

"What has Miss Polly Day to do with the Derby?"

"Everythin'. She—she's the kind of girl who gets what she wants."

"Most clever girls do. Go on—when did you first see Madison and her together?"

"I seen 'em out at the Downs one Sunday mornin'. There was half a dozen Derby candidates all workin' that mornin'. Slenk, he was gettin' Red Moon out, and he was late. So he was waitin' till he got a clear track.

"I was standin' by Red Moon's head, and we was over by the six-furlong gate to the track, and Madison and that girl—I didn't know her name then—they drove up in Madison's roadster. They stop right by us and I hear her say, 'Oh, isn't that a lovely creature!' And Madison says, 'That's one of the Derby candidates. That's Red Moon.' And she says, 'What a beautiful name,' and she gets out and comes over and she pats Red's neck. And Madison comes over too. Madison, he didn't like me—"

"I know that. Go on—tell us about the girl."

"Madison, he says, when she keeps sayin' how pretty Red is, 'If you like him, Polly'—that's the first time I hear her name—'if you like him I'll buy him for you.'

"He must-a spoke too quick, for she took him up in a flash. She says, 'Oh, will you? Thank you so much, Henry, and we'll run him in the Derby, won't we?'

"Then Madison, he starts to crawfish—not at gettin' Red Moon for her, but at runnin' him in the Derby."

"Why should Madison crawfish at the idea of running the favorite?"

Barton didn't answer. Austen waited. Not a word came from the jockey.

Austen stood up. "I'm through." He spoke to Hunt: "Take him back—book him on suspicion of murder." Austen started toward the doorway.

"Please! Wait a minute, Major." Barton was promptly vocal. "I'm going to tell—"

"I don't want to listen, Barton. You haven't brains enough to know who's your best friend in this mess. I wash my hands—"

"Wait, please wait! I'll tell you, but I—I'm scared."

Austen stepped back to him. "Scared of who, what?"

The boy's answer came in a half whisper: "I'm scared of—of Nick the Dago."

Austen sat down again.

"Nick the Dago—the New York betting manager for Colonel James Pigler?"

The jockey's head nodded.

"Why are you afraid of him?"

"I—I'll tell you. It's this way." Words poured from the frightened rider:

"About a week before that Madison, who didn't have a entry named for the Derby, he made a whale of a bet in Nick the Dago's future book."

"You mean in Pigler's future book."

"Nick handled the money—in New York."

"Go on. But Madison said he never bet."

"Huh! He lied. He made bets on the quiet, sir."

Austen nodded. "I know it. Now about this bet."

"Nick the Dago, he comes to the Downs and looks me up. He wanted to know what was Red Moon's condition. Wanted straight dope. I says, 'We are carryin' him along slow and sure.' Then I shut up. Wouldn't say nothin' more till he come across."

"What do you mean—come across? With cash?"

"No sir—but till he told why he wanted to know so much. He finally says he's got a chance to pick up a juicy bet—he calls it—on Trumpet Call. That colt then was second choice to Red Moon in the future bettin'. About eight to one.

"I knew, from talk around the stables, that Madison was sweet on Trumpet Call. That he had tried to buy Trumpet Call and been turned down. So I figgered it was Madison who was wantin' to make the bet. So I says, 'Well, why don't you go on and take Madison's money?'

"Nick thinks I know everythin' 'cause he spoke right up. He says, 'Because I think Trumpet Call's better than he looks to be.' I says, 'Sure, but Red Moon's better, too, and I'm the best rider in the race. How much you takin' from Madison?'

"He says, 'He wants to put ten grand down,' and I says, 'Why don't you take it?' And Nick says, 'You sure you goin' to win with Red Moon?' And I says, 'Sure. I'm the only boy what can win with him too.' Nick don't say nothin' else. He goes away an' he talks with Guy Slenk. I think he must-a slipped a piece o' change to Slenk. Slenk was always busted, you know."

"Do you know what Slenk told Nick the Dago?"

"Yes sir. Slenk told me he told Nick he was goin' to ride me on Red Moon in the Derby. The next day Nick comes out an' we have a early workout. The colt does fine. We step the Derby distance in 2:05 4/5, and Red doesn't draw a hard breath. He's fightin' for his head. While they're coolin' him out Nick comes over to me and says:

"'Boy, you swear to me you're goin' to win with this horse?' I said, 'You see what I did a while ago, didn't you? You timed him in 2:05 4/5.'

"He looks hard at me, says, 'I'm just 'fraid you might fall dead before the race. Nobody else might get speed from him.'

"I said, 'I won't fall dead and I'll get speed from him.'

"He says, 'All right,' that he'll take Madison's bet. I says, 'What's in it to me?' And he says, 'Plenty jack,' and I asks, 'How much?' Nick looks straight at me, and I know he ain't lyin'. He says, 'Boy, you win with Red Moon, an' I give you two grand—two thousand dollars as a little present.'

"Nick laughs. He says, 'Kid, it won't be our jack—it'll be Madison's. He wants to make a still bigger bet, and I'll sweeten the pot for you if he does.' Then—" The jockey broke off, shuffled his feet.

"Go on—what next?"

"The smile leaves Nick's face, and he says, soft-like, 'Kid, if you ever tell anybody about this I'll cut your heart out.' And, Major Austen, that—that's why I was holdin' back on you."

"So Nick took a whale of a bet from Madison," Austen said grimly, "Madison betting that Trumpet Call would win."

"Yes sir. That's why Madison didn't want to get Red Moon and have to start him in the Derby. He might lose that bet. He always ran his horses to win, and he'd-a run Red Moon that way—"

"But if he was so sure Trumpet Call would win, why should he be afraid to send Red Moon out?"

"Because every horse race's a gamble. I might win with Red Moon—or another boy might win with Red Moon. It would upset everythin'—far as Madison's bet was concerned. He stood to win eighty thousand dollars! But—if Red Moon didn't win—don't you see?"

"See what?" Austen demanded.

"The fix it put Madison in? I—I didn't like him, but he was honest in racin'. Ran his horses to win. And—of course he'd want his colors to win, even if it cost him half a million dollars. But if Red Moon didn't win—well, Polly

Day would be on his neck, mad. And people would hear about his bet on Trumpet Call. They'd say he hadn't tried to win with Red Moon. No sir!" The jockey was emphatic. "Madison didn't want to have nothin' to do with Red Moon. Red Moon complicated things. And that girl—" He broke off, shuffled his feet again.

"Yes, that girl. What about her?"

"She kept wantin' Madison to buy Red Moon and run him. She and him come to the track several times in the mornin' to see me work him. Slenk says she's Miss Polly Day, a actress, that Madison's fell for her.

"Last Sunday in April they was out again. They ride up just as I'm takin' Red Moon on the track. She runs over, and he comes after her. She says to me, 'Can I pet him once for luck?' And I says, 'Yes, miss.' She does, and she turns to Madison and says, 'Henry, you promised me you'd buy this colt and run him in the Derby for me. Don't you keep your word, Henry?' And she says, slow-like, 'I like men who keep their word, Henry.'"

"What did he say?"

"Didn't hear," the jockey answered quickly. "He took her by the arm and led her away, and I went out on the track with Red Moon. But two days later Madison's agent comes to Slenk and demands the colt. Offers a cert—cert'fied check for five thousand. Slenk cusses him and refuses. The agent says Madison has a option to buy at that figger. Slenk says there's nothin' in writing. The agent goes away hoppin' mad, and then all of a sudden Rock Doyle shows up.

"Him and Marge Maxwell. They been comin' out to the Downs too. She's been tryin' to work on me. I told you about that, Major Austen."

Austen nodded.

"I got scent of what was up. Rock Doyle—his Chicago book—they'd taken plenty of big bets in Chicago on Red

Moon. They—the Chicago book—didn't want me to win with Red Moon. The New York book that took plenty of big bets of Trumpet Call—they did want me to win."

"Gambler against gambler," Austen said with a grin. "East against the West. What happened?"

"Rock Doyle—he brings a paper with him and demands the colt. Slenk, he feels that Red Moon will win, sure. So he swears nobody's goin' to take the colt from him.

"Slenk—he calls me and the stable foreman. Tells the foreman to start the colt and gives him the startin' money. Says I'm to ride; explains he's goin' across the state line, will stay there till after the Derby's run, so no court papers can be served on him. That ain't all, neither."

"What else?"

"Slenk wanted to win the Derby for himself, and he wanted to win for Nick the Dago. He's scared of Nick. He heard about that big bet on Trumpet Call. He was scared if Madison got the horse—well—" The jockey shrugged shoulders. "See what a mess it all was?"

"Yes—a mess ending in murder. And you blamed for it."

"I know, Major." Barton stopped a moment and then went on: "Well, Madison gets the colt and turns me down. Tracey—I could see—hear—that he was doin' his best, but he didn't know how to ride that entry. Madison kept his word with that girl all right, but if it hadn't been for her I'd have had the leg up on Red Moon. I'd-a won with Red Moon. And I bet you Madison would be alive—that's all I know."

"Who is this Polly Day, Barton?"

"I don't exactly know, sir—a actress; I understand she's playin' here in Louisville."

"Very well. Now if Rock Doyle had got the colt—what would have happened?"

"That's easy, Major. He'd have scratched Red Moon out of the race—so the Chicago future book could-a kept all the money bet on Red Moon. But, Major?" the jockey spoke expectantly.

"Yes?"

"Doyle knew he couldn't get Red Moon. He figgered Madison's option would be rec'nized. That's why he sent Marge Maxwell after me—to get on the good side of me. Well, I just laughed at Marge Maxwell."

"Which was pretty smart. Now tell me this: Why didn't Madison exercise his option on Red Moon sooner? He could have scratched the horse—"

"He warn't the kind that would scratch a good horse out of a race." Barton was firm about Madison's turf probity. "But still—I don't know why he didn't try to get Red Moon sooner."

"I can tell you," Austen said. "Barton, you never had a chance of riding Red Moon."

"How's that, sir? Slenk promised me—"

"You never had a chance," Austen repeated. "Madison had an option, but he didn't want the horse, having made that big bet on Trumpet Call. He knew Doyle had an option—those things are noised about—so he was planning to hold off and let Doyle take the horse. He must have known of those big bets Doyle's book was taking on Red Moon. He knew Doyle would scratch Red Moon from the Derby at the last minute—"

"And along comes that girl—that Polly Day!" Barton spoke with heat. "Polly Day wanted to see that horse run in the Derby. So Madison had to take up his option to keep in good with the girl!"

"Now you understand a few things, don't you, Barton?"

"Yes sir! But if Madison hadn't been pigheaded, kept me off Red Moon—"

"Enough of that," Austen said shortly. "I wish you'd told me about this girl last night, Barton."

"I—I was scared, Major Austen."

"I know. And Madison was killed. And Pigler killed. And Red Moon runs in the name of a man dead but not yet buried." Austen turned to Hunt. "Sergeant, have Barton taken back."

"Listen, Major, can't I get a lawyer?"

"I guess you can, tonight, Barton."

"But won't you still look—look out—for—?" He hesitated.

"Take it easy, Danny," Austen said, speaking once more in a friendly tone. "I'm sort of interested in this case, you know."

As the jockey was being led out the desk sergeant called from the outer room:

"Say, Major, that Chicago newspaper feller askin' for you. That Shep feller. Take it in there?"

Austen did. The nonchalant voice of the reporter came over the wire. "How much money you lose on the Derby, Major?"

"What?" Then Austen grinned. "Listen, fellow, you missed a big yarn—Pigler killed last night. That's what you get for high-hatting me in that wagon diner."

"Did I do that? Tsk-tsk! Too bad. Funny, I don't see my friends when—when—"

"When you're with a pretty girl?"

"When I leave my specs at home! But say, Major, how'd you like to meet her tonight?"

"Same girl?"

"Same girl, Major."

"Swell. Who is she?"

"An old friend."

"What's her name, Shep?"

"Her name, Major? Rather a pretty one—Polly Day."

33

Austen listened to Shep Thomas' voice for another minute, then put the phone down as Hunt returned to the room.

"Major," Hunt said, "that jock, he—how'd his tale sound to you?"

"The same as it did to you, Hunt." Austen smiled at him. "Now for some news." He looked from Hunt to Trigg. "Shep Thomas is going to take me to dinner," he said, "and after that he's going to introduce me to a girl—"

"I'll bet—" Trigg interrupted excitedly, then stopped.

"—a girl named Polly Day," Austen finished.

Sergeant Hunt whistled, snapped his fingers.

"Major"—Trigg was rubbing his lantern jaw in excitement—"I'll bet she tells everythin'!"

Austen laughed. "Trigg, you know horses and jockeys," he said, "but girls are something else again. Chances are she tells exactly nothing. But I'm interested in Marge Maxwell. See what her condition is, Hunt."

Marge Maxwell was tossing nervously in bed, the hospital reported by phone. It would be better to delay further questioning for some hours.

"That's that," Austen said shortly. "Now find when Doc Campbell will have a report of his autopsy ready."

The toxicologist reported it would be sometime after eight o'clock. "Trigg, camp on his doorstep. Hunt will tell you where to go. When that report's finished bring a copy to Hunt."

"Where'll you be, Sergeant?" Trigg turned to Hunt. Hunt looked at Austen.

"Hunt, you stand in the lobby of the Mercury Theater tonight," Austen said. "Trigg will join you there. Seems that Shep Thomas and I are going to take this Polly Day to see a show. I'm to meet 'em for dinner at the Brown Hotel. I'll come out, get the report from you. And if I learn anything from this girl—well, both of you will be handy. Now scram!"

The Brown Hotel was jammed with after-Derby throngs as Austen pushed in at seven o'clock. Celebrities were pouring in from the track, demanding drink and food. Celebrities were shouting to one another over the shoulders of the crowd. Bellboys were paging celebrities. Celebrities were checking out for special planes and trains; porters were shoving the luggage of celebrities out of the main doors. Drunken celebrities were trying to seize the lobby walls for support.

Austen caught Shep Thomas' eye as they went up the grand stairway. The newspaperman, cigarette drooping from his lips, reached out a thin, strong hand and drew Austen to one side of the landing. "Look at 'em, Major." He grinned, dropped his cigarette, and heeled it. "Half the stuffed shirts of America are here; half of 'em are drunk—"

"And half the real people who count—they're here too, Shep." Austen spoke warmly.

Shep Thomas, rebuked, nodded. "Guess you're right. But say, you missed a great race today."

"Yes? And I missed meeting a beaut of a girl last night, Shep."

"You know, it's funny," Shep Thomas drawled, "when I'm with a beautiful girl—like Polly Day—well, I—I just couldn't admit knowing a man hunter—one out looking for Madison's murderer." The reporter said it with a grin.

"I get you, Shep"—Austen grinned back—"but it's too bad—you let yourself be scooped on Pigler's murder."

"Huh! Seems I did read something about that. But that broke on afternoon-newspaper time—after the morning sheets were put to bed."

"You mean that's when the reporters first got wind of it!"

Thomas nodded. "What about telling me about Pigler," he said, "in forty-five seconds? Then we eat."

In swift phrases Austen told him all the essential facts but said nothing of grilling Barton an hour ago. Now and then Thomas asked a question; then, the tale finished, he said:

"Come on—I got a table in the grill for us at this very split second." He verified the time by his wrist watch.

"Where's the girl?" Austen asked.

"She won't be here for dinner. Come on—you meet her soon enough."

When they had found their table Thomas said: "I've already ordered—know what you like. Got a French chef doing a back somersault over fried apples, country sausages, Southern style, hominy, stewed tomatoes, and corn bread. Now tell me more about Brutus. I refuse to talk about the girl till you meet her."

"Brutus?" Austen spoke quickly. "He knows who killed Pigler. Though of course he said he only saw a back—"

"That wouldn't be much help," Thomas broke in.

"No? Should be the best in the world!—if you know how to read 'em. Remember, Brutus can neither hear nor speak. He depends on his eagle eye. He can read backs, I'll wager! Shep, ever think that backs can be more expressive than faces?"

"How come?" the reporter asked, starting to eat.

"Many a man has a poker face, Shep. You never heard of a poker back. Why, it can be the most expressive part of the anatomy—"

"Oh yeah?"

"It expresses dejection, elation, anger, sadness, defeat, victory—reveals it automatically as the emotion is felt."

"Go on—you're good, boy." Shep Thomas grinned.

"I am going on! Backs differ as faces do—in contour and in character. There are weak and strong backs, wide and narrow ones, straight and crooked ones; some one shoulder high and another low—"

"And a tailor at a hundred and twenty-five dollars a suit fixes—"

"Don't interrupt me!" Austen grinned, went on, "There are the backs of bums and the backs of aristocrats—"

"And the backs of twenty-dollar bills!"

"Sure—but the hundred-dollar ones are prettier! Now the back of this man is tossed on the top of the pile—the pile of jigsaw-puzzle pieces:

"Two murdered men, three or four good motives, three or four suspects, one man killed by accident fleeing the city, one pretty girl badly injured, the voice of a girl—your pretty girl, she's mixed in it somehow, Shep," Austen said meaningly, "a deaf-and-dumb black man, a dumb-acting chief of detectives who's not so dumb when he doesn't want to be, a non-practicing physician who reads the detective tales, Nick the Dago and Rock Doyle's Chicago bunch scrapping against each other, and—" Suddenly Austen changed his tone, asked abruptly:

"Shep, who's this Polly Day? How does she fit in the puzzle?"

Shep Thomas looked up from his plate, a blank look on his face. "Yes sir, it was a great Derby," he said. "Course a lot of money was lost on Red Moon and won on Trumpet Call." He shrugged his shoulders. "It was a great spectacle.

I've already written my yarn. It's on the wires now. To-night, old-timer, we're going to a show. We're going to see a whale of a clever actress—"

"Thought we were going to take her to a show!"

"Nay, nay! She's the show—leading lady in a stock company playing here for the Derby season. Take you back to meet her after the show's over. I'll make up for last night's cut."

Silence between them for a moment. "You've known Polly Day some time, haven't you, Shep?"

"Polly Day? Oh, sure. Wrote a feature yarn about her in Chicago—year ago."

"Who is she?"

"That's funny," Thomas answered quickly, "everybody who's ever seen her asks that question, and she won't tell. Polly Day—stage name, of course." He laid down his fork an instant, went on, "Honest to goodness, Major, I don't know who she is. Clever girl, though. Keen head for publicity. Once told me she was the offspring of a French brute and something or other. Japanese butterfly, I believe. Was born when the cherry blossoms bloomed."

"Makes a good yarn."

"Ought to—I wrote it." Thomas grinned again. "That's when she came to Chicago, playing a Broadway success. Romantic comedy. Refused to tell me where she got her start or where she'd played before being on Broadway.

"Next I hear of her she's in Canada. A wild tale comes over the wires she's searching for a long-lost brother. Seems this time—"

Thomas stopped speaking for a moment and hummed a tune from a musical comedy of another generation. "It seems," the reporter continued, "that this time she was born on 'the banks of the Saskatchewan.' Doesn't matter. She's one beaut of a girl."

"Clever?"

"I'll say! I was passing the theater last night. Saw her picture in the lobby. Went backstage. She had a dinner date with some chap. Playwright, name of Grant Hayes."

Thomas' manner sobered, became thoughtful as he went on: "He's a fellow of twenty-seven or -eight, Major. Had a big success on Broadway last year. A comedy. I'm pretty sure he's fallen for Polly Day. Anyway, he's down here writing a play for her. Wait a minute. The play's already written. Fact, they're playing it now—trying it out. I told you she's clever, didn't I?"

"You did. Go on—you're getting good."

"I'll show you how clever she is. I'm a reporter. Gave her a batch of publicity once. And here I drift in a year later, unannounced—"

"I get you," Austen broke in. "She broke her dinner date with this Grant Hayes."

"Righto!" A grin spread over his homely features. "Not because I'm so darn handsome, either," he admitted, "but because I can be of use—someday. Hayes came in the dressing room while I was talking—after I had asked her out for a bite. She told him she was sorry, couldn't go out with him. I was an old friend, and all that."

"How'd this Grant Hayes take it?" Austen asked sharply.

"Not nicely. He'd been drinking, y'see. She told him to quit being a baby, put him out of the room. She said"—Thomas' eyes narrowed in thought, and he finished slowly—"she said, this Polly Day said to me:

"'Shep, you mustn't mind Grant Hayes. He's an awfully dear boy. I'm terribly fond of him, but he's a bit jealous.'"

Another silence between them. Austen rubbed a hand through his hair a moment, then asked quietly:

"You get a good look at Grant Hayes?"

Thomas nodded.

"Was he in white tie and tails?"

Another nod.

"Have on gloves, Shep?"

"He—did. Light-colored gloves—and he was slightly drunk and terribly jealous." The men looked at each other, said nothing. Then Thomas spoke: "I wanted to take her to a first-class place. She said, 'I want some chili, Shep. There's a wagon diner behind the theater—the chili's scrumptious. Let's go there.'"

"That wasn't the reason she chose the wagon diner?"

Thomas shook his head. "She knows I don't make a million a month. She was letting me down light. Clever girl— nice girl."

One more silence. "Shep," Austen said as their coffee was served, "I didn't tell you about Marge Maxwell this morning." He described the hospital visit in detail. "And this afternoon we grilled Barton, and he told us—"

Shep Thomas' eyes widened when Polly Day's name entered the recountal.

"Madison must have been wild over her—maybe Pigler was too," Austen finished.

"Yes—maybe, but Grant Hayes is," Thomas said firmly. "And Hayes is a jealous man." He lowered his voice, leaned over the table, and looked Austen in the eye, said: "Grant Hayes' clothes were disheveled, as though he'd been wrestling with somebody, or maybe had pushed through briars—and"—his voice dropped still lower as he repeated —"Grant Hayes was wearing light gloves!"

34

For a moment both men sat without speaking.

"More coffee, sir?"

A waiter was hovering over Austen. "Oh—no, thanks."

Thomas, too, waved the coffeepot aside. He leaned back, relaxed.

"Shep, does Polly Day know you are going to take me backstage tonight?"

"I never mentioned you to her," he said easily. "I never mentioned Madison, either."

"Did she?"

"Yes, seems as if she did." Thomas drawled his answer. "Said she had just heard Mr. Henry Madison had been murdered. Said it was a terrible thing. That she had met him— that he was a very charming man."

"Did she seem worried?"

"That gal? I'll say not! But—didn't I tell you she's a clever actress? But come on"—looking at his watch—"it's almost curtain time. Let's be in when the lights are lowered."

Twelve minutes later they were in aisle seats; then the lights dimmed.

The curtain rang up. They were viewing the living room of an English manor house after an air raid: a room gay in red-and-tan chintz but with an ugly fresh crack up a side wall. Stars could be seen shining through a casement at the right. Shep Thomas nudged Austen, said behind his hand: "Forgot to tell you, if this goes over Polly will be starred when they hit Broadway. Watch—she makes an early entrance."

A few moments of play between minor characters, then an elderly man was left standing, musing, beside the crack in the wall. An instant later a peal of laughter off stage.

The casement opened. Through it stepped one of the loveliest girls Roderick Austen had ever seen—the girl of the wagon diner. Slightly above medium height, willowy and strikingly beautiful, she gave the impression of being vibrantly alive.

Long golden hair was done low at the neck, and not even the loose tweed sport things she wore could conceal the graceful lines of her figure. Eager, intelligent eyes swept the room, then rested on the man by the wall. Her opening lines rippled forth:

"You didn't expect me to come in this way, did you?"

Roderick Austen sat immobile. Not a muscle in his face twitched. At last he turned his head. Shep Thomas was watching him, a question in his eyes. Austen looked blankly at him, then back to the stage.

Austen was listening to one of the most musical voices he had ever heard: a voice that ran the range of emotion, now soft and pleasing, then inquiring, again with a note of doubt in it. A well-trained voice coming from a beautiful and superbly poised actress.

It was a short first act. When the curtain fell Austen turned to Shep Thomas. He spoke one word only: "Yes."

A big sigh of relief came from Shep Thomas, and he said, "I thought so. Let's go in the lobby."

Outside Austen said: "That's the voice, Shep, and the girl who knew in advance that Henry Madison was going to be killed. It's the girl who phoned me, begging me to act for her. I'd swear it's the one."

"Had a suspicion it was," Thomas said casually. "Especially after seeing Grant Hayes, the jealous sweetheart."

At that instant Austen saw Hunt, waved him over. "Trigg show up with the autopsy?"

"Not yet."

"Watch for Trigg. And now—know who backs this company?"

Hunt shook his head. "Been open just a few weeks."

Austen lowered his voice. "Then find out. I want to know who the angel is—understand?"

Hunt nodded, moved off.

"What do you want to know that for?" Thomas asked with innocence in his eyes.

"You know what I want to know, Shep—and why. I want to know if any man has a hold on this girl. Sometimes a theatrical angel—well, he gets a strangle hold on a pretty leading woman if he can. That's human nature. And he bristles like a gamecock if another man comes around."

"Bristles—and stabs," Thomas added.

"Or shoots."

"Yep. True. Now Hayes is handsome as the devil. If I were Hayes and somebody were putting up the coin to feature this girl—" He broke off as a bell sounded and ushers called:

"Curtain going up!"

"Never mind the thinking," Austen said. "Let's go in."

"Just a minute." Shep Thomas spoke quickly. "You grilled Marge Maxwell this morning. What'd she say about not being Madison's girl?"

"She said, 'Get Madison's real girl—she knows all about it! Make her talk.'"

"Think she was speaking the truth—about Madison's real girl?"

"I do."

"Then I'm putting out a short snappy story: *Marge Maxwell Reveals Unknown Beauty in Madison's Life.* And I'm going to predict that I'll name the beauty in twenty-four hours. Do I get it exclusive—if it's Polly Day?"

"You bet. But don't go off half cocked. Maybe it isn't Polly Day."

"Maybe! See you after the act. I'll get my yarn off in thirty-two minutes."

Austen took his seat as the house lights were lowered, then the footlights went on. For forty minutes—during most of the act—Polly Day was on stage. Austen marveled at the girl's speaking voice, at the range of emotional tones. Not since he had seen Ethel Barrymore had he heard such flutelike tones.

The production, too—nothing shoddy or cheap about settings, costumes, or direction. It was a Broadway production all right—trying out during the Derby season. Someone had put up a pot of money—for the play or for Polly Day.

The act, a long one, was over shortly after ten. As Austen went into the lobby Shep Thomas came off the street. "Made it, but where's Hunt with his report?"

"Here!" Hunt was at their elbows. "I got it. Henry Madison backed this show, put up the jack to bring a corking good director down to handle this special production; they put on two plays before this one. But this—Hayes' play—hasn't seen Broadway yet."

"Thanks."

"A question, Major. Isn't this—this Miss Day—the unknown girl who telephoned you?"

Austen smiled. "Your guesses are good, Hunt. You stay out front—wait for that autopsy report. I've a hunch it's going to reveal a lot. After the show you wait outside.

Shep and I are going to see Miss Day. If we come out don't recognize us unless we speak first."

Hunt nodded and moved off. Again the call, "Curtain going up!" Austen and Thomas went inside. Again the loWering of house lights; then the soft glow of footlights against a red-wine curtain. A swish! The curtain rose, revealing a pensive Polly Day sitting by an English hearthstone in the twilight's glow. Austen drew in a breath. The girl—and the scene—was indescribably beautiful. The house broke into spontaneous applause. . . . At last the curtain fell.

A great roar came from the audience. The curtain rose and fell swiftly, rose again, the entire company bowing to the audience. Still more applause. Once more it rose, revealing Polly Day and her leading man. Again—and Polly Day alone. Still applause welled up; she had caught the crowd's fancy. Finally she stepped out on the apron and said in her rich, throaty tones:

"I thank you. I do—I do!"

"Beautiful?" Shep Thomas asked.

Austen nodded, said nothing.

"The devilment a beautiful woman can cause—" Thomas didn't finish the sentence. "Come, let's go," he said in a different tone.

Three minutes later they were on the stage, where grips and clearers were striking the last-act set. They dodged a papier-mâché sundial that the property man was shoving into a corner, stepped aside as an imitation tree trunk was swung against the wall.

"Look out!" the electrician warned. "Don't stumble over those cables. You'll tear 'em and hurt yo'self."

Gingerly they made their way through the orderly disorder, coming to the dressing rooms on the other side. One room was apart from the others. On it was a silver star, gleaming with rhinestones. The newspaperman grinned, pointed his thumb at it.

"Somebody put that star up for Polly. Getting ready for Broadway."

He rapped on her door.

The lovely voice called: "Who's there?"

"Shep Thomas and a friend."

"One minute, Shep, please."

"Shep, as a favor to me"—Austen spoke quickly—"after you introduce me you vanish. Get me?" He added, "You've got to get another yarn on the wires tonight."

Shep grinned. "Sure—but remember, I want to be in at the kill. Sometimes I write pieces for the paper."

"You know me, Shep. Just cool your heels with Hunt."

Quick footsteps sounded inside the dressing room. The door opened.

There stood Polly Day—still in costume. A very clever Polly Day—a girl keen enough to step back quickly into the lights from her dressing-room table. The first view of her should not be in shadows.

"Oh, hello!" she called, holding out both hands.

Shep Thomas stepped forward, followed by Austen. Thomas took her hands, turned toward Austen.

"Polly, here's an old friend. Saw you from out front tonight. Threatened to kill me dead if I didn't bring him back." Then in a flash his tone changed, became touched with gallantry:

"Miss Day, let me present Major Roderick Austen." Austen was not sure if he imagined a slight dilation of her expressive eyes, an imperceptible stiffening of the graceful form. Shep Thomas went on, "The title's genuine—see War Department recommendations for gallantry."

"I take your word, Shep!" Smilingly both her hands now were extended to Austen. "Major, I'm so glad you came back! You see, I've read about you! I know you made

a great record in M.I.—that's military intelligence, eh?"
Her eyes were dancing. "And now you—you are keeping
racing straight for us poor dubs who try to pick the winner. Come in—do!"

Austen smiled. "If I could get the crowds cheering for
me," he said, "as they did for you tonight—"

"Bah! Mere mass psychology!" she scoffed, but the
dancing light did not leave her eyes. "It's an actor-proof
part in a swell play. Any *ham* could put it over."

"Exception to that! Wait till you hear the roar of Broadway, Miss Day—that is, if you ever hear it."

"What do you mean?" She drew her hands back, then
smiled with a touch of hauteur. "Why, just ten minutes
ago it was decided to close the season—to go straight on
to Broadway. We are to open there Monday at the—"

"I hope you get to Broadway—I certainly do," Austen
said gravely.

The girl's beaded eyelashes lowered as if in a puzzled
manner. Before she could speak Shep Thomas broke in:
"The two of you excuse me? I've got to get another yarn
off. See you later."

"Wait, Shep, you can't desert an old friend this way,"
she protested.

"Who's the old friend?" he demanded, grinning. "Rod
Austen or yourself?"

"The idea—asking such a question!" Gaily she waved
him from the room, closed tightly the door after him.

"A dear chap," she was saying as she pushed a chair forward for Austen. "Nice of you to come back, Major."

"You take the chair." Austen spoke quickly. "I'll take
the trunk." He sat upon a flat-lidded theatrical trunk.
Polly Day slipped into the chair, crossed her ankles grace-
fully.

"You've seen many shows," she was saying. "You must
tell me what you think of ours."

"You were gorgeous in your part. That's the word to use—gorgeous—isn't it?"

She smiled and nodded.

"We pick up a word like that now and then, but I'm getting away from business." His face sobered. "I really came back, Miss Day, to—" He stopped, peered intently at her. She sat still. A hand—her right one—went up to her throat. Casually it touched a slender gold necklace.

She got to her feet. "You were saying, Major—"

"I came to make a formal report to you, Miss Day."

"A report to me? I don't understand!"

"No? I want to report—" He broke off as a sharp knock sounded on the door.

Her eyes darted from him to the wooden barrier. Clearly and in poised tones she called:

"Who's there, please?"

The answer came in deep, masculine tones. "It's I—come in?"

"One minute!" She stepped forward, grasped the doorknob. Her head turned to her visitor. "You'll pardon me, Major Austen?" She flashed him a smile. He nodded, got to his feet. Then she opened the door, stepped into the corridor, and closed the door behind her.

Two pairs of footsteps, heavy steps and light steps, moved off.

A moment later she was in the room again, was saying with another smile, "Just a business talk—about our play. I know you'll excuse me. I must change. Shall we have our chat another time? And it's been—enchanting!—to have seen you. Do come and see us in New York, won't you?"

Her hand was extended to Austen, but he didn't take it.

"Expect me to fall for that?" he demanded.

"Major Austen, I'm shocked!" She drew back from him. "I don't understand you!"

"You will!" He spoke sharply. "Go on—have your business talk, if you must, but you better come back and talk to me."

"My dear man—"

"Stop it!" Austen commanded. "I see you are trying to bluff out. So"—he smiled at her, went on—"I'll give you exactly ten minutes, Polly Day, to change into street clothes. Then I'll be back. Knock on your door. Understand?"

Her lips half parted, but she stifled a retort. Her hand, again at the necklace, grasped it. The chain broke. She turned her back on him. Austen caught a glimpse of her face in the dressing-table mirror. There was terror in it.

"I'll be back in ten minutes," he said. He went out the door, closed it after him, stood on the stage, now bare and lighted only by a pilot light. The man who had knocked on Polly Day's door evidently had gone. A couple of property men were lashing a set for shipment, and the stooped stage-door keeper was idly standing by.

Austen looked at his watch. In ten minutes the hands would point to eleven o'clock.

35

In exactly ten minutes Major Austen rapped on Polly Day's dressing-room door. Her voice called, "One minute, please." He waited.

The door opened within fifty seconds. Austen replaced the chronometer he had been holding in his hand. As it touched the bottom of his watch pocket he stepped forward across the threshold. In front of him were costumes hanging from wall pegs. Then the door closed, and Polly Day stepped from behind it.

This was a different—or rather *the*—Polly Day. The other had been the actress, in costume and make-up. In ten minutes and fifty seconds she had swabbed her face of all cosmetics, had changed into a short blue skirt and coat, shining golden hair held down by a jaunty beret. She looked—well, make it twenty—till you looked closely at the oval face drained of color, at the dark blue and troubled eyes behind drooping lids. Maybe she was twenty-three.

A cape, lined with deep crimson, was thrown around her shoulders. She wore dark pumps with brown buckles and stockings of a lighter shade.

The girl tossed her head back, smiled at him fearlessly.

"Sorry to have kept you waiting," she apologized in her flutelike tones. She smiled. "Now will you tell me what it's all about?"

When in the trappings of a character she was a different creature—one who fenced with men. But Polly Day, the girl, was straightforward in manner.

"What is it, Major Austen?" she asked as he stood gazing at her.

"I came to make a report to you, Miss Day." He spoke in businesslike tones. "A report on my activities since you retained me last night."

"Since I retained you? For what, please?"

She stood tall and straight and was looking at him levelly.

"You called me on the phone—"

"I called you?" The blue eyes were enormous.

"Yes. You said Henry Madison was going to be killed; you were afraid an innocent man would be arrested, charged with his murder. You—"

"Are you insane?" she broke in.

"Please—don't interrupt. You wouldn't tell your name—nor see me. But you said if I'd wait a few minutes at my house you'd prove it was no joke. You did. You sent me this envelope and contents."

He pulled the envelope from his pocket. "You sent me these two hundred and eleven dollars in bills—as a retainer. I found out who you were—never mind how. You are my client"—he smiled—"and I seem to be your private investigator—at least I have your money. If you want to call things off—and I think it better—why, here's your money. I've earned none of it. Fate handled the matter."

He held out the money. She drew back against her make-up table.

"No—no—I don't know what it's all about." She shook her head firmly. "That isn't my money. What are you talking about?"

"Will you take the money, please?"

"Certainly not! It is not mine. Are you—insane?" She repeated the question. "What possible interest could I have in Mr. Madison—a man I only knew casually?"

Austen put the envelope and money back in his pocket. "I'll give you till tomorrow morning to claim your money, then it goes to feed stumble-bum jocks and trainers." Polly Day said nothing, her face a lovely blank.

"To answer the question about your interest in Henry Madison," he continued, "he's the angel of this show—he's putting up the money to star you on Broadway. You deny that?"

She made no answer, stood motionless. At last she said: "Please—go on with your fairy tale."

"Call it a fairy tale if you want to"—Austen's voice was hard—"but the fact is Madison was your angel. So you only knew him casually! Most angels—need I say more?"

She caught her breath sharply. Then her tone was mocking: "How elegant you are! Since I am alone, I presume I must stand your insults."

"If you'd rather have me say this to you before witnesses—"

"Not necessary," she said with an icy smile. "You began this little play in my dressing room. Suppose we finish it here, Major Austen."

"All right. Here goes! You say you knew Madison only casually. Those were just casual trips to the Downs, were they?"

For the first time deep color came into her cheeks, as if they had been slapped with a rouge puff.

"Remember the day you saw Red Moon for the first time? Danny Barton was waiting to work him out. You said, 'Oh, isn't he a beautiful horse!' You got out of Madison's car—a roadster. Remember? Madison followed you. Both of you walked over to Red Moon. You spoke to Barton, then you petted the colt. You remember that!"

Her lips twitched slightly, but her eyes were steady.

"Madison told you Red Moon was nominated for the Derby. You were out there several times looking at the colt. You did your darnedest to persuade Madison to buy

Red Moon and run him in the Derby, yet you knew him only casually!"

Now the color was draining from her cheeks, and her lids were drooping heavily.

"Henry Madison was killed last night. Colonel James Pigler was killed last night." Austen's words came clearly —slowly. "Down in the police station a poor fool of a jock, an innocent boy, is facing the charge of murder. And there's a trainer down there facing a murder charge; he's innocent too. Understand?"

"Please"—she moistened her lips—"go on."

"The jockey and the trainer—no friends, no influence. And caught near the scene of the crime after making fool threats against Madison. So—they'll be put to death, Polly Day, unless you do a decent act—"

"What do you mean?" Her shoulders straightened.

"Tell me the name of the man you tried to protect."

"Tell you what?" Her tone was incredulous. Now she was mistress of herself. "If Shep Thomas hadn't presented you—well, I'd call for the police. You are mad!"

"Mad? We'll see. When you phoned me the last time you didn't know Madison had been killed. I did. I told you so. And I told you something else too." Stepping closer, he smiled again at her. "I told you, 'Sure, I'll take that case,' because one of our jockeys, Danny Barton, had been caught at Madison's—was facing murder charges. You were surprised and you said, 'Who?' And I said, 'Danny Barton.' And you said—and I'll never forget the relief in your voice —'Oh, thank God!' And you hung up."

He turned away from her a moment. When he looked back she was still standing motionless, but with every nerve on guard.

"The man who killed Madison got away," Austen went on. "That's the man you wanted me to protect. You didn't care if an innocent man was caught—so long as your man went free."

His right hand shot out, caught her right wrist.

For a split second the girl was still—still as a statue. Not even her eyes twitched. Then with a mighty effort she jerked her wrist back. And jerked Austen with it.

He caught himself just as he was crashing against her. "You're strong, but not stronger than—" He stopped.

"Than what?" She spat the words out like a creature at bay.

"Not stronger than the law."

"You let me go!" She spoke the words in a tense whisper.

"Come on!" He started pulling her toward the door. She screamed.

Austen dropped his hand, stepped closer to her. A sudden pounding on the door behind him, and someone called:

"Hey! What's trouble?"

In a flash the girl seized the manuscript of a play lying on her dressing table, thrust it into his hands, said swiftly:

"Here, hold that."

Then she opened the door.

The stage-door keeper stuck his head and stooped shoulders into the doorway, looked at Austen, then at Polly Day.

His jaws worked, as if shifting a cud. He stuck his left thumb at Austen, said:

"This guy hurtin' you?"

Polly Day laughed. "I'm surprised at you, Jim. You've been in theaters all your life. Don't you know we sometimes rehearse our lines? Major Austen, here, was kind enough to cue me. It's a new scene that's been written into our play, Jim"—she smiled at the old fellow—"and if you come to New York with us you will hear that scream in the second act six nights and two matinees weekly."

"Well, I—"

"It's all right, Jim." She stepped forward, touched his left shoulder lightly. "You're a dear and I thank you for looking out for me."

Jim shifted from one foot to another. His jaws worked again. He walled his eyes at Austen, then looked again at Polly Day.

"All th' same—you call me"—he turned his head, spat over his shoulder—"if you need me, Miss Day."

"Thanks, Jim."

The man withdrew head and shoulders, shut the door tightly behind him.

36

Polly Day and Roderick Austen again were alone together. He held the manuscript out to her. She took it and tossed it onto the dressing table.

"Pity," Austen said, "to take a girl—clever as you—down to the jug. But you are going."

She gazed at him without saying a word. She was still standing with her back to the door.

"You could be a star tomorrow," he went on, "this play—tailor-made for you. It will be a smash hit. You'll be a sensation *if* you reach Broadway." He emphasized the *if*.

"You mean *when* I reach Broadway," she corrected.

"No, if," he repeated. "Only chance you have now to get there is to come clean. It's little I ask."

"What are you asking?"

"The name of the man you are hiding."

"What?"

"The man you thought was going to kill Madison—and—"

She shrugged her shoulders. "This is positively silly," she said indifferently.

"Silly? I don't think so. I know a lot, Polly Day. I even know you telephoned me twice from the wagon diner behind the theater." She made no move, no sign. "If you are not the girl who put in those calls—if you are not the

person who sent me this money"—he touched his coat—
"then you'll be willing to clear yourself."

"Clear myself?" she laughed nervously. "Major Austen,
I feel I must ask you to go."

Austen ignored her words. "The wagon diner is open
still. Come across the alleyway. If the cashier says you
are not the girl who came in there twice in costume, with
make-up on, once at eight and once at eight forty-five,
and telephoned"—he hesitated and went on—"if the old
delivery man at the telegraph office says you are not the
girl who brought the envelope to be delivered—well, I'll
call it off. Come on, let's go."

He picked up his hat from the trunk.

"What an absurd idea."

"Come on—I'm playing fair. You'll make the test or
you'll go to the station."

"Major Austen"—she rested one knee on the low bench
facing the dressing table—"if I had a real friend in this
city you wouldn't dare speak this way to me."

"You have one."

"Who?"

"The man you're shielding."

Instinctively she straightened up. "You are a madman!"

"No, just a fellow trying to keep two friendless fools
from burning, trying to keep racing clean. You see, Polly
Day, I don't believe those murders—well, I don't think
they were turf murders."

"No?"

"No."

"Then what are they?"

Lines came into his forehead. "Want to hear me do
some thinking out loud?" he asked.

She shrugged, spread her hands in a gesture of indiffer-
ence. "Go on!"

"After you made that call to me—at eight o'clock—you could have hopped into a fast car, driven out to Madison's home, shot him—"

"For what possible reason, pray?"

"Don't interrupt. You could have come back—you were already made up; you had time enough before the first curtain. Either you did it—or the boy friend did."

She glared at him, turned her face away an instant.

"Boy friend—ugh! You are coarse, aren't you?"

Austen watched her, not bothering to retort. Outside the noise of approaching steps sounded in the corridor, sounded loudly now that all theater activity was stilled. The steps stopped on the other side of the door. Someone rapped upon it—sharply, as if he had a right to knock.

The girl stepped to the door, grasped the knob, looked once at Austen.

"Why don't you open it?" he asked.

She did.

The stooped shoulders and head of the doorkeeper stood out in the gloom of the passageway.

"Note for you, Miss Day." He gave her a folded slip of paper and looked curiously at Austen. He waited, as if for a reply.

Polly Day opened the folded sheet, glanced at it. Her penciled eyebrows went up slightly, then fell.

"Thank you, Jim. There's no answer."

She closed the door, carefully placed the sheet on the dressing table. Then, ignoring Austen, she took from a shelf a small spirit lamp, one used to heat wax for beading the eyelashes. Casually she lighted the lamp, then took a tiny pan filled with wax from the table. It slipped from her fingers.

"Oh!" she gasped as it struck the table, fell to the floor.

Austen stooped to retrieve it. Her hand shot out, seized the note, thrust it over the tiny flame. It flared into blaze.

Austen jumped up, seized her wrist. With his free hand he slapped the burning paper.

"Ouch!" she exclaimed. "Now you've burned me!"

He released his hold. The charred paper, half consumed, fell to the floor. She put a finger into her mouth an instant.

"Oh, it hurts," she said. "I didn't think you'd do a thing like that."

He paid no attention to her, reached down for the paper. Evidently the message had been only a few words, for the top of the paper was burned off, and the rest was blank. But on the edge of the charred portion he saw the letters *a n t.* Carefully he put the paper in his coat side pocket.

"How's the finger now? Let's see it."

She let him take her hand.

"Not a blister—not even red." He released his hold. "Where did it burn you?"

"Here." She pointed to the top of her first finger.

"Funny, you didn't even put that finger to your lips. It was the inside of your little finger. I saw you." He shook his head. "That piece of acting wasn't so good. You overdid it. And you put the note too carefully on the table."

"Really?"

"You did. If you had carelessly thrown it over there I'd have thought nothing of it. But you didn't. That aroused my curiosity. Then—"

"Oh, a psychological detective!"

Austen ignored the taunt. "Then you tried to trick me and burn it. Again not well done." He watched her closely. "That's something you should have rehearsed first. And on the charred edges of what was left I saw the letters *a n t*—part of a word. You call him Grant, don't you? Grant Hayes, the playwright?"

When Polly Day spoke now she was mistress of herself. "Look here, Major Austen, let's quit this foolishness.

You've made a terrible mistake, but I can understand that. Naturally it's your duty to follow up every idea—I believe you call 'em clues?"

"Clues is good enough. Go on, please."

"If you must know it, that was a note from the author of this play—Grant Hayes."

"So I presumed."

She smiled at him. "Were you ever an actress?"

"Not yet."

"Even so—you may understand: we receive hundreds of notes and letters, mainly from strangers. If we kept them—even those from friends—we'd need warehouses to store them in. I burn mine immediately after reading. And that's that." She smiled again.

"Good tale," he conceded. "But getting to the point—"

"Please, please, Major Austen!" The wide eyes were frank now, almost pleading. "Let's have done with all this! I'm playing—in a new show. We're nervous—excited. A friend brings you backstage, and all of a sudden you begin walking the floor, pointing the finger at me. Now is that nice?"

"Whoa, there! There has been no floor walking, no finger pointing—but there may be," he added meaningly.

"Oh well, you understand. You made me nervous, but I'm willing to forget all that. Now it's getting awfully late. I took an apartment for the season. Won't you be sporting and drop me there? If you're chilly I can shake you up a spot, but you'll have to run quick." She smiled. "I really must get some sleep. We leave for New York tomorrow, you know."

For a long moment he was bathed in her smile.

"Wait—you got a note from Grant Hayes—the boy friend—"

"Now, now, don't be vulgar," she chided.

"Well, call him your fiancé, if you like that term better."

"It's truer," she said, so softly that it was a rebuke.

For a moment the color rose in his face.

"Hayes wants to see you tonight."

"Any harm if he does? We've business to discuss—business of the production. You must realize that we work while you sleep."

"I know. But he's coming here, so"—he sat on the trunk against the side wall—"I imagine he said he's coming back in a half-hour. Well, I'm waiting for him."

She leaned against the door, a chagrined look on her face. "I wish I had a friend to appeal to," she said.

"You've got plenty. There's the doorkeeper, or—" He broke off as a sharp rap sounded. "There's one—open and see."

She made no move. Another rap, an insistent one.

"Go on. Open it."

Still she refused. "If you won't," he said, "I will." He got to his feet, brushed her aside from the door, flung it open. Someone was standing a foot from the threshold—a slim chap, twenty-eight or thirty, dressed in heavy gray tweeds, and looking as if he hadn't slept for days.

"Hello, Hayes," said Austen. "Come in—we're waiting for you."

The man crossed the doorsill, slammed the door behind himself. First he looked at the girl, then at the man with her.

"What are you doing here?" he demanded. And before giving Austen time to answer he turned on the actress. "Every time I come around I find another man in your dressing room."

She put a hand on his arm. "Now, Grant, you're tired. Go to the hotel and get some rest."

"Rest? Not till this man gets out of this room."

"Suppose I don't get out?" Austen asked.

"Then I'll throw you out."

"Oh no, you won't," Austen said quietly.

"Won't, eh? Why won't I throw you out? I've thrown bigger men than you out of this room."

Austen smiled. "One of them was Henry Madison, wasn't he?"

"Henry Madison?"

Grant Hayes was a playwright—not an actor. He showed he was startled by the name.

"Yes, and that's not all you did to Madison, either," Austen said. "I am leaving this room, Hayes, but you are leaving with me. So is Miss Day. After we get outside"—he spoke slowly—"you can go where you please, but she— goes—with—me."

37

The playwright glared at Austen for a moment, then his mouth went open. He looked toward Polly Day; her face was expressionless. He turned and glared at Austen, now standing by the dressing-room door. "Going to come with you!" Hayes exclaimed. "Pol—Miss Day coming with you, and I can— Say, what in hell do you mean?"

Austen's right hand reached into his trousers pocket. He brought something out—opened his hand. "See it?" It was a badge.

Grant Hayes looked. "What's that?" he demanded.

"Chief investigator—State Racing Commission."

"What's that got to do with Miss Day?"

"Plenty! I'm taking her to the station in connection with the murder of Henry Madison."

Hayes straightened; his fists clenched. "Say, you got a search warrant?"

"Search warrant?" Austen laughed. "Buddy, I don't need one. I've authority to arrest any person suspected of a crime—and this girl is suspect—plenty."

"Suspected of what?"

"Of killing Henry Madison—that clear?" He looked at the girl. "Ready, Miss Day? I'll take you down in a taxicab."

Once more blood drained from her face; her lips trembled. Then the playwright, his hands shaking—shaking from liquor—stepped between them. "Look here, you—whoever you—you are!" He glared at Austen. "You can't arrest this girl!"

"Can't, eh? Well, I'm going to!"

"I tell you, you can't."

"And why not?"

"Because—" He hesitated, swallowed nervously, looked at the girl. Her face was still blank.

"I'm ready, Miss Day." Austen turned toward the door.

"Dammit, man, you can't take this girl!"

"Come on, Miss Day." Austen hesitated, his hand on the doorknob.

"You can't take her because—because"—Grant Hayes stepped between Polly Day and Roderick Austen, gripped Austen's shoulder with his right hand; there was a glaring light in his eyes—"because she didn't kill Henry Madison—because I killed him myself."

Austen reached up, took Hayes's hand from his shoulder. The girl's breath came in sudden gasps. "What?" she exclaimed. Her hands went to her throat for a moment.

"Oh," said Austen, looking first at the man, then Polly Day. "I thought I'd dig the truth out." He turned again to Grant Hayes. "So you killed him. Will you tell me why?"

"Sure, I killed him." Hayes spoke with desperation. "I warned him to keep away from Polly—"

"So," Austen broke in, looking at the girl, "you just knew Madison casually!"

"I—I—" The hands dropped from her throat.

"Shut up, Polly," Hayes commanded. "I—warned that s.o.b. to keep away from you. He wouldn't do it. And that gabbing mouth of his. He kept—kept bragging—"

"Grant!" the girl exclaimed.

"Never mind, Hayes, save it," Austen warned. "Tell it in court. You'll need all of that. If you say you did it—

well, Polly Day can go free. Unless—well, I won't take her
in tonight. Come on, Hayes—let's move."

He put a hand on the playwright's arm. "Come on!"
Austen swung the playwright around. The girl sprang forward, tore Austen's hand from the playwright's coat sleeve.

"You can't—I tell you—you can't do that!" she said
between gasps.

Austen wheeled on her. "I've had enough from you. You
keep out of this," he advised.

"But I tell you, you can't arrest him." She spoke tensely. "I know you—you won't arrest an innocent man."

"What do you mean, an innocent man?"

"Hush up, Polly," Grant Hayes said. "You keep out of
this. You don't know anything about it."

"Oh, I don't?" She looked up into his face. "You're the
one to keep quiet, Grant Hayes." She turned to Austen.
"I tell you, Major Austen, Grant Hayes is innocent. He—
he had nothing to do—to do with it. He was drunk last
night—too—too drunk to kill anyone."

"That's untrue," retorted Hayes. "I—I was cold sober.
I—I didn't start drinking till it was over."

"Cut it, both of you. Come on, Hayes!" Austen again
took his arm. Once more Polly Day pulled Austen's hand
off the playwright's sleeve.

"You can't—you shan't arrest him, because"—she
stopped, caught her breath, closed her eyes an instant; she
spoke in a half whisper—"because, you see, I am the one
who killed Henry Madison. I—I did go out to his house
between those two phone calls."

"Polly!"

An astounded Hayes spoke the name.

The girl threw her shoulders back, smiled fleetingly.
"The truth had to come out, Grant," she said tonelessly,
"but it's going to be all right." She turned to Austen:

"You see, Henry—he—well, he broke his word, and—well—yes"—she spoke hurriedly—"I'll wait and tell it in court—every bit of it. Let's go, Major Austen. Let's go quick!"

She stopped as suddenly as she had started talking. Grant Hayes, his mouth half open, stared at her. Neither spoke. No one moved.

Austen broke the silence, but first he looked at the girl, then at the man, and turned the knob of the door.

"Both of you—beautiful liars!" he said. "Good night!"

He opened the door, passed out, closed the door behind him.

As Austen went out the stage door he saw two figures in the alley shadows: Shep Thomas and Sergeant Hunt.

"Let's go," he said to them. They walked down the alleyway and to the street on which the theater faced. Across the street was a large tree with overhanging branches in front of a darkened house.

"We'll wait under the tree," he said. A cruising taxi approached.

"Get it," Austen ordered. Hunt stopped the cab. It backed into the shadow of the tree. "Put your flag down," Austen said. "Wait here. We'll need you in a few minutes."

"Okay, boss."

The driver turned the meter on. It began clicking loudly in the still city night—a city beginning to sleep off its Derby debauch.

Austen stepped back against an iron fence bordering the pavement. Hunt and Thomas drew close to him. From where they stood they could observe the entrance to the theater alleyway without being seen by anyone leaving or entering it.

"What happened, Major?" Hunt asked in low tones.

"Tell you in a minute. Where's Trigg?"

"Doc Campbell hasn't finished that Pigler autopsy—or hadn't an hour ago," the detective explained. "I had Mr. Thomas keep watch for both of us while I phoned him. Gave me a royal bawling out too. I gathered, between cuss words, that it'd be ready by midnight."

Austen pulled out his watch, stepped from under the tree so rays from the corner light would strike it. "Midnight now." He replaced it, stepped back into the shadows.

"What did you learn, Major?" Shep Thomas was anxious.

"Plenty—and nothing," Austen snapped. He was tired, now irritable. "Grant Hayes, the playwright; Polly Day, the actress—each confessed to killing Henry Madison."

"What?" from Hunt.

"I be darned!" from Shep Thomas.

"First Hayes confessed—when I threatened to arrest the girl. He came in as I was grilling her. Then the girl confessed when I started to take him to the station house."

"What did you do—say—Major?" The reporter was eager.

"Told them they were beautiful liars, said good night, and walked out."

"But one of 'em must have done it!" Hunt exclaimed.

"Yes? Don't forget Danny Barton and Slenk, Brutus and Marge Maxwell—and maybe a half-dozen others," Austen snapped. Then he spoke more slowly: "Hayes could have done it. He had reason to. He's in love with the girl. And Madison—the angel of the show—had been trying to make her. Been bragging about going to do it too. That's enough to send any decent lover on the warpath."

He drew in a deep breath, went on: "Then the girl could have done it. She had time—between phone calls to me—to rush to Madison's place, beg him to lay off, quit bragging. He could have started some funny business; she could have shot him."

"But which one did it?" Shep Thomas asked the question.

Austen peered at him in the gloom. "You tell me," he countered. His voice was hard. "I know who killed Madison and I know who killed Pigler." He paused. Then, "But I can't prove it—yet."

Silence again among them. Hunt and Thomas both shuffled their feet. Then Austen spoke:

"I mentioned Pigler's murder only once—didn't want to diffuse my fire. Both were high-strung. The girl on the border line of hysteria, yet she gave a great performance—in that dressing room. The man's suffering from heebie-jeebies. And both willing to lie dramatically to save a sweetheart. Now that I've left, the tension's broken.

"They'll be out—in a minute or two. We'll follow them. I've a hunch—" He left the sentence unfinished, turned his back, walked off a few paces as if he didn't wish to talk.

They waited five, maybe ten minutes. The night was still, save for an owl car clanging over distant rails, a motorcar passing, a drunk weaving his way against the building across the street, a drunk moaning loudly. Then the ticking of the taxi's clock was heard once more.

A few minutes, and another cab swerved around the corner and slowed to the theater's curb. A little chap hopped out and said, "Take a nickel for your trouble, driver. You made it in five seconds flat."

It was George Trigg—one shoulder jutting forward. As the cab moved off he looked around. Hunt whistled softly. Trigg turned his head, listened and looked. Hunt whistled again. This time Trigg located the sound. He shuffled across the street.

"Oh, there you are, Major!" he called, spying the group under the tree.

"Shut up! Want to wake the town?" Hunt cautioned. Trigg lowered his voice to a loud whisper. He gave the envelope to Austen. "Here 'tis—that autopsy. Doc Campbell says it's completed, and he's plenty sore 'cause we rushed him."

Austen took the envelope. "Thanks," he said. He stepped into the taxi, switched on the overhead light, then sat back so he could not be easily seen. "Hunt, you and Thomas keep an eye on that alleyway," he directed.

He tore the envelope open, unfolded the medical sheet, began reading it—a report written for a layman. Halfway down it a paragraph caught his eye. He read it slowly, then reread it, and whistled to himself.

Austen finished reading the report. He held it in his hands a minute, then said to the taxi driver: "Buddy, suppose you get out of the cab."

"Huh? Me?" The man whirled around in his seat.

Austen grinned. "This is no stick-up. We just want to have a private talk, but watch for a signal from us."

"Huh? All right—okay!" He got out, moved off a few paces.

"You, Hunt, Shep!" Austen called in low tones through the window. "Step inside—read something. You, Trigg, keep an eye on the theater alleyway. If a man and woman, together or alone, come out—say the word."

38

"Lean back so you won't be seen," Austen said as Sergeant Hunt and Shep Thomas got into the taxi. They leaned back.

"Now take a look at this report." He folded under the paragraph that caught his attention.

"H'm'm—ordinary report," Thomas said.

"Sure, but what's folded under, Major?" Hunt asked.

"Now look at this next paragraph." Austen turned the paper over. This was the paragraph:

"Pigler evidently was a dope addict, as multiple punctures were found in his left arm. One was of recent making, as there was discoloration and swelling around it. Possibly made a few moments before his head was smashed open."

A little further down a sentence read: "Thorough analysis revealed three grains of morphine in the body; enough to cause death if there was no other agency."

"So the old bird was a dope fiend!" Hunt exclaimed. "That explains his fishy eye—and why he lived alone with a black man who couldn't tattle."

"Explains something else too," Austen said in low tones. "Pigler would have killed himself if he hadn't been murdered. He knew, when Madison took Danny Barton off Red Moon's back, that Trumpet Call was a Derby standout, was sure to win—barring the unforeseen. And

Trumpet Call did win! Pigler had taken thousands in bets on Trumpet Call—through Nick the Dago in New York."

"And at long odds, too, I bet," Shep Thomas broke in.

"Yes, he did," Austen went on. "Trumpet Call wins—Pigler sees himself bankrupt. You'll have to understand the psychology of a race-track gambler to understand, but remember, a race gambler's word is about the only thing sacred in the world. To him. Pigler saw himself bankrupt—he'd have to renege—to welsh. That's the most detested word on a race track—to welsh: not to pay a gambling debt.

"Pigler wouldn't be the first gambler to take the suicide route to avoid welshing. So he shot himself full of morphine, then his head was hacked open while going into his last stupor. He—"

Austen broke off; he saw something through the taxi window. "Here they come, Major," Trigg whispered. Austen saw two figures—a girl and a man—emerging from the alleyway's gloom.

Trigg signaled the driver. The man got behind his wheel. Trigg squeezed in with the others.

"No, don't turn it off." Austen stayed Trigg's hand as the little man started to switch off the light. "It would look suspicious."

Footsteps clacked across the way, the theater's wall acting as a sounding board.

Polly Day and Grant Hayes came out of the shadows, stopped under a street lamp a few feet beyond the alley. Neither glanced across the street. Their heads were close together. At that moment another taxi came cruising by. The playwright waved it down. The cab stopped. Hayes put the girl in it, got in himself. The door slammed. The driver's voice was heard:

"Where to, mister?"

A muffled answer was given. The car moved off.

Austen leaned forward, directed: "Follow that cab, buddy—but not too closely."

"I get you, boss."

They drove off. "When that car slows down and begins to draw up to the curb you slow down too," Austen went on, "but drive past it. Slowly. Understand?" The head on the front seat nodded. "Then pull up to the opposite curb a half block beyond it."

"I gotcha."

Not till then did Austen switch off the overhead light.

They drove from the quiet business section across Broadway and, turning, went into a street that once had been the home of aristocracy—before the movement to the Shore Road. Drove past two- and three-story houses of stone and brick set back among trees—houses now decaying.

The roadway was rough; the residents lacked the political power which results in smooth paving, smooth living. Hunt cursed under his breath as the jolting taxi threw him against Trigg. "Hey! I wanna live!" the ex-jockey muttered, elbowing the larger man off him.

Suddenly the car ahead slowed up, then so did Austen's.

"That driver's looking for a number," Hunt said.

"Nope," said Austen. "If he was looking for a house number he wouldn't be driving in the middle of the road; he'd cruise nearer the curb. Nothing to prevent him—no cars allowed to park here at night."

"I should have figured that out," Hunt admitted.

"We've crawled along for more than a block," Austen said. "That means they are going to pay a midnight call on some one, and they are trying to decide what to do and say when they get there.

"If they were going to Grant Hayes' hotel or Polly Day's apartment," Austen continued, "they'd go straight there— and talk once they were inside the door."

"You're right, Major." Hunt seemed eager to agree. "And I can guess who they're going to call on."

"Who?" Shep Thomas demanded.

"A lawyer—of course," Hunt snapped. "It's the first thing a suspect does—shouts for a mouthpiece."

For another block they crawled—and still another. Then the first car picked up speed.

"Huh! They've agreed on what they'll say," the reporter said. "What kind of houses along here?"

"Old places, mainly owned by estates," Austen said. "This is a town of sentiment and tradition, Shep. They hold onto these old houses—nearly every old Louisville family has an old house—keep it closed, filled with huge furniture made especially for it. The furniture won't fit in the average new house. Many of these places the owners open up for the Derby season, then open them in the fall too. For entertaining. They—"

He broke off as their driver slowed down; now they were passing the first cab. It was drawn up against the curb on the right.

Outlined in the new moon's rays was an old structure on a terrace shadowed by ancient trees.

"And this is one of them," Austen said. "Hey, buddy, this is far enough."

Their car slowed to the opposite curb. Austen gave the driver a bill as they got out.

"Thanks, boss. Want me to stay?"

"Stay if you want to," Austen said. Then to his group:

"All of you, we're going to follow them in. Once inside, let me do the talking. Understand?" They nodded. "And if I call for handcuffs I want them quick, Hunt."

"Yes sir."

"You, Trigg, and you, Shep, stand by and say nothing. Let's go."

The sidewalk was lined at the curb's edge by drooping maple trees. They walked under the shadows. Across the way Grant Hayes and Polly Day hesitated on the steps leading up the terrace from the pavement.

"Sh-h-h!" Austen stopped his group.

The couple was arguing. In the moon's gleams the playwright was waving his hands and arms abruptly. Evidently the girl agreed to what he was saying, for suddenly she nodded her head and turned toward the house. He took her arm. They went up the terrace steps together, crossed the lawn on flagstones, stepped onto the stone veranda.

Not a light showed in the house.

Now Grant Hayes and Polly Day were lost in the veranda shadows. The quietness of the night was broken by the muffled clangor of a distant bell. Still no lights inside. After a wait the bell was again heard. Lights flashed over the door's transom and through small, high side windows.

Slowly the door opened—ever so slowly. A shaft of light shot across the veranda.

The door was swinging wide, as if someone behind was pulling it back, someone not seen by Austen and his group.

Grant Hayes and Polly Day crossed the doorsill. Noiselessly the door closed behind them.

"Come on—let's go," Austen commanded.

39

Austen was the first of the four to reach the shadowed doorway. "We'll give them a minute," he said, standing by the doorbell at the right. "Grant Hayes and Polly Day weren't expected, or porch lights would have been on. We're not expected either."

They waited; then Austen jabbed his finger against the bell button. There was no immediate answer, no sound of movement inside. They waited several minutes. Once more Austen pressed the button, held his finger on it. The clangor echoed in the rear of the house. Austen lifted his finger, stepped back.

"Look, Rod," Shep Thomas said under his breath.

"I see it," Austen whispered. A sliver of light was showing along the right doorjamb. Someone had started to open the door, then stopped. Evidently it had not been latched after the entry of the playwright and the actress, for no sound preceded that sliver of light.

Now the sliver increased, became a bar of light. The door was swinging open slowly, as if by itself; then muttered words were heard behind it. Whoever was opening that door was cautioning someone—perhaps in a room adjoining.

Now the door was fully open, revealing a small, square hallway, a portion of the rear wall hung with crimson velvet drapes which half concealed a Juliet balcony of the nineties.

Without hesitation Austen stepped across the threshold, and a slender gentleman of middling years, a lavender dressing gown belted around him, came from behind the door.

The man was Dr. Ralph Fellowes.

Austen smiled. "Good evening, Doctor," he said easily.

The physician, hands in dressing-gown pockets, raised his shoulders an instant. "Why, ah—hello, Austen." He seemed bewildered.

"Sorry to disturb you, Doctor."

"Oh, used to being disturbed tonight," Fellowes interrupted. "Came here half an hour ago—this our old house, opened for the Derby season—and I find someone's broken in: a rear window jimmied open. Then two friends dropped by moment ago—"

"We won't keep you long," Austen said and called over his shoulder, "Come on, boys." Shep Thomas and Sergeant Hunt and George Trigg shouldered into the square hall. Trigg closed the door behind them.

Fellowes stepped back. "Austen! What's this?"

"We'll go in for just a minute, Fellowes. We came for Henry Madison's murderer." He looked toward an opened doorway leading into a large drawing room at the right.

"What?" The physician's hands came out of his pockets. "Madison's murderer? I've an idea there's a thief hiding in the house—somewhere—unless he went back out of that window. But there are no murderers around here."

"Didn't you just admit someone? You said you did."

"Certainly I did—two friends. But the idea of looking for Madison's murderer in my house—it's absurd!"

"I don't think so. Who's inside?" Austen nodded toward the opened doorway. Fellowes stepped back again till he stood squarely in front of the velvet crimson drapes hiding the alcove.

"In there?" Fellowes demanded. "My guests—of course."

"Tell them to come out!" Austen spoke sharply.

"Look here, Austen, this is too much!"

"Who's inside—the names, Fellowes!" Austen commanded.

Fellowes drew himself up with dignity, looked coldly at the intruders.

"You going to tell me who's in there?" Austen repeated.

The two men glared at each other.

"Austen, you put a veiled threat into that question," Fellowes said. "I'm going to answer you because I have nothing to hide, but you may know this"—he stepped angrily away from the crimson drapes and toward the investigator—"tomorrow I shall report this sorry episode to the Racing Commission and demand an apology." His jaws snapped shut

"Suppose you answer my question." Austen's voice had the ring of iron.

"Two of my friends are here," Fellowes said stiffly. "They are in the theater—consequently keep ungodly hours. Which explains their arrival a moment ago. They are as innocent of murder as you or I."

"How do you know?"

"Just a minute—I'm still answering your question. The servants I had here went home hours ago. I opened this old place for Derby entertaining, and now the Derby's run. Tomorrow the house will be shut again. Any more questions, sir?"

"I'm waiting for the names of your visitors, Fellowes."

The physician looked at him a moment. "You know you have no right here," he said, "grilling me like a common prisoner. I can only think, Austen, you have lost your balance worrying over this case." He drew the dressing gown around him closely. "My guests are Mr. Grant Hayes and Miss Polly Day," he said. "Now"—with a gesture of dismissal—"I'll thank you and your men to leave."

"Just as I expected," Austen said, ignoring Fellowes' request. "In that room, boys." He indicated the open doorway on the right. "Follow me."

He led Shep Thomas and Sergeant Hunt and George Trigg into a long drawing room extending from front to rear of the house. Before a mantelpiece against the inner wall stood Polly Day and Grant Hayes. The girl's lips were half opened in soundless protest against the invasion; Hayes, a sullen scowl on his face, stepped in front of the girl.

"What in hell!" he exclaimed.

"This is a damnable outrage," Dr. Fellowes protested, following Austen and his men in. "You have no search warrant; you can't invade my house."

"You opened your door; you let us in yourself," Austen flung over his shoulder.

"I'll call the police!"

"Save your breath," Austen snapped; "we're the police." He held up his hand. "Wait a minute, boys. Dr. Fellowes is right." He looked around the room. "There's no one else here. Guess we'd better go."

"Indeed, you had," Fellowes said, trying to control himself. "The door is behind you."

"Thanks, Fellowes. But wait—Hunt, bring out those handcuffs."

Steel clinked as Hunt whipped them from his belt.

"Snap them on Grant Hayes!" Austen ordered.

Click! Click! Before the dumfounded playwright could protest a cuff was snapped on each wrist. He looked like a man awakened to find a nightmare true. The girl stepped around to his side, looked at the glinty steel holding the playwright's wrists together, looked at the physician, looked at Austen.

"What—is this?" she managed to say.

"Come on, Grant Hayes." Austen spoke sharply. "I arrest you for the murder of Henry Madison and for the murder of Colonel James Pigler." And to the physician, "Sorry to have disturbed you, Doctor, but you understand—have to be a bit rough at times."

He about-faced and started toward the hallway. Hunt gave the playwright a shove. "Get a move on!"

"Oh, my God!" the girl screamed. "You can't do it! You mustn't do it!" There was horror in her tone. She seized Hunt by the arm, tried to hold him off Hayes. "You can't do that, I tell you."

Austen, at the hall doorway, turned around. "Quit that foolishness," he said. "Sergeant Hunt, bring the man out. But first get his hat; he has a right to it—for a while."

Hunt reached a free hand out and took Hayes's hat from a console. He slapped it on the playwright's head. Polly Day, clinging to Hunt's arm, raised her voice in hysterical protest: "You can't—you can't do this!"

"But we are going to," Austen said. "Come on."

Hunt gave Hayes another shove. The girl released her hold on the detective, wheeled about and faced the physician. Her tone changed to one of deadly calm:

"You! Are you going to let him be arrested for a murder he didn't commit?"

Dr. Fellowes stood like a graven image; the rest stopped and were still. The girl's lip curved upward. She said—and every syllable sounded sharp as the crack of a gun:

"And you call yourself my father!"

"Polly!" It was Grant Hayes's first word since being manacled. Sergeant Hunt looked astounded. Trigg was rubbing his jaw in excitement. Shep Thomas' eyes were widening.

Austen looked at the physician. The blood was draining from his face. His hands shook; now his face was the hue of light ash. He stood staring at the actress—just staring.

The girl turned on Austen, said: "I tell you Grant Hayes didn't do it—he killed no one. He was miles away. He may have wanted to, but he didn't. Now I'm going to talk if"—she again faced her host—"if Dr. Fellowes won't."

No word from the physician.

"It was—it was—" Polly Day's words stumbled. Fellowes took one slow step, then two, toward her.

"Oh, you're going to make me say it!" she cried suddenly, passionately.

"No," said Fellowes, "you don't have to say it, Polly." And to Austen, "Have those handcuffs taken off Hayes."

"For what reason?" Austen asked. "Why take them off?"

Fellowes stepped to the group. A wraith of a smile played across his face. "Let Hayes go," he said, "because—I am the man who killed Henry Madison." He threw his shoulders back, added, "And I have no regrets."

Austen threw up his hands. "What? Another confession? You're the third person tonight who's confessed to killing the horseman. Sorry, it's no use; you had no motive, Fellowes. This playwright had plenty." He motioned to Sergeant Hunt. "Let's go." He stepped through the door.

Hunt seized Grant Hayes's right arm, pulled him on out into the square hall. Shep Thomas and Trigg followed, then the girl and Fellowes.

"Wait—wait!" the girl pleaded. Austen, near the front door, stopped and turned around. The four men were at his right. Fellowes was slowly walking into the room; he stopped abruptly and faced Austen, his back to the crimson drapes hanging in front of the alcove. The girl paused in the center of the hall. "What is it now?" Austen asked.

"One minute, please, Major Austen." She turned her back to him, faced Dr. Ralph Fellowes. "You know you killed Madison! You threatened to kill him—if he didn't leave me alone. I tried to stop you. You went out and killed him anyway—came in and told me so. Now poor Grant's charged with that killing, and you—you—you say you are my father!"

"It's no use, Miss Day," Austen called out. The girl turned to him.

"What do you mean?" she asked.

"Dr. Fellowes—your father! He's a bachelor," Austen told her.

"Yes? He married my mother secretly twenty-seven years ago in New York. Didn't you?"

Fellowes nodded his head slowly. A stricken look hung on his features, and he seemed as one deprived of the power of action.

The girl talked on with fierce earnestness: "His people were rich, socially prominent, ashamed when they learned he had married a working girl. They bought my mother off, threatened her, made her let him have a secret divorce. Oh, they paid her! And you"—she whirled on Fellowes—"you were weak—ashamed of what you had done. You kept track of me—especially after Mother died and I had gone into the theater. Now that you're getting old and lonely and I'm—I'm becoming a success you want to claim me. Isn't it true?"

Fellowes' lips moved, but no sound came from them.

"I'm young, and Grant's young," she went on while the others stood still, "but you've lived your life! Grant has a right to live—a right to me!

"When this—this person"—she turned for an instant toward Austen—"accused me of killing Madison tonight Grant took the blame, said he did it. But you did it—you told me so! If you want me to—to acknowledge you, then admit the truth! You can't ruin Grant's life and you're not going to ruin mine."

She stopped speaking, reached out, caught the back of an old mahogany wall chair. She almost fell into it.

"All right, Fellowes," Austen said, "you better talk fast or I'm taking Hayes to the police station."

"You shan't!" The girl jumped to her feet, ran to the physician, pounded her fists against his chest. "You are the man who's going behind bars. I've protected you all I could. You go—not Grant."

Fellowes stepped back from her bombardment of blows. He shook his head as if to clear it of the confusion that was upon him. "All right," he said with a deep breath. "It's the easiest way out. Let me get my hat." He stepped to an old-fashioned hat-rack.

"Just a minute, Fellowes," Austen cautioned, "your confession doesn't free Hayes."

"What!" The man wheeled around—his right hand reaching back to touch a littered table, beside the hat-rack. "Why doesn't it?"

"I'll take you down for Madison's murder, but I'm taking Hayes for the killing of Pigler."

"O God!" the girl cried, stumbled back to the chair again, sank onto it, hands pressed against her face.

Fellowes glanced at her, then looked toward Austen. "You damn fool!" he said. "I killed both men. Didn't you know it? Now let Hayes go."

"Oh, you did!" Austen grinned at him. "I think you're a damn liar!"

The physician moved swiftly forward to the middle of the square hall. His right hand was pointing straight at Austen, and Austen was looking into the muzzle of an automatic pistol.

Fellowes had had the gun concealed in the litter of papers on the wall table. He had seized it while near the hat-rack. He said, leveling the weapon at Austen's face:

"No cheap race-track detective can call me a liar!"

40

"That's right!" A strange note came into Fellowes' voice.
"Keep hands out of your pockets—all of you. If anyone
moves I kill Austen—so keep still. Now you, city detective"—he waved his pistol at Hunt—"step to the wall this
side of the drawing-room door and face the wall."

"Do as he says—the man's going batty," Austen warned
in an undertone. Hunt obeyed.

"And, you, go beside him." The command was to Shep
Thomas. The newspaperman grumbled and obeyed.

"And you, little runt"—to Trigg—"get in line with
them."

"Say! I ain't no—"

"Shut up!" Austen commanded. "Do as he says; we're
covered." Trigg went to the wall.

Austen was standing with his back to the front door,
the manacled Hayes at his right side. Polly Day, sitting as
still and erect as a person in a trance, was in the chair on
Austen's left.

Fellowes was speaking: "Anyone moves—I kill Austen.
The first man was hard to kill. The second not so hard.
This one will be"—he waved the point of his pistol in a
circle and smiled—"will be easy."

The girl, her face deathly white, got to her feet.

"Put the gun down," she pleaded.

273

"Hush—sit down!" He rasped the words at her. She sat down.

"Now, mister race-track detective, you men at the wall, I'm keeping my eye on you; don't move your hands. You, Austen, apologize for calling me a liar."

Austen looked at him steadily. "Don't you recall the lie, Doctor?" He forced himself to ask the question with a smile on his face. "That little tale of Madison stealing Piglet's girl—I thought it a joke."

"Ha! I fooled you!"

"You didn't expect me to believe you, did you? Your friend wasn't cold, and you tell an amazing tale of illicit intrigue involving his honor."

"You didn't believe me?"

"No, I didn't." Austen forced himself to smile. "I suspected you from the first, but I could prove nothing—not even a motive."

A cackle of a laugh came from Fellowes. "Ha, not even you, the great Major Roderick Austen, could find a single clue!"

"Yes, I did find one clue, but then you were too smart."

"Eh? First—the clue."

"It's psychological. You'll appreciate it, Fellowes. When in my rooms Madison told you he, was going to throw a party for her—I couldn't help overhear it. I didn't hear your answer, but your face was a dead giveaway, Fellowes. You didn't like the idea at all. Then—"

"Bah! That's no clue!" Fellowes spoke scornfully, still waving the pistol.

"No? It was a key that fitted a lock."

"What lock?"

"The lock was your statement in the club. You said:

"'People seldom kill over money down in this section, Austen. Usually a woman is at the bottom of our murders.'"

"And so they are—so they are! Go on—tell me more! What about my being too clever?"

"In going to Pigler's with us. You seemed a little bit too carelessly anxious to go along."

"That's no clue!"

"No? But when you were here and I wanted to find the phone you were too quick to suggest the room that had a phone, though you claimed never to have been in the house—"

"Bah—no clue!"

"No, but when you add all these things up, Fellowes, you get an answer. The answer is *you.*"

"Tell me some more!"

"All right. You walked in the front door of your club; then you walked around that turn in the hall and out the back door into the club parking lot, got your car, drove out, and killed Madison; then killed Pigler, returned, put the car in the lot, came into the club by the back way."

Surprise came into Fellowes' eyes. "How did you know that?" he demanded, still keeping his gun leveled at Austen, and adding in a different tone, "Keep still, everybody, or I shoot."

"I didn't know"—Austen tried to sound nonchalant—"just figured it could be done when you offered to take us to Pigler's in your car. See? You were too smart in wanting to go out with us. You started around the turn in the hallway; I saw the glass rear door, lights in the club lot beyond. I guessed you could do it that way, and I'd never have figured it if you'd kept still. You did it that way, didn't you?"

"Of course!" There was braggadocio in his words.

"You made two or three other mistakes too."

"Name them—name them—and remember, I've got you covered! You can talk, and then—then—" He waved the pistol once more.

"Well, you were clever enough to agree with me that Danny Barton seemed innocent. But then you tried to throw the blame on too many people. You blamed everyone concerned but yourself."

"Go on—go on."

"You tried to lay Pigler's death at the feet of poor Brutus, who worshiped his master as a god." Austen shook his head. "If you know the blacks as I do you should know they don't kill and remain with the body. You were clever, though—I admire you."

A cackle came from Fellowes' lips. Again he waved his weapon.

"Listen—I want—"

"Shut up!"

Trigg, against the wall, wished to protest something. It was Austen who hushed him.

"That's right—keep your men quiet," Fellowes commended. "I'll say just a word, then leave all of you here."

He smiled blandly at Austen, then his face sobered. Out of an eye corner he saw the playwright, still manacled, standing by Austen's side.

"Unshackle that lad," he commanded.

"Sorry, I haven't the keys. You'll have to let Sergeant Hunt step away from the wall."

"No, no, he stays there—till I leave." Fellowes' voice rose. "Yes, I'm Polly Day's father! What she says is true, but that's in the past. For years there's been an ache inside. And when Polly grew up—"

For the first time the girl interrupted him: "Please finish!"

"Quiet, Polly! When that skunk Madison bragged to me, when drunk, that he was going to possess you—how do you think I felt, when I couldn't acknowledge you?"

"It must have been tough, Fellowes," Austen broke in soothingly. "When Madison boasted he was going to give a

party for a certain girl—to celebrate getting Red Moon—
that was Polly, wasn't it?"

"Miss Day—no. Miss Fellowes to you, sir! *Miss Fellowes!*"

"I'm sorry!"

"Yes, it was she! When Madison dropped me at the club
he again bragged he would have her. That drove me mad. I
hadn't played fair with Polly's mother, but I would protect
the child.

"So I went through the club—just as you guessed—went
to Madison's, found him in the office, told him if he ever
spoke to my child again I'd kill him! I'll kill any of you—"
He stepped back until his body touched the crimson velvet
drapes in front of the alcove. The heavy curtains rippled.

"Madison laughed. He called my child a name I can't
repeat. When he said that one word I lost my head. On his
desk was a pistol. I grabbed it—I shot him. I ran out the
back door, drew it after me. Now, you believe me, don't
you, Austen, and you'll let Grant Hayes go free?"

Austen said nothing. The links of Hayes's handcuffs
clinked. Hunt shifted his feet. Shep Thomas murmured,
"What a story!" Polly Day sat as if frozen to her chair.

"You believe me, Austen?"

The investigator answered thoughtfully, "You might
explain—were you wearing gloves?"

"When I killed Madison? Of course!" Another cackle
came from the man. "But for those gloves I would never
have killed Pigler—never!"

"How's that?" Austen asked in a loud tone. Then, in a
half whisper, "Keep still—all of you."

"I ran out the back way from the office. You, Austen,
keep still—I saw your hand move!"

"Sorry—a mistake."

"I ran through the hedge, scratched and tore those
gloves, and ran into Pigler. He had heard the shot. He

lived right behind Madison. The fool! His curiosity—he came down his driveway to see what had happened.

"I told him nothing. He saw the gloves in the light from my car's lamps. He said they were torn, that I must go in. I went into his house. He wanted me to take the gloves off, said I'd scratched my hands, wanted to put iodine on them. When I refused he said, 'I think you shot Madison just now.' I told him he was a liar—a damn liar. I leaped at him—he at me. I snatched up the battle-ax by the suit of armor. I brained him—but that isn't all. I wanted to make sure he was dead, for he had accused me of shooting Madison. Pigler took dope. I know why—shan't tell—violation of medical ethics. Understand, Austen?"

"I do."

"Pigler kept morphine in the vizor of that suit of armor. I knew it! I took it out, shot him full—he'd never come to life—never, never, never!"

Fellowes burst into a mad laugh.

"Why don't you laugh—all of you?"

"I'd like to laugh, but you fooled me—that morphine," Austen said, trying to keep his voice calm. "I got sentimental—bad mistake!—and said Pigler had probably doped himself—to die—because he couldn't make good betting losses on the Derby."

"Ha, but I did it! I went back to town, changed my clothes, was in the club when police phoned and asked me to act as Madison's best friend—notify relatives. Ha, best friend—ha!" Suddenly the man's mood changed. He became dignified and aloof. "If you think you're going to arrest me, disgrace me, you're wrong." He moved sideways, to his right. Now he was standing at one edge of the alcove drapes.

"You—you're not going into the alcove and hide?" Austen asked the question in the tones he would use with a child.

"No, I'm going to the moon instead! I—"

He stopped speaking. But still his gun was leveled at Austen.

"I think I'll kill you before I go, Austen." He said it in a matter-of-fact voice. Again he raised the gun till it pointed squarely at Austen's face.

41

The crimson drapes in front of the alcove bulged momentarily.

"Look!" The exclamation escaped from the lips of Grant Hayes. Fellowes saw the direction of the manacled playwright's gaze. He turned his head a split second, saw what Hunt and Thomas and Trigg saw as they wheeled around:

A huge black hand and a huge black wrist poised on the edge of the curtain. Then the curtains flashed apart and a giant black man hurled himself on Fellowes, knocking his pistol arm upward. The weapon exploded. Hunt leaped forward, but his leap was too late. Brutus, the black, crashed Fellowes to the floor, in a split second had his knees on the man's stomach, and his great hands were choking the breath of life from the physician.

"Pull him off!" Austen commanded, seizing the gigantic arm and tugging. Hunt, Trigg, Thomas—it took all to pull the giant loose. Suddenly Brutus relaxed, sat back on his haunches, licked his lips fast for a moment.

Hunt wheeled around on Hayes. "Here—let's take 'em off." He whipped a key from his pocket, took the cuffs off the playwright.

Fellowes was gasping on the floor, was trying to push himself upward on one elbow. With a hand he was rubbing his middle.

"On they go!" Hunt exclaimed. He snapped one on Fellowes' right wrist; he pulled the left wrist over, snapped that one. The man's head and shoulders fell back on the rug.

Fellowes rolled from side to side, one elbow, then the other, hitting the floor. Then he raised his cuffed hands before his face and laughed. It was a loud and hilarious laugh.

"He's cuckoo!" Trigg exclaimed.

"Better notify the station, Hunt," Austen suggested.

"Wait—let me get to that phone first!" Shep Thomas strode forward. The drapes, shoved back from the alcove, had revealed a phone on a stand.

"Long distance! . . . Chicago. . . ."

A moment later his voice was booming over the wire:

"Shep Thomas speaking. FLASH! Dr. Ralph Fellowes confesses he murdered Henry Madison and Colonel James Pigler—reveals himself as father of Polly Day, the actress. . . . Yes, Polly Day! Get your art out; you got plenty. Now take a bulletin—by Shepherd Thomas, and don't forget my by-line. . . ."

The girl herself, hands gripping the chair for support, sobbed, "That's—publicity—I—I don't want!"

Grant Hayes was by her side, now on his knees, was soothing her: "Don't worry, honey; it'll be over in a day. Nothing can hurt you. You've played a real-life role—"

"I don't want drama in my private life!"

"It's all right!" He was holding her hand. "You played the role of a thoroughbred."

"Ha-ha-ha-ha!"

Delirious laughter burst from the handcuffed physician, rolling from side to side on the floor. Hunt was watching him.

The girl sobbed afresh. "My father—to go—"

"No, he won't." Austen was in front of her, spoke quickly. "He's insane, Miss Day. Even I can tell that. His repressions—they burst through"

"But to know—my father—in a madhouse—"

"It's better that way," Austen said.

"I know, yes, but—he's my father!" Long-dormant affection for a parent she had never known was breaking through. Or was it pride? Austen asked himself.

"That black man"—she stopped sobbing; her face became stern—"he almost killed my father."

Austen shrugged, tried not to smile sardonically. He did say, "Brutus saved my life, Miss Day. Your father's trigger finger was crooking—"

"You knew the black was here?" she demanded.

"No, he was a surprise. He must have seen Dr. Fellowes arguing with his master, so he took the law into his own hands. He knew Fellowes was staying here during Derby week. Brutus is the one, of course, who broke in; he was laying for Fellowes; he timed his attack to the split second. An instant later—" Austen shook his head.

The girl dabbed her eyes again.

Austen's hand touched something in his coat pocket—a bulky, small envelope. He remembered. He took it out, said:

"Oh, this is yours, Miss Day. I didn't earn it, and I couldn't take it—the Commission pays me." Austen gave Polly Day the envelope containing two hundred and eleven dollars. "Yours, of course."

"Yes." She took it. "Thank you. Yes, I did telephone you. I—I was desperate, Major Austen. I was trying to save Grant." She looked up, smiled at the playwright. He patted her shoulder. "He—he was drinking and threatening to kill Madison. Madison was—"

"Pursuing you." Austen supplied the words.

"That's putting it—mildly," she said. "For business reasons, he being the show's backer, I—I had to be—be civil to him—"

"The s.o.b. bragged, you know," Hayes broke in.

"I know," said Austen.

"Grant—was drinking," the girl went on, "and he—he loved me enough to—to kill the s.o.b.!" She said it with a faint smile. "I didn't know which way to turn. I wanted to protect Grant; I had no friends here, but I knew—had read—all about you. I—I thought you could save him. If I'd had time to see you—but I called between rehearsals, and the show—"

"I know," Austen said. "Odd, I had to take the tack I did toward you. But you see, I'm a racing man first. My job's to see that racing is run on the level—that it's kept clean.

"So when a poor dumb jockey, then a dumb and friendless trainer were being charged with the crime I had to find out who was guilty. Now the matter's closed."

"Come on," Hayes said to her, "I'll take you in the drawing room. You can rest a minute, then we'll go." He took her hands, lifted her to her feet, led her through the doorway.

"Hunt, I've an idea," said Austen.

"Yes, Major?"

"Suppose we let Brutus go home. I sort of feel obligated to the fellow—that's why I'm glad we didn't let him kill Fellowes. I could see Fellowes' trigger finger flexing—one second more—"

"And blooey!" Hunt grinned. "Yep! We don't know ourselves that he broke in—let him go." He thumbed Brutus toward the door.

The black, who had been sitting impassive on his haunches, looked up. His face came alive. He looked at Hunt, then at Austen. Pointed a thumb at himself.

Austen smiled, nodded, and pointed to the front door. Then he reached down, clasped Brutus' right hand, pulled him up.

A big grin, revealing a splendid set of ivories untouched by gold, spread over the giant's face. A friendly, cooing sound came from his lips.

"Thank you, Brutus," said Austen softly.

Brutus seemed to understand. Austen walked beside him to the doorway. Brutus hesitated, his hand on the knob. Austen nodded. The door opened; Brutus went out into the night.

Austen turned around as Shep Thomas came from the phone in the alcove.

"Look at Fellowes—like a man in a daze now," Thomas said. Fellowes had subsided. Lying on his back, he weakly moved his chained wrists, stared at the ceiling.

"Get your stuff in?" Austen asked.

"Sure did"—Shep grinned—"thanks to you. I scoop the world on this. Now for the follow-up tomorrow, Major. Do I still have the inside? I mean—about this big bluff you pulled, the bluff that made good. Say—that's a phrase, the bluff that made good!"

Austen grinned at him. "I don't talk much, Shep. Trigg doesn't talk at all. Sergeant Hunt—" He looked at the city detective.

"The captain talks for us," said Hunt.

"Thanks, all of you. Now, Major, how'd you figure it out—that Fellowes was the guilty guy?"

"Know your Bible, Shep?"

"Huh?"

"'*The wicked flee when no man pursueth,*'" Austen quoted. "I went to Fellowes to find out what I could about Madison's associates. And Fellowes started alibiing himself. Oh, in a very casual, clever manner, but he did it purposely. Then I saw how he could go out the back way to the car lot without the front doorman seeing him. And Fellowes—he was too quick, tying up his dead friend in scandal. It's just not done. Don't forget, Shep, he blamed everyone but himself."

Shep Thomas grinned. "Go on—let's see the wheels in your head go round."

Austen smiled back. "Everything added up—the answer was Fellowes. My main trouble was to find a motive that pointed straight to him. Strong motives pointed to Danny Barton and Guy Slenk and Rock Doyle—motives too good to be true. I guessed jealousy. I thought Fellowes was a little too anxious to paint himself Sir Galahad. Madison bragged about planning a party for some girl. Fellowes' face showed he didn't like it. Not at all! Well, they did clash over a girl, but not for the reason I thought. That's all. It was easy."

"Oh yeah?" Shep Thomas grinned again. "Now I know why you draw a fat pay check."

"Forget it. And listen: I promised the captain we'd give the credit to the police department. Give credit to Sergeant Hunt—"

"Shucks!" Hunt broke in. "I didn't break this case. You did, Major."

"No," said Austen, "credit goes to you. In fact," he drawled, "I'm no longer interested in this matter."

"How come?" Thomas demanded.

"I cleared racing of any connection with it," Austen said, "and that's my job—to keep racing on the level. This was an odd scrap over a girl. Racing doesn't enter the picture, so I'm going home. Hunt, you'll see that the cap lets Slenk and Barton out?"

"Will I? And I'll let 'em know they'd better come around with a batch of thanks to you tomorrow."

"I'll go to the station with you," said George Trigg. "I'll tell 'em a few things, I will! Especially that Slenk!"

Austen grinned. "Forget it! Guess you'd better call the wagon, Hunt. I'm going to get some shut-eye. Shep, want to ride downtown with me?"

"You bet! I got a batch of questions—"

"Skip them! All this is in the past." He walked to the door, opened it, said as he stepped outside:

"There'll be a big Derby next year—the biggest in history. I just hope no girl gets my telephone number—the day before!"

THE JINX
THEATRE
MURDER

ALEXANDER WILLIAMS

Details at
CoachwhipBooks.com

Available from your favorite online retailers

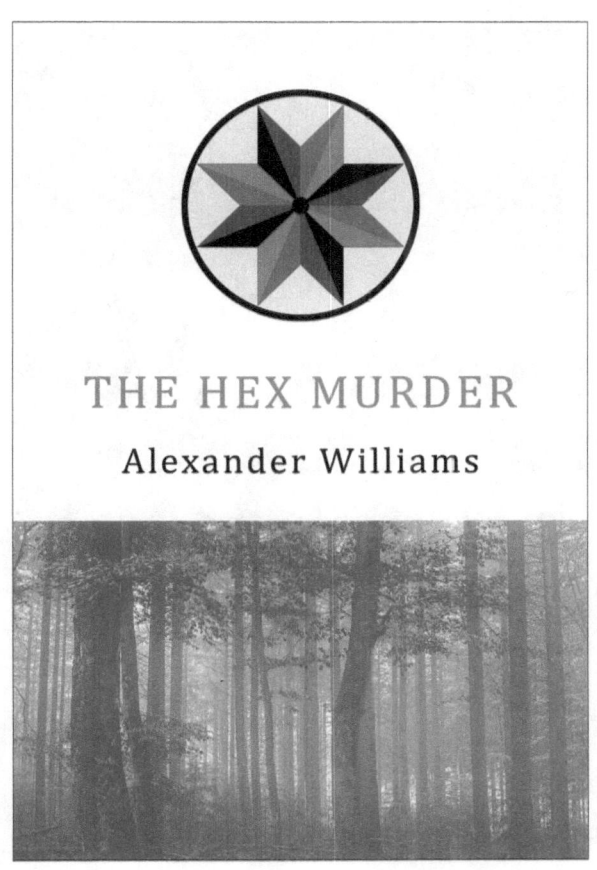

THE HEX MURDER

Alexander Williams

Details at
CoachwhipBooks.com

Available from your favorite online retailers

Details at
CoachwhipBooks.com

Available from your favorite online retailers

Details at
CoachwhipBooks.com

Available from your favorite online retailers

DEATH
BEATS
THE
BAND

IDA SHURMAN

Details at
CoachwhipBooks.com

Available from your favorite online retailers

DESIGN
for MURDER

Frederic Arnold Kummer

Details at
CoachwhipBooks.com

Details at
CoachwhipBooks.com

Available from your favorite online retailers

Details at
CoachwhipBooks.com

Available from your favorite online retailers

THE
THING
IN THE
BROOK

PETER STORME

Details at
CoachwhipBooks.com

Available from your favorite online retailers

Details at
CoachwhipBooks.com

Available from your favorite online retailers